PRAISE FOR ROSE IN BLOOM

This is a beautiful love story between two people who weren't ever supposed to be together. The story moved along and didn't drag at all... Great read for those who love historical romance, and even if you don't, I say try this series.
~Delightfully Dirty Reads

Helen writes these books with such grace and finesse that you feel as though you've been transported back in time and are walking among the characters. You feel every bit of passion, anguish, and love emanating from the pages. It envelops you and leaves you grasping at the hopes that these two wonderfully in love couples get to have the HEA they both deserve.
~Bare Naked Words

ROSE
IN BLOOM

A Sex and the Season Novel

HELEN HARDT

WATERHOUSE PRESS

ISBN: 978-0-9905056-8-6

ROSE
IN BLOOM

A Sex and the Season Novel

HELEN HARDT

For everyone who has ever believed in me…thank you!

PROLOGUE

London, 1806

"I'll have you yet, little one." Beau had sneaked up on the pretty young housemaid while she was making up one of the many guest rooms in the London terrace home. Now she stood across from him as he backed toward the door and turned the key in the lock. "I'm not leaving for university before I have a taste of those treasures under your dress."

Joy frowned, but then giggled and tossed her copper curls. "A few stolen kisses are one thing, my lord. You may think I have no choice to resist you, but I shall."

"Come here," Beau said, as he sat down on the unmade bed.

"Absolutely not. You touch me and I shall scream."

"Who would hear you, dove? I sent everyone else away this afternoon."

"You sent an entire household of servants away? 'Tis not possible."

"I'm the master's son." Beau winked at her. "My command makes anything possible."

Joy smiled demurely. "You think you can command me?"

He grinned. "I know I can, little dove," he said, "and I'll have you begging for it by the end."

Joy backed slowly away from the bed, into the alcove created by three windows. "I will never beg for anything."

"We shall see about that."

Beau crawled slowly across the bed and lunged at Joy. She ran toward the door of the chamber, but he was too quick for her. He grabbed her and whirled her around, throwing her on the bed.

"My lord," she said, "not like this."

"Like what?" he asked breathlessly, his black hair falling into his eyes as he looked down at her sweet innocent beauty, her full lips the color of rubies. He had to have her.

"You...you wouldn't force me, would you?"

He smiled. "No, sweet dove, I won't force you. That I promise." He crushed his mouth down on hers and coaxed her lips open, yearning for a taste of her sweetness.

He had coveted Joy since she first came to the London house two years ago. Her coppery tresses and rich blue eyes enraptured him. A shy lad of sixteen at the time, Beau had worshiped her from afar and had only gained the courage to steal a kiss a mere three months ago. Joy had responded, so he stole another one, and then another. The newfound knowledge that he was attractive to women had led him to steal kisses from a couple of other young servants and a few girls in town, but none were quite so luscious as Joy and her honeyed lips. As they parted for him now, he knew he would have her before he left on the morrow. Damned if he would arrive at Oxford as an untried lad of eighteen.

He fumbled clumsily with her bodice, the weight of his body imprisoning her beneath him. She wriggled under him, trying to push him off of her, but to no avail. She was trapped, just the way he wanted her.

"My lord," she said breathlessly, "you said you wouldn't force me."

"And I shan't," Beau gasped. "I won't take you unless

you beg me to. But that doesn't mean I can't have a taste of your delights." He freed her young plump breasts from their restriction. Perfection.

"How lovely you are, little dove." He clamped his mouth onto a tight nipple. He wanted to be gentle, really he did, but his passion overwhelmed him. He pulled at her roughly, squeezing and kneading her breasts, panting and puffing as she writhed under him.

"My lord! Oh!"

"Yes, yes," Beau said. "Just a little. You're so beautiful. Does that feel good?"

"Aye, my lord." She panted against him. "So good."

He glided his lips over her bosom. "I'll make it good for you, dove." He pressed tiny kisses over her milky skin and then returned to her nipples, licking them tenderly, until he felt her body relax beneath him. "Is that better?"

Joy didn't answer. She moaned softly, and then inhaled sharply as he stroked her private parts.

"Such sweet wetness," Beau whispered against her soft flesh. "Do you want me to fill the emptiness inside you?"

She sighed. "I want... But I'm afraid."

"Don't be, dove. Let me touch inside of you." Beau entered her slowly with one finger. So sweet, so tight.

Soon she was writhing under his touch, wanting more, wanting *him.*

"Oh, my lord," she moaned.

"Do you want me?" he asked huskily.

"Aye, my lord. I want you." Joy arched her hips.

Beau added another finger, stretching her. "Are you begging me?"

"Aye. Yes. I want you. Please!"

Beau ripped the buttons from his trousers, sending them plunking across the wood floor. He freed his aching arousal and plunged it into her, taking her maidenhead with more force than he had intended. She screamed from the pain, but the pleasure he felt overpowered his concern for her.

"Oh," he groaned. "Oh my God. Joy. Joy!" He shuddered as he climaxed, spilling himself into her, welcoming the release of his seed.

He collapsed onto the bed and rolled off of her, too exhausted to move.

Joy remained silent for several moments. Then, "My lord?"

He turned to look at her beautiful face flushed like a ripe raspberry. "Yes?"

"I... May I go now?"

"No, don't go." Beau took her delicate hand and lightly brushed his lips over it. "I'm sorry. I just couldn't... It will be better for you the next time. I'll make sure of it."

She smiled. "Aye, I know, my lord."

But a next time never came. When Beau came home from Oxford on holiday, Joy was gone.

CHAPTER ONE

Laurel Ridge, Lybrook Estate, Wiltshire County, England
Wedding Ball for the Duke and Duchess of Lybrook, 1853
Cameron Price downed his fourth glass of champagne and cursed the day he'd ever laid eyes on Lady Rose Jameson. Watching her waltz with Lord Evan Xavier for the fifth time this evening was more than he could stomach.

When the Duke of Lybrook had approached him six weeks earlier to compose a wedding waltz for his bride, Cameron had no choice but to take the commission. His family, tenants on the Lybrook estate, needed the money badly, and the sum of two hundred pounds also offered him the opportunity to hire a man to work his family's farm so he could devote more time to his music.

The duke had insisted that he work closely with Lady Rose, a talented pianist, while composing the waltz, so she would be adequately prepared to play it at the wedding. The many hours of sitting next to her at the piano, working out measures and harmonies, their elbows grazing as her fingers danced across the keys... He'd nursed many a cockstand afterward. Fighting his attraction to her had become a loathsome burden, a constant duel between his head and his heart. Her sapphire eyes haunted him. Even in slumber he found no peace. Rose's beautiful visage tormented him in his dreams.

No one played as Rose did. She made the pianoforte sing, giving Cameron's music a power and seductiveness it didn't otherwise possess. The waltz had been well received tonight, but he had no doubt that Rose's interpretation, not his talent as a composer, had made the difference.

Watching her now, in the arms of Xavier, who was courting her, felt like a punch in the gut.

No.

More like a stampede of heavy-hoofed stallions trampling him.

Xavier had been an oarsman at Weston and was consequently a big man, tall and blond with friendly brown eyes and a pleasantly handsome face. Surely a perfect match for the quietly virtuous Rose.

Cameron disliked him on principle.

Cam had bedded his share of females in the past, but never before had he felt such an intense attraction to a woman as he did for Rose. He ached inside. She was meant for parties and high teas, silk gowns and diamonds. He had nothing to offer her.

He set his champagne glass down on the refreshment table and walked out of the ballroom.

"You're not leaving yet, are you, Mr. Price?"

Cameron turned to face the duke's mother, Morgana Farnsworth, the Dowager Duchess of Lybrook.

"Yes, Your Grace," he said. "I believe it is time I got back to my family."

"We'll be serving a small meal at midnight. Won't you stay and join us?"

"I'm sorry. I couldn't impose."

"Nonsense. The duke and duchess would never forgive me if I let you leave. Everyone here is dying to talk to you about your compositions. You have an exciting career ahead of you."

"Thank you for the compliment, Your Grace." Cameron bowed politely. "However, I don't think it would be appropriate for me to stay. After all, I'm one of the duke's tenants."

"You're an invited guest," the duchess said.

Cameron sighed. If these people wanted to speak to him about his music, he couldn't afford to leave yet. Perhaps it might lead to another commission, and he needed the money to provide for his widowed mother and two younger sisters. "Thank you, Your Grace. I would be honored to stay."

"Wonderful, Mr. Price. Please make yourself welcome." She touched his arm in a maternal fashion and then hurried off to speak to another group of guests.

Cameron headed back toward the refreshment table, inhaled another glass of champagne, and strode toward the ornate double doorway that led to the back terrace. He needed some fresh air.

★ ★ ★ ★

Rose thanked Evan for the waltz and hurried to the ladies' retiring room to check her appearance. Her pale green satin gown was in fairly good shape, considering she had been wearing it since early afternoon. She fussed with her blond tresses a bit, which were swept atop her head in an elaborate coiffure of cascading curls, and then bit her lips and pinched her cheeks. The midnight meal was only minutes away. Rose was not hungry, but it would be bad form not to attend. She smiled in the looking glass as she thought of her sister, Lily, who had already left the ball with her new husband, Daniel, the seventh Duke of Lybrook. They would no doubt be missing the repast, as well they should. To have a wedding night with the man she loved—Rose envied her sister's good fortune.

Seven weeks ago the sisters had come to Laurel Ridge with their parents, the Earl and Countess of Ashford, and their brother, Thomas, Viscount Jameson, for a pre-season house party hosted by the Duke of Lybrook. Lily had caught the eye of the duke soon thereafter, and the two had fallen deeply in love. The way they looked at each other took Rose's breath away. She couldn't imagine feeling that intensely for someone.

Well, she could. Just not for Lord Evan Xavier. She cared for him and she enjoyed his company...and his kisses. But they didn't share the ease together that Lily and the duke—Daniel—did. It was still difficult for Rose to call her new brother-in-law by his Christian name. Then again, she and Lily were two very different people. Perhaps Lily, with her disdain for convention and the dictates of the peerage, was just more comfortable using Christian names than she, Rose, would ever be.

Rose took a few deep breaths and walked to the back terrace for some air before the midnight meal. Several couples hid in the shadows, chatting intimately. Some were embracing each other and laughing softly. She walked swiftly away from them, looking for a dark corner where she could be alone with her thoughts for a few moments. She finally settled on a spot against the railing, outside the glimmer of the torchlights. She inhaled the fresh night air, expanding her lungs as much as her corset would allow.

"Good evening, my lady."

Rose turned, squinting in the dark shadows. About ten feet away from her, concealed in the nightfall, stood Cameron Price. Rose's skin erupted in tiny bumps and her breath caught. He never failed to affect her, and this evening, dressed formally, he was an intoxicating vision.

Cameron drained the glass of champagne he was holding and shuffled toward her.

"A wellborn lady such as yourself shouldn't be out here unescorted," he said, the aroma of alcohol on his breath unmistakable.

"Mr. P-Price," Rose stammered. "I...I was just getting a breath of fresh air."

"Won't Xavier miss you?"

"I don't know... I...I'm not wholly his concern."

Cameron snorted. "He certainly monopolized you on the dance floor this evening."

Rose's cheeks warmed. She was thankful for the darkness. "Not many others asked me for a dance."

"How could they, with him breathing down your neck? He's the size of a mountain, for God's sake."

Rose wrinkled her nose. "You're inebriated, Mr. Price."

"Slightly." He chuckled. "Tell me, would you have danced with another man if he had asked you?"

"Of course," Rose said. "I danced with my father and my brother, and my cousin's friend Mr. Landon."

"You danced with a mister?" Cameron shook his head. "You mean you'll dance with an untitled gent?"

"Why wouldn't I? Mr. Landon is an impeccable gentleman. He owns land here and in the Americas, and he's a cousin to His Grace."

"Ah, I see." Cameron lifted his champagne glass to his lips. "Damn, it's empty." He set it down loudly on the railing. "Money is the issue then, as well as blood."

"Mr. Price," Rose began, unable to look at him, "I fail to see what—"

"My lady," Cameron interrupted, "would you have danced with me, had I asked you?"

Rose turned. His silver eyes penetrated her flesh like daggers. She felt defenseless. All those heart-wrenching hours spent at the pianoforte with him, fighting her attraction to him and telling herself they had no future, flooded into her like a tidal wave. He had treated her with such disdain, never missing an opportunity to make a snide comment about their different stations. Was it possible he felt an attraction too?

"You're foxed, Mr. Price," Rose said, forcing herself not to stammer. "This conversation would be better served if we were both in our right minds."

Cameron tentatively reached toward her arm and touched her lightly with his finger. A spark shot through Rose at the contact.

"I may have imbibed a bit more than usual, my lady," he said. "But I assure you, I am in my right mind. I asked you a question. Would you have danced with me?"

"I...don't know. It wouldn't really be appropriate."

Cameron snorted again. "Of course. What would the other peers have thought if you, the daughter of the Earl of Ashford, were seen dancing with a commoner? Pardon, not just a commoner, but a tenant on your brother-in-law's land." He turned away from her. "Good evening, my lady."

Rose's heart hurt. She *had* wanted to dance with him. She had dreamed of more than that. Of kissing him the way she kissed Evan. Of doing...*more* than kissing. "Wait, Mr. Price."

He turned. "What is it?"

"Yes," she said.

"Yes, what?"

She gulped. "Yes. I would have danced with you."

He walked back to her and brushed back a stray curl. Her skin burned where he touched her.

"Will you dance with me now?"

"It's nearly time for the meal." Rose swallowed. "The orchestra is taking a break. I...we should go in."

"Please. Dance with me."

Her heart hammered against her chest. "There's no music."

He cupped her cheek. "We don't need music. You and I together have it in our souls."

"Mr. Price..."

"Come with me." He took her arm and led her to the stairs of the terrace.

Rose looked around quickly. They were alone. Completely alone. The other couples on the terrace must have gone in to be seated for the meal. Cameron pulled her down the stairs and out onto the soft grass of the lawn. He led her away from the torchlights to a dark crevice where only the light of the crescent moon veiled them in a lustrous cloak.

"Dance with me," he said, taking her into his arms. He led her left hand to his shoulder and pulled her to him. "Look at me."

She gazed up into his sterling eyes, the moonlight illuminating his handsome face and casting highlights into his coal-black hair. He looked like a pagan god come to earth to deflower an innocent maiden. Her heart raced and fear coursed through her, but she didn't look away. He began moving in a slow waltz, leading her around the lawn in intricate steps that surprised her.

"You dance very well, Mr. Price," she said.

"Yes, we common folk dance too," he said, a bit

sardonically.

"I didn't mean—"

"Shhh." He pulled her closer.

She laid her cheek on his shoulder and inhaled his salty cinnamon scent. She closed her eyes, the pulse of his throat racing against her forehead, her own heart thumping madly. Being in his arms at last felt wonderful. Too wonderful. She started to pull away.

"No," he said, resisting her. "Stay with me. We haven't finished our dance."

She relented, melting into him. He stopped waltzing and simply swayed gently. To finally embrace him, feel him against her, filled Rose with joy and agony. If only this moment could last a lifetime.

Slowly he pulled away from her, just slightly. With one hand, he tilted her chin up and gazed into her eyes. Her lips trembled, but she knew what he wanted. She wanted it too. His mouth descended until his lips were on hers.

Rose knew how to kiss. Evan had taught her well. She parted her lips and Cameron's tongue invaded her mouth, tasting her gently, slowly. He withdrew his tongue and brushed it delicately over her lips. She sighed softly and tentatively reached her own tongue out to explore the fullness of his lips. They were softer than Evan's, and she felt a surge in her womb that was new to her. Frightened, she turned her head away. His lips caressed her cheeks, her neck, nibbling and nuzzling her until she shivered.

"We should go in."

"No. Not yet," Cameron said. "I know I can never have you. I need at least this much of you. Please."

She turned and sought his mouth with her own. This time

the kiss wasn't gentle. Cameron clamped onto her, absorbing her. He swirled his tongue with hers, tasting her, taking her. He tasted of champagne and tea, passion and lust. She wanted to kiss him forever, to lose herself in his strong body. He moved from her mouth to her ear, tracing its outer edge with his tongue and dipping into its cove just enough to wet it. When he caressed the wetness with his breath, the tingling made her shudder.

"Do you like that?" he whispered.

"Oh, yes," she breathed. "Yes."

He nibbled on her earlobe and then moved to the other ear, tantalizing it as he had the first. Rose squirmed, her body possessed by new and exciting feelings. Evan had never kissed her ears. Her skin blazed and her heart raced wildly, her blood like molten lava in her veins. Cameron caressed her cheeks with moist kisses, moved down to her neck, her pulse throbbing as he licked her in little circles, blew softly on the wetness, and kissed it.

"Oh, Rose," he whispered. "Rose, Rose. You're so beautiful."

He nibbled down below her neck to the sensitive skin above her breasts. Rose buried her hands in his hair, pulled out the queue that bound it, and laced her fingers through the thick black locks. Cameron kissed the tops of her breasts, tracing his tongue around the neckline of her gown. She moaned as he forced his tongue between her breasts, down into her cleavage, retreated, and did it again.

"Goodness," she said. "We shouldn't...."

"I know." He moved his lips upward. Gently he eased the sleeve of her gown down and kissed her shoulder, his hands cupping her breasts.

Even through her corset, Rose felt her nipples tighten. She gasped.

Cameron tore his mouth away from her arm. "Are you all right, sweetheart?"

The endearment surprised her, and her pulse quickened. "Yes, yes, I'm fine. I just feel so..." She panted, trying to catch her breath. "We really should stop."

"Do you want to stop?" he asked, running his finger up and down her bare arm ever so lightly, giving her the chills.

"No...I mean, yes..."

But his mouth was on hers once more, their tongues mating and swirling, feasting on each other.

His lips found her ear again. "Your kisses are magic, Rose," he whispered.

"Yes," she sighed. "Magic."

"Do you want me, sweetheart?" Cameron's voice was rough and smoky. "Do you want me to touch you?"

"Oh, yes," Rose whispered, the ache in her womb nearly more than she could bear. "Touch me, Cameron. Please touch me."

He pulled her into a shadow. Gently he lowered her to the ground, positioning her into the crook of his arm, and kissed her mouth again as his free hand fumbled with her bodice. He eased her gown down around her arms and loosened her corset, freeing her full breasts, which glowed incandescently in the moonlight.

"You're more beautiful than I imagined," he rasped, gently kneading them, brushing his fingers over her taut pink nipples.

She moaned his name softly.

"Do you want me to kiss you here?" he asked.

"Yes," she pleaded. "Yes, please."

He lowered his head and licked one pink circle, gently kissed it, and sucked the nipple into his mouth, tugging and then releasing it slowly, and tugging again. Rose closed her eyes and arched her body toward him, reaching for something elusive that she couldn't imagine, but that she wanted more than anything.

"Please, Cameron."

He sucked her nipple harder, and then moved to her other breast and licked her, kissed her, his breath coming in rapid pants against her flesh. With one hand he reached under her dress and tugged at the ribbons of her drawers.

"Sweetheart," he said, "you need to stop me now."

"What?" she rasped.

"If you don't stop me now, I'm going to take you."

Take her? Make love to her? Her skin was tight around her body, and her only thought was how she wanted him. "Yes, take me. Please, Cameron."

"Dear God," he said, exploring her flesh with his fingers. "You're dripping wet." He rubbed against her slick folds and then brought his hand to her mouth. "Taste." He traced her lips.

She darted her tongue out and licked the musky sweetness from his fingertips.

"Your ambrosia," he said. "You made it for me."

He glided his fingers under her skirts again, finding her sex and touching her wetness. He brought them to his own mouth this time. "Sweet," he said. "So sweet."

Rose thrashed against him, arching her hips wildly.

"Do you want me to touch you again?"

"Yes, yes, again."

He complied, reaching under her skirts, finding her swollen nub, and teasing it with his fingers. "Does this make you feel good?" he whispered.

"God, yes, Cameron. Yes," she sobbed, grabbing his hand and rubbing it harder against her.

She moaned, writhing beneath him, running toward something—she didn't know what—until her insides exploded in a wave of pleasure that sent stars into her body, crashing her into a wall of joyful euphoria. When her shuddering finally slowed, Cameron released her.

He lowered his head to hers, kissed her mouth lightly, and whispered, "Does Xavier make you feel like that?"

"No," she said, breathing heavily, seeking his mouth with hers.

"Who makes you feel like that, Rose?" he asked, his breath tickling her neck.

"You, Cameron."

"Who do you want to take you? Who, Rose?"

"You, only you." And she meant it. She wanted him inside her. Now.

Cameron brushed his hand down her arm, making her shiver, taking her hand and leading it to his groin. "Do you feel that?" He moved her palm over his arousal. "That's for you, sweetheart. Only for you."

Rose explored the hardness through the silky fabric of his trousers. "Cameron," she whispered. "My goodness."

"I ache for you, Rose." He groaned. "Only you can ease my suffering."

"I want to. I want to, Cameron."

"Are you sure, sweet?"

"Yes, yes. Take me now."

"Do you...understand what will happen?" He panted in her ear. "Do you?"

"Of course. And what I didn't know my sister told me. I just didn't expect you to be quite so...engorged."

Cameron laughed softly. "Perhaps I'm better endowed than the duke."

"What?"

"Never mind, my darling. Are you sure you want to do this?"

"Yes, yes, please. I want it more than anything." Rose sat up and tugged at Cameron's black formal coat. "I want to touch you."

★ ★ ★ ★

Rose's face was flushed in the moonlight, her eyes shimmering with passion and promise as she looked at him, her shoulders creamy white as a new-fallen snow, and her bare breasts hanging gently, their tips rosy and puckered. God, she was lovely, and Cameron wanted her, hungered for her. She was his for the taking. He could have her once and remember this night forever.

"Damn it," he said gruffly.

He couldn't do it. She was a virgin, a lady of the peerage, the daughter of an earl, for God's sake. Cameron removed her hands from his coat. "Rose, we're going to stop now."

"No, no." She pulled at his hands, trying to release her arms. "I want to, Cameron."

"Sweetheart, I need to leave you while I still have a shred of sanity left." He pulled her to her feet. "You'll regret it if I take you this way, outside, in the grass. You deserve to be loved in the comfort of a bed. Your first time shouldn't be like this."

"No," Rose said. "If...If this is all we'll ever have, I want it now. Please."

"You deserve more. You deserve better. Better than..."

"What?" she asked, toying with his cravat. "Better than what, Cameron?"

He looked down at the grass, at his feet shod in shiny leather boots. His formal wear had cost more than he normally paid for clothing in a year, yet he had used a portion of the money he had earned from the duke's waltz, money that could have helped his family. The duke had requested his presence at the wedding ball as composer of the piece, and Cameron had bought the garments so he wouldn't look like a mere peasant. He had bought them for Rose. To impress her. He knew he was attractive to women. He knew he looked elegant in his black courtly clothes. He knew she would notice him, and she had. But he was still a tenant on the duke's land. The expensive suit didn't change that. He was nothing.

"Better than *me*, Rose," he said quietly.

Rose reached up and touched his cheek. "You're the one I want. The one I've always wanted. Perhaps we can't be together for the long- term, but—"

"Then what is the point of this?" he asked gently. "I'll ruin you."

"I don't care." She reached for his arousal through his trousers. "You still want me."

"God, yes."

"Then take me, Cameron. I'm yours tonight."

God forgive him his weakness. He pulled her to him and kissed her passionately, easing her down to the grass once again. He reached under her skirts and stroked her. She was still wet for him. He hastily unbuttoned his trousers, freeing his aching erection, and moved on top of her.

"It may hurt a bit," he said. "I'll try to be gentle."

"Yes, I know. It will be all right."

He nudged the head of his cock through the slit in her drawers, rubbing it against her juices. "Oh God," he groaned. "Oh God, Rose." He teased her entrance, braced himself to begin his descent.

"No!" Rose pushed against his shoulder, her eyes suddenly icy and full of terror. "No! I changed my mind. I can't, I can't!"

He moved away from her quickly, the unsated hunger almost unbearable. "Damn you," he said between clenched teeth. "I gave you two chances to stop me, you little cocktease. Damn you!"

Rose began to weep quietly, hurriedly tucking her breasts back into her bodice. She stood. "Please forgive me," she said, her gaze cast downward. She ran away, sobbing.

"Damn it," Cameron said under his breath, and then, loudly, his voice strained with remorse, "I'm sorry, Rose. I'm so sorry. I didn't mean it. I didn't mean it! Come back, sweetheart. Please!" He would hold her and comfort her, tell her it was all right, that he would wait for her.

But Rose ignored him and ran toward the mansion, disappearing into the vacant ballroom.

Cameron buttoned his trousers, his arousal still burning. "Fuck you, you stupid idiot. How could you believe she actually wanted you?"

He walked away from the house. He couldn't go in and join the party for dinner. If he missed out on a chance for another commission, so be it. He couldn't see Rose again. Never again. It was over. Hell, it hadn't even begun.

It never could.

He trudged home to his cottage on the Lybrook land. The sun was edging over the horizon when he finally fell into his bed, exhausted, his feet blistering from the long walk in his new boots.

CHAPTER TWO

Rose entered the ballroom from the back terrace. Several servants were cleaning up, but they paid her no heed, thank goodness. She hurried to the back stairwell and made her way to her bedchamber on the second floor of the east wing. She longed to fling herself on her bed and cry herself to sleep, but she couldn't miss the midnight meal. Her parents would never forgive her. She wished for a moment that she were Lily, who wouldn't think twice about defying convention and doing what she wished. But she wasn't Lily. She was Rose, and Rose always did what was expected of her. Lily would have slept with Cameron tonight, on the grass, if that was what she had desired. Rose, however, knew her place.

She strode into her dressing room and sat down in front of the looking glass. Her eyes were puffy, her cheeks streaked with tears, her lips dark and swollen from Cameron's kisses. Cameron's kisses, so different from Evan's. Evan's kisses were gentle and sweet, and Rose enjoyed them. But Cameron's... She had never imagined... Kisses that took as well as gave, kisses that made her womb ache, that changed the very composition of her soul. She went to the basin, splashed cold water on her face, and returned to the mirror. She pinched her cheeks until they had regained their peachy rosiness and began to work on her hair. When she was satisfied that she was presentable, she rang for a maid to tighten her corset. She moved to the full-length looking glass and smoothed her gown as best she could, tucking in her swollen breasts.

As she walked down the hallway toward the stairwell, she hesitated for a moment, tempted to go up instead of down and find Lily. But her sister was no doubt in bed, making love to her new husband. She would never forgive Rose for disturbing her wedding night.

Lily and Daniel were leaving early the next day for London to begin their wedding trip. Rose would rise early tomorrow, no matter how exhausted she was, and catch Lily before she left. In the meantime, she had no choice but to venture downstairs and partake of the midnight meal. She was already unfashionably tardy.

Lord Evan Xavier stood when Rose entered the dining room. "Where have you been?" he asked. "Your mother has been concerned."

"Please forgive me, my lord," she said. "I was feeling a bit poorly so I went to my chamber to rest for a bit. I didn't mean to cause anyone needless worry."

Evan furrowed his brow. "Are you better now?"

"Yes, thank you. I hope I haven't missed too much."

"Only the appetizers. The soup is being served now." He led her to her table with the rest of the wedding party. The chairs for the duke and duchess were conspicuously vacant. "I see Lybrook and your sister decided to forego the feast," Evan said, chuckling. "Not that I blame the bloke."

Rose's cheeks warmed. "I'm sure they didn't mean to be disrespectful."

"Who said anything about disrespect? Here you are." He held out her chair and sat down next to her. Her brother, Thomas, was on her other side, and her cousin Alexandra next to him.

"Where have you been, dear?" Alexandra asked.

"Just resting a bit. I was feeling poorly, but I'm much better now." Rose took a taste of the winter squash soup set before her. "This is delicious."

"Yes, it's divine," Alexandra said. "Guess what? The most wonderful thing has happened!"

"What?" Rose asked.

"Well," Alexandra said, "you know that Mama and Miss Landon have renewed their childhood friendship during the past several weeks."

"Yes, of course," Rose said. Lucinda Landon, sister to the dowager duchess, and Rose's Aunt Iris had been best friends as girls.

"They've so enjoyed each other's company," Alexandra continued, "so Miss Landon and the dowager duchess have invited Mama and Sophie and me to stay here at Laurel Ridge for the summer! Isn't that amazing?"

"It sounds lovely," Rose said.

"Just wait. The best part is that they've asked that you join us! Mama will be here to keep an eye on you, and then we'll all be here to welcome Lily and the duke home when they return from France. Mama has already spoken to Auntie Flora and she says you may stay if you wish. What do you think, dear?"

"Oh, goodness." Stay here? And possibly see Cameron? She couldn't....

"That way you can continue to...you know." Alexandra winked and nodded toward Evan.

Evan's estate was only a few hours away by carriage. If Rose returned to the Ashford estate in Hampshire, continuing Evan's courtship would be difficult at best. No doubt her mother, Flora, the Countess of Ashford, was in favor of keeping the relationship going.

"If the two of you are going to continue to talk over me," Thomas interjected jovially, "perhaps we should exchange seats?"

"Yes, Thomas, that's a marvelous idea," Alexandra said, rising. "Here you go."

Thomas held out his chair for Alexandra and then took her vacant seat.

"But what of the season?" Rose asked. "We were all to be presented for the first time this year."

"Yes, yes, I know," Alexandra said, "but we're all young yet. We can wait until next season. Sophie and I have discussed it at length and have decided we'd like to stay at Laurel Ridge."

Rose didn't doubt it. Her cousins, Sophie and Alexandra, had both met men they fancied at the Lybrook house party. Alexandra had been keeping company with Mr. Nathan Landon, the duke's second cousin, and Sophie had caught the eye of Lord Marshall Van Arden, heir to an earldom and a very amiable fellow, if not the most handsome one. They were both having a wonderful time, and Rose was happy for them. They hadn't had easy lives. Their mother was Lady Ashford's older sister, Iris, the Countess of Longarry. She hadn't received an offer of marriage on her own, so her parents had married her to a brutal Scottish earl when she was twenty-five years old. He had mistreated her and the girls, and had died two years earlier, his reckless spending leaving them penniless. The Earl and Countess of Ashford had taken care of them since then, setting them up in a townhouse in Mayfair and bestowing dowries upon the girls.

"I'll think on it," Rose said.

"Oh, you must stay," Alexandra urged. "We'll have the

most fun. Miss Landon, who has asked that we call her Auntie Lucy, by the way, and the duchess—er, the dowager duchess— wants us to call her Auntie Maggie. Isn't that a hoot? Anyway, what was I saying? Oh yes. Auntie Lucy says there is the most wonderful Midsummer festival in that lovely little village outside of Bath. Won't that be fun?"

"Yes, I suppose so," Rose replied. They had all enjoyed the May Day festival several weeks before. It was unlike anything Rose had ever experienced, as her father, Crispin, the ninth Earl of Ashford, was a devout Christian and frowned on anything with pagan origins. The earl and Thomas had returned to Hampshire to conduct estate business before the wedding, but the countess and Rose and Lily, along with Aunt Iris and the cousins, had stayed at Laurel Ridge, and the duke had escorted all of them to the festival. It had been a merry day, and Rose smiled slightly. Cameron had won the archery contest, besting even the duke himself, who came in second.

Cameron. If she stayed at Laurel Ridge, she would no doubt see Cameron. Just the thought of it made her heart skip a beat, even though he must be terribly angry with her at the moment. She wanted to see him more than anyone, but they had no future. They both knew that. And if she stayed, Evan would still court her. She cared for him, but he didn't evoke the passion in her that Cameron did. Perhaps leaving would be best. She would leave both Cameron and Evan, and hope that she could find someone else in Hampshire or during the London season.

But no need to upset Ally right now. Rose would tell her tomorrow that she was returning to the Ashford estate.

She would also tell Evan.

★ ★ ★ ★

A young housemaid rapped on Rose's door at six in the morning. Rose was exhausted, having not gone to bed until after two, but she had asked to be wakened early so not to miss Lily before she left. She rose from her bed and went to the door.

"It's six, milady," the maid said.

"Yes, thank you. Do you know if the duke and duchess have left the estate yet?"

"No, not yet, milady. The staff was told they were coming down to breakfast at seven."

"Perfect," Rose said. "Could you ready a bath for me please?"

"Yes, milady."

Rose bathed quickly, dressed in a morning gown, and descended. The house was silent. No one would be about yet this early. Lily and the duke sat in the informal dining room, smiling at each other. Lily was radiant in a light brown traveling outfit, her dark hair plaited and piled on her head. She looked up to see her sister enter the room.

"Rose, dear, what on earth are you doing out of bed this early?"

"Good morning, Lily, Your Grace." Rose nodded to her new brother-in-law.

"Please, no more of this Your Grace," Lily said. "She may call you Daniel, right?"

"Of course," the duke replied. "I get a little tired of all the formality anyway. We're all family, now."

"Yes, of course...Daniel. Th-Thank you," Rose stammered. "Lily, I'm so sorry to interrupt your breakfast, but I need to talk to you. It's...urgent."

"Goodness, is anything wrong?" Lily asked.

"No, not exactly. But I desperately need a half hour of your time. When are you leaving?"

Lily gestured to her husband, who replied, "In about an hour. Our baggage is being loaded into the carriage now."

"Since I'm all packed, I'm yours," Lily said. "Do join us, will you?"

"No, I couldn't. I'll wait for you in the ladies' sitting room. I need to speak to you in private."

"Lily," Daniel said, "I need to see to some...arrangements for our trip. Why don't the two of you breakfast together in here while I take care of matters."

"No, I couldn't possibly—" Rose began.

"Nonsense," Lily said. "That is a spectacular idea, Daniel, and you're a darling for thinking of it." She gave him a loving smile as he strode from the room.

"Is there anything he wouldn't do for you?" Rose asked.

"If there is, it hasn't come up yet. He's a gem, isn't he?"

"Yes, you're very lucky."

"I know exactly how lucky I am, dear. Now what is troubling you?"

Where to begin? Rose took a deep breath. "Oh, Lily, I don't know what to do!"

"About what, Rose?"

"I...I did something very foolish last night. Something I can't take back. I...I don't want to take it back, but I... I nearly slept with...with..."

"Evan?" Lily asked.

"No," Rose said. "If only... Not Evan. Cameron Price."

"Mr. Price? Oh, Rose."

"I know. He's completely unacceptable. He's a commoner,

a tenant, for goodness' sake. But Lily, I...I'm attracted to him."

"Yes, I know you are."

Rose rubbed her forehead. "Oh, you can't imagine how hard it was. While he was writing your waltz, he and I had to work together so I would have it ready to perform for the wedding. We spent hours together, working at the grand piano in the conservatory. It was wonderful...and terrible. And of course I couldn't talk to you about it because the waltz was a surprise, and I didn't dare talk to anyone else either, for fear they might divulge it. He's brilliant, Lily. His music is so poignant and touching. It made me want to weep sometimes. It's that beautiful."

"Yes, the waltz was lovely. He's quite a talent."

"He's amazing," Rose said dreamily.

"What about Evan? Do you still care for him?"

"Yes, I've always cared for him. He's a kind man, and he's been a perfect gentleman but for a few stolen kisses, which I gave permission for. We get on well, and I enjoy our time together. But with Cameron...that is...Mr. Price...oh, I don't know how to explain it."

"You don't have to explain it to me. I know what that kind of attraction feels like."

"I know you do, but it was different with you and Daniel."

"How so?"

"Lily, he's a duke! A perfect match for a daughter of the Earl of Ashford. But Cameron is... Well, he's nothing." An invisible thud hit Rose's gut. "God, I didn't mean that. He's not nothing. He's...*everything*, actually."

"Tell me what happened last night," Lily urged.

Rose's pulse fluttered at her neck. "I went to the terrace for some fresh air, and he was out there, alone in the dark. He had been drinking, but he seemed sincere. He was upset that Evan had monopolized me, and he asked me to dance with him on the lawn."

Lily smiled. "That sounds heavenly."

"It was." Rose closed her eyes and inhaled the smoky scent of Lily's morning tea. "I always thought he found me attractive, but he treated me with such scorn while we were working together. He made snide comments about my being above him, and the like."

"No doubt he was fighting his attraction for you, hoping it would go away because he thought you and he had no future."

"Perhaps. Yes, that would make sense. Anyway, we danced, and it was lovely. It felt so right to be in his arms, Lily. Do you know what I mean?"

"Yes." Lily winked. "I know."

"Anyway, we stopped dancing after a while and simply swayed together, and then...he kissed me."

No hint of shock graced Lily's face. None at all. Well, of course not. She'd had a passionate affair with the duke only weeks before.

"It was unbelievable. He said he knew he couldn't have me, but he wanted at least that much of me. It was so romantic. I melted."

"But, Rose, how did you go from a kiss to almost sleeping with him?"

"I don't know. One thing led to another, I guess. He told me I should stop him. In fact, *he* tried to stop it twice. He was a dear, actually. He said I deserved better than to have my first time on the grass. But I wanted him. I wanted him so much. I never imagined that I could want another person like that. It was nearly...uncontrollable."

"I know exactly what you mean."

"I know. That's why I wanted to talk to you about this before you left for a month. There's absolutely no one else who would understand."

"Rose, you said you *almost* slept with him. What happened?"

Rose bit her lip. "I got scared, Lily. The emotions were... *overwhelming*."

"Lord," Lily said, frowning. "He didn't take it well, did he?"

"No, he didn't."

"Men are built a little differently than we are, Rose. They reach a point where it is actually...*painful* to stop."

Rose's heart sank. She never wanted to cause Cameron any pain. "God, Lily, I didn't know."

"There's no reason why you should have, dear."

"But I told him I wanted him to take me. That I was his. Oh, he must hate me!"

"No, I don't think he could ever hate you."

Tears misted in Rose's eyes. "I ran away from him in tears. He called for me, and he said he was sorry, but I kept running."

"You poor thing. Are you in love with him?"

"I don't know. How do you know when you're in love?"

"Good question." Lily paused a moment. "I'm not sure I could tell you exactly when I fell in love with Daniel. Once I realized it was love, I felt like it had been there from the beginning. Does that make any sense?"

"No. Yes. I don't know."

Lily took Rose's hand. "You'll need to figure this out, and I'm sorry I won't be here to help you. But I'll be back in a month. What can happen in a month?"

Rose stared into her sister's warm brown eyes. "Lily, you and Daniel were betrothed after three days."

"God, you're right."

"And here's another thing. Miss Landon—who wants us to call her Auntie Lucy, as if I'll ever get used to that—has invited me to stay here with Auntie Iris and the girls for the summer. Sophie and Ally have decided to forego the season and stay. If I stay, I'll have to see both Evan and Cameron, and if I don't, I won't see either of them."

"What do you want to do?"

"Last night I thought I had made up my mind to return to Hampshire. To forget both of them and start again. Maybe have a season by myself. But now, talking to you, I just don't know."

"I think you should stay."

"Really. Why?"

"Because you can't run away from your feelings, Rose. Lord knows I tried. It doesn't work. You need to sort this out and decide whether you want Evan, or Cameron, or neither."

"But what if it's Cameron? Papa and Mummy would never let me—"

"Nonsense. It's *your* life. You have a generous dowry. You'll want for naught, no matter whom you marry."

"Papa could disown me. He could take away my dowry."

"He wouldn't do that."

"He might."

"I don't think so, and even if he did, Daniel would give you a dowry."

"Oh, I could never—"

"Hush. It's unlikely it would come to that," Lily said. "The fact remains that you need to work this out. And if you stay, you'll be here when I return and we can spend the summer together!"

"Don't you want to spend the summer with your new husband?"

"Of course. But he sees to estate matters during the mornings. That leaves me free to spend time with you."

Rose sighed. "All right. I'll stay. My, what have I done?"

"You've done nothing wrong."

"I've been compromised, Lily."

"Yes, but no one knows, and Cameron won't tell anyone."

"No, I don't think he will. I think he...cares for me."

"Of course he does. Anyone could see it from the moment he first laid eyes on you."

Rose smiled. "I felt something the first time I saw him too. It was a...well, almost a stab, in my...you know."

"Yes, in your womb." Lily smiled. "I know the feeling well."

"And then, last night, he did something to me, with his fingers. It made me feel... I'm not sure I can describe it, except that it was the most sensational feeling ever. Something I never imagined."

Lily giggled. "It's called a climax, dear. It's heavenly, isn't it?"

"Yes," Rose sighed. "Yes. Have you ever...with anyone other than Daniel?"

"No. He's the only one who made me come."

"Come?"

"That's just another word for it."

"Oh." Rose warmed and her insides tingled. "How can you talk about these things so nonchalantly? I don't feel at all like a lady right now."

"Of course you're a lady. Ladies can enjoy the bedchamber as much as gentlemen can, Rose."

"Still, it makes me feel a bit...*wicked*."

"Rose, need I remind you that you aren't the same person you were before we came to Laurel Ridge. You've engaged in some scandalous behavior since we've been here. We got foxed together celebrating my betrothal, and you punched a woman in the nose."

"Yes, that's true." Rose laughed, recalling the antics. "And I nearly slept with a commoner, and had a...a..."—she lowered her voice—"a *climax*."

"You don't have to whisper," Lily said. "It's not a bad word."

"I suppose not. Anything that feels so good can't be bad." Rose giggled. "So Daniel's the only one who made you...*come*, and you married him."

"Yes, but that doesn't mean you have to marry Cameron."

"I suppose not," Rose said. "But I would like to have that feeling again."

"You will."

Daniel entered the room, clearing his throat to announce his presence. "I'm sorry, love," he said to Lily, "but we need to be going."

"Yes, of course." Lily rose and gave Rose a quick kiss on the cheek. "I am going to miss you, Rose. Please don't worry. Stay here, and follow your heart. I'll be back in a month, and we'll talk then."

"Yes, Lily. Do have a good time, both of you."

"We will," she said, smiling and taking the arm of her handsome husband. "There is no doubt about that."

★ ★ ★ ★

After Lily and Daniel left the estate, Rose returned to her chamber and slept for a few more hours. She rose at eleven, dressed in an afternoon dress, and went down to join the others before luncheon. She found her cousins lounging on the front terrace.

"Rose!" Alexandra called.

"Yes, Ally, what is it?" Rose asked.

"Lord Evan has been looking for you. None of us had a clue where you were, so we sent him to the stables. We thought you might have gone riding."

"No, I slept late," Rose said. "I was fraught with exhaustion from yesterday's excitement."

"I know," Sophie chimed in. "Can you believe our Lily is married, and is a *duchess?* It's too romantic for words."

"Romantic, yes," Ally said. "But who cares about being a duchess? The duke is rich, rich, rich, and Lily will never want for anything for the rest of her life. What I wouldn't give for that kind of security."

"I've told you before," Sophie said, "that there are more important things than money."

"Yes, yes, I know." Alexandra rolled her eyes. "And I've told you that money is paramount as far as I'm concerned. I couldn't care less about a stupid title. The man I marry will be loaded with gold. I don't ever want to have to worry about money again."

"You don't have to worry now, Ally," Rose said.

"Only because your parents are supporting us," Ally replied. "It sticks in my craw, it does. I hate being a charity case."

"You're no charity case," Rose said soothingly. "You know that."

"What else would you call it? Father left us penniless. If it weren't for Uncle Crispin and Auntie Flora, we'd be living in the gutters. Poor Sophie and I would probably have had to sell our bodies to support mother."

"Ally, really!" Sophie admonished.

"I doubt it would have come to that, Ally," Rose said.

"But you can't say for sure, can you?"

"We're family," Rose said. "We would have never let anything so terrible happen to you."

"Yes, yes, I know. But I'd like to know for sure that my future is secure, and the only way to do that, for a woman anyway, is to marry money."

"What about love, Ally?" Sophie said.

"We've been through this before," Ally said. "Love is an illusion, Sophie."

"I think Lily might disagree," Sophie replied.

"Yes, I suppose so," Ally said, "and I couldn't be happier for her and the duke. But then again, Sophie, Lily also made a great financial match. The duke is one of the richest men in England."

"She's so happy, too," Rose said dreamily. "If only someone that wonderful could love me."

"I've no need for love," Ally stated. "Only money."

"You may change your mind about that," Rose said.

"Yes, of course you will." Sophie smoothed her dress. "What if you could make a match with an incredibly rich man, but he mistreated you, the way Father mistreated Mother? Would you still marry for money?"

"Probably not. But I'm not Mother. She has a weak spirit.

I don't."

"How can you say that about Mother?" Sophie cried.

"Because it's true, Sophie. You know I adore Mother and would do anything for her, but she never fought back. I would."

"A married woman has little or no legal rights," Sophie said. "What could Mother have done?"

"She could have left."

"And spent her entire life running? What would that have been like for her? Or for us?"

"For God's sake, may we end this drivel?" Ally demanded. "I want to marry money. The end. Case closed."

"The two of you go round and round on this subject," Rose said. "Perhaps you should just agree to disagree."

"Never," Sophie and Ally said in unison.

The three of them broke into gales of laughter. They were still chatting and giggling when Evan approached.

"Good morning, Rose," he said, bowing.

"My lord, good morning," Rose answered.

"I've been looking for you," Evan said. "Could we walk a bit?"

"Certainly. Would you excuse us, Sophie, Ally?" She took Evan's arm and strode with him toward the stables.

"Rose," Evan said. "There's something I would like to ask you."

Oh, no, not marriage. He had been courting her for over a month. "Yes, what is it, Evan?"

"Well, I've grown quite fond of you Rose, and..."

"Yes?"

"My father has asked to meet you. Would it be all right if he came along with me next weekend when I come to visit?"

"Of course." Rose breathed a sigh of relief. "I'd love to

meet your father, Evan."

"Then you'll still be here?"

"Yes, I've decided to stay at Laurel Ridge for the summer, along with Aunt Iris and Sophie and Ally."

"Oh, that's splendid," Evan said. "I was hoping I could continue to see you."

"Of course."

"My father asks about you so often. I was afraid you might not want to meet him this soon."

"Why wouldn't I? I'm sure he's just as fine a gentleman as you are."

"Yes, of course, he's a fine man."

"Tell me a little bit about him."

"He's a widower, as you know. He enjoys horses as much as I do, so perhaps we can all go riding. I know he'll be impressed with your riding skills."

"That sounds lovely. I do look forward to meeting him."

"He'll adore you," Evan said. "We should get back for lunch now. Would you care to take a short ride this afternoon, before I leave the estate?"

"Of course, that would be wonderful."

"After lunch then. Come on, let's get back."

Cameron's head throbbed when he finally rolled out of his bed only slightly before noon. Thankfully, the man he had hired was working the farm, so he didn't have to rise with the sun anymore. He raked his fingers through his long, thick hair and cleared his throat. He was hungry, and unbearably thirsty. He had never been prone to drink excessively, and he never would again. The water in his basin was stale and warm, but he used it to brush his teeth anyway, and then he pulled on a clean shirt and pair of trousers. He headed out the back door, avoiding his mother and sisters, and walked briskly to the creek behind his cottage. There he stripped off his clothes and plunged his body into the cold water, cleaning off the remnants of the previous evening. The coldness helped ease his hunger for Rose, but did not abate it altogether. He toweled himself off quickly, dressed, and decided to pay a visit to Eloise Warren. She was always good for a tumble.

Eloise was a young widow who lived on the Lybrook land. Cameron had bedded her a few times, as had many other men. She was pretty and clean, and all she asked in return was a few kind words and a chore or two around the house. Cameron had money this time, though. He wouldn't have to stay and make small talk while he cleaned her barn or milked her spotted cow.

He saddled his stallion, Apollo, and trotted to the Warren cottage. Eloise sat on the porch, stitching a sampler, her bare feet visible beneath her apron and skirt. Her blond hair was light, lighter than Rose's honey locks, and it was plaited into a long braid hanging down her back. Though not as tall as Rose, whose above-average height seemed to fit Cameron's lean build perfectly, Eloise was well-figured and pleasing to the eye. A smattering of freckles veiled her nose, giving her a fresh look.

"Afternoon, Cam!"

He dismounted Apollo and bowed to her politely.

"What brings you this way today?"

As if she didn't know. When had Cameron come to call for any reason other than a tumble in bed? "Just out and about. I was hoping you might have some...time before dinner?" His neck warmed.

"For you, of course. Come on in."

Eloise stood and entered her small dwelling. Cameron followed.

"I've been hoping you would come by to see me."

"You have?"

"Yes. I think you're the most attractive of all the single men around here. I've been yearning for you ever since you beat the duke in the archery challenge on May Day."

"Oh?"

"The way you stared down your arrow. You had so much concentration and focus. It was *powerful*, that's what it was."

"I don't know that anyone has ever described archery that way, Mrs. Warren."

"Cam, call me Eloise. We don't stand on ceremony here."

"Of course, Eloise."

She moved toward him, loosening the strings on her peasant blouse. She wore no corset, and soon her round breasts were tumbling free. She took his hands and cupped them around her bosom, as she wrapped her arms around his neck and pulled him to her. Her lips were soft and wet, and she knew how to kiss. She plunged her tongue into Cameron's mouth. Her mouth felt different than Rose's. Eloise was fresh cotton where Rose was silk. He turned away from her and lowered his mouth to her neck, nuzzling her soft flesh. She smelled of soap, where Rose had smelled of strawberries. Slowly he lowered his head farther, to kiss and suck her breasts. Her nipples were paler than Rose's, and the circles not as large. He brought one into his mouth, tugging gently.

"Oh yes, Cam, that's the way," Eloise sighed. "No one

sucks my titties like you do." She lowered her voice. "No one eats my cunny like you, either."

He stiffened at her words, lusty words that Rose, a lady of the peerage, would never say to him. He tugged on her nipple, moved to the other, biting, sucking.

"God, yes, Cam. I can't wait to have your cock in my wet pussy again." She lifted her skirts. "I'm slick as warm honey for you. Care to take a taste?"

He let her nipple go with a soft pop. Rose had been slick as warm honey. Ambrosia, he'd called it. Ambrosia she'd made only for him. While Eloise's heat might ease the physical ache, it wouldn't take away his yearning for Rose.

Rose.

He wanted Rose. No substitute would suffice. He raised his head and looked into Eloise's fresh pretty face as he tucked her breasts back into her blouse and tied it. "I'm sorry, Eloise. I don't want to do this after all."

"What's the matter, Cam? Did I do something wrong?"

"No, no. You did nothing wrong." He pulled a one pound note out of his pocket and handed it to her. "I want you to take this. It will cover your expenses for a few weeks."

"I couldn't."

"Yes, please take it," Cameron said. "And, Eloise, I would consider it a favor if you would not tell anyone I was here today."

"Of course I won't, Cam. My word's as good as gospel. You know that. I do miss you, though. Are you sure you don't want—"

"I'm sure." Cameron strode toward the door, but then turned back toward her. "You don't have to do this, you know. You deserve more."

"Oh, Cam, this is my life. I've resigned myself to it." She smiled weakly.

"You could marry again."

"Who would marry me? I'm damaged goods."

"There's someone out there for you, Eloise. There's someone out there for everyone."

"I had my time, Cam. Lionel is dead. We could have had a good life. We were on our way, but he died young, leaving me without provisions. With my parents both dead and no brothers and sisters, what more is there for me?"

"I know life dealt you a bad hand. But there are options. Think about it, will you?"

"Sure, Cam." Then, "I do wish you would stay."

"I can't. I'm sorry." Cameron strode out the door, untied Apollo, mounted him, and started toward home. The May breeze blew through his hair as he thought about Rose. Sweet, beautiful Rose. He could never have her. Thank God she had stopped him last night. He was treading water in an ocean with no lifeboat. If he pursued her, he would surely drown. He still had most of the money left from his commission for *Lily's Waltz*. He would leave the majority of it with his mother and sisters, and he would go to London and try to make a living doing what he loved most, composing music. He had two published songs to his credit, and even though neither had enjoyed a wide distribution, it was at least a start. He would pack up and leave on the morrow.

As he neared his cottage, he was surprised to see an ornate carriage out in front. He didn't recognize the crest, but the horses hitched to it were beautiful, a perfectly matched pair of chestnut Morgans. Cameron stopped Apollo for a few moments to admire the horseflesh, and then rode to the stables and put him in his stall. He walked into the house from the back.

Mrs. Clementine Price sat on the sofa, but Cameron couldn't see the visitor who was sitting in one of the chairs by the window of the small parlor. Cameron strode in nonchalantly, making deliberate noise.

His mother looked toward him. "Oh, here he is now, my lord." Then, "Cam, you have a visitor."

Cameron followed his mother's gaze to the large man sitting opposite her. He sighed heavily. It was none other than Lord Evan Xavier.

CHAPTER THREE

"Good God," Cameron said under his breath. Xavier must have found out about his tryst with Rose. He had no desire to be pummeled by this mountainous man. He looked up. "My lord?"

"Mr. Price, good afternoon," Evan said. "I'm sorry to barge in unannounced, but I'm leaving for my estate and wanted to speak to you as soon as possible."

"About what?" Cameron asked, a bit rudely.

"I have...er...a business proposition for you."

Mrs. Price rose. "I have work in the kitchen, so I'll leave you two gentlemen to your discussion."

Evan stood up gallantly. "Of course, Mrs. Price. It was delightful to meet you."

"The pleasure was mine, my lord." She made a quick exit.

"What can I help you with, my lord?" Cameron asked.

"Well," Evan began, "you know that I'm courting Lady Rose Jameson."

"Yes," Cameron said dryly.

"She is a great admirer of your music."

"She is?"

"Of course, didn't you know that? I was under the impression that you worked closely with her on the waltz for the duchess."

"Yes, we worked together," Cameron said, thankful that Xavier hadn't come to throttle him. "She never mentioned any particular taste for my music."

"Well, she has mentioned it to me."

"I'm flattered. But what do you want from me?"

"I'd like to commission a song for Rose. Not a waltz necessarily. Perhaps a ballad."

"I don't write lyrics, my lord," he said, although for Rose, he probably could.

"You don't? Well, that's not a problem. I'm more interested in the music. I think it would mean a great deal to her. I...I'm planning to propose marriage to her, and I would like to serenade her with a piece of your music."

An invisible knife stabbed Cameron in the heart. "You're proposing?"

"Yes. Not right away. I want to have the song first."

Cameron sighed. He could write a song for Rose. He could write a whole symphony or opera about her. About only one part of her. He could compose an entire piece on her lips alone, or her sapphire eyes, or her peachy satin skin. It would be the easiest commission ever. He could do it in his sleep.

But he would not. Not if it was to be a gift from another man. He couldn't.

"I'm sorry, my lord, but I'm leaving for London on the morrow."

"When will you be back?"

"I won't. I'm moving there permanently."

"You could still write the piece, could you not?"

"I'm afraid not, my lord. I'm taking a job that won't allow me the time for private commissions."

"Could you postpone your departure? I assure you that you will be handsomely compensated."

Cameron sighed again. He had no job lined up in London,

and he needed money. "How much are you offering?"

"What is your going rate?"

"Two hundred pounds."

Cameron expected Xavier to laugh at him. To say there was no way in hell he was going to pay such an exorbitant amount to some amateur composer. But he didn't.

"Two hundred it is, then," Evan said. "Surely you could see fit to postpone your departure for that sum."

Two hundred pounds was a ridiculous amount of money. The duke had paid it, but he was one of the richest men in England. Xavier was the second son of the Earl of Brighton. He would never come into a title of his own. His father must provide him with a generous allowance.

With another two hundred pounds, Cameron wouldn't have to worry about his mother and sisters for a year, or even two or three. He could go to London and make a name for himself in the musical world, knowing his loved ones were cared for. But to write a song for Rose, for another man to give to her? He'd sooner scoop out his heart with a pitchfork.

But Rose was only a dream. His family was reality, and the money would mean they could live better lives.

"You've convinced me, my lord," he said. "I'll require at least a quarter in advance."

"Of course."

"I assume time is of the essence?"

"Yes, I'd like it done by the solstice."

"That's little more than three weeks, my lord."

"I know. Is it possible?"

"I suppose, but I can't do a full orchestration in that amount of time. I can only arrange it for the pianoforte."

"That's perfect," Evan said. "Rose loves the pianoforte, as

you most likely know."

"Yes," he said dryly, "I know."

"Very well then, Price." Evan rose and held out his hand.

Cameron shook it, his large long-fingered hand dwarfed by Evan's ham-sized one.

"I'll see myself out."

"Good day, my lord." Cameron sank down onto the sofa, running his fingers over the worn satin brocade. *What the hell have I done to myself?*

★ ★ ★ ★

The next day Rose went riding. Although her two mares were still in Hampshire, the duke had a stable full of beauties, including Begonia, a mare he'd bought for Lily. When Begonia was saddled, Rose mounted and took off down the southern trail.

Rose kept Begonia to a trot for a bit to warm her up, moved her into a canter, and then a full-blown gallop. She diverged a little from the trail to check out the duke's jumping course. Rose adored jumping, but she hadn't tried this particular course before. She looked over it carefully, decided she could handle it, and proceeded. The jumps got progressively harder, but Rose managed them expertly, the pins falling from her hair as she and Begonia leaped into the air again and again. By the time she had completed the course, her hair was falling over her shoulders and neck. She laughed aloud and patted Begonia's black mane.

Finding the trail once again, Rose and Begonia trotted past the fairy garden, where she and Evan had shared their first kiss—Rose's first kiss ever. Dear Evan. He had kissed her and asked if he could court her. Giddiness had consumed her that day. Evan was a good man, a man who would take care of her always. She considered herself lucky. Perhaps they would never have the passion or the ease with each other that Lily and Daniel shared, but that type of relationship was rare.

Rose continued riding, enjoying the lush green of the countryside in spring. She breathed in the fresh air. When she came to a small stream, she stopped so Begonia could drink. Rose pinned up her riding habit and looked around while Begonia quenched her thirst. She didn't recognize the scenery and hoped she could find her way back to the main house. Deciding to let Begonia rest for a while, Rose sat under a tree and closed her eyes. Her thoughts hammered in her head, as she recalled her first kiss with Evan in the fairy garden.

★ ★ ★ ★

Evan led Rose through a small winding path, picking blooms and handing them to her until she had a small bouquet, and then placed one behind her ear. "There," he said. "You look just like a fairy princess."

Rose laughed. "A fairy princess in a brown riding habit."

"My lady, you would be devastating in anything."

"Thank you, my lord."

"Won't you use my Christian name?" Evan asked. "It would mean a great deal to me."

"I'm afraid it's not proper, my lord."

"Lybrook and your sister use each other's names. In fact, I don't think I've ever seen Lybrook quite so animated as he has been today with her."

"My lord, they're just...good friends. Neither His Grace

nor my sister are interested in courtship."

"Are you, my lady?"

"I don't know..."

"Let me see if I can convince you."

He leaned toward her, touching her face with both hands. His lips brushed hers lightly, sending a delicious tingle through her whole body.

"Would it be acceptable to you if I asked your father for permission to court you...Rose?" He stroked her cheeks gently with his thumbs.

Rose closed her eyes, his smooth fingers tantalizing her skin. "I would be...honored...Evan."

He brushed his lips against hers again, coaxing them open. His tongue entered her mouth slowly, softly, taking only the smallest taste. Oh yes, Lily was right. Kissing was heavenly. Then she couldn't think at all, as Evan found her tongue and swirled his own around it. She sighed into him, dropping her small bouquet of flowers as he led her arms around his neck.

★ ★ ★ ★

Rose had nearly swooned at Evan's first kiss. It had been unlike anything she had imagined. But though she cared for him deeply, she didn't love him. When she slept at night, Evan didn't hold her in her dreams. When she woke in the morning, Evan's face wasn't stamped in her mind. It was Cameron who haunted her thoughts. Cameron, with his thick black hair, his calloused hands, his soft full lips. He had consumed Rose's thoughts since she first saw him. Her skin tingled, her heart thumped, her belly fluttered every time his image appeared in her mind. Working with him on the waltz had nearly unnerved her. He had treated her with disdain for the most part, seeming to resent her and who she was. But one time, his guard had come down and they had connected.

★ ★ ★ ★

Rose and Cameron sat together at the grand piano in the Lybrook conservatory. The waltz for Lily was about half complete, and Cameron had brought the sheet music to Rose so she could begin preparing it for the wedding. As her fingers lightly touched the ivory keys, the hair on the back of her neck rose slightly. Cameron was watching her. She couldn't see him, but his steely grey gaze burned into her. She was used to stammering and making mistakes in his presence because he unnerved her so, but this time, she swallowed and summoned all the power within her. She turned and looked at him, staring into his silver eyes as she continued to play.

"You play beautifully, my lady," he said.

"Thank you, Mr. Price. I do appreciate the compliment." She finished the piece.

"Don't stop," Cameron said. "I could listen to you play all day."

"I've played through all that you have completed," Rose said. "It's brilliant. I wouldn't change a thing."

"Actually, I'm thinking of making a few minor changes. A key change here, perhaps." He reached over her arm and pointed to the music. "Perhaps to D minor? What do you think?"

Rose began playing again and transposed to D minor where Cameron had indicated. "Yes, I like that. It gives the waltz a more melancholy feel there."

"The duke wants a joyful tune," Cameron said, "but I think it will still be gleeful even with the change. You see, love isn't always wine and roses. The key change represents the anguish of love."

"The anguish of love?"

"Yes."

"Whatever do you mean by that?"

Cameron stared straight into Rose's eyes. "I mean that love—real honest to goodness true love—is as much anguish as it is joy. It hurts to love that much."

"How on earth can it hurt to love?" Rose asked. "Love is wonderful."

"Because, my lady, the more you love someone, the more you have to lose. And that creates fear. And if the loss comes, sorrow."

Tears welled in Rose's eyes, but she blinked them away and cleared her throat. "How do you know so much about love, Mr. Price? Have you ever been in love?"

"No." Cameron looked away from her. "But I've seen the anguish of love. When my father died, for example. It was unexpected, and my mother still pines for him after seven years."

"But the duke loves Lily beyond reason," Rose said. "There's no anguish there."

"But there is." His gaze penetrated hers again. "There is always a little bit of torment in love. When they are separated, they will pine for each other. And even when they aren't separated, there is always that fear in the back of the mind that someday the person you love will be taken from you. That is what this part of the music represents. It's only a few measures, and then we go back to the original key."

Rose nodded, understanding perfectly, and wondering how Cameron could have such a keen knowledge of love. "It's a brilliant change, Mr. Price. It makes all the difference in the piece."

"Thank you, my lady. Could you play the entire piece again, including the change?"

"Of course."

Rose began, the burning sensation of Cameron's gaze on her again. She made several errors and her neck heated. Relief swam through her when she played the final note.

"It's beautiful," she said. "I'm afraid I didn't do it justice that time."

"You were wonderful. You play with such emotion. Would you play something else for me?"

"Well, I—"

"Surely you have a repertoire. Any musician as talented as you would."

"I suppose I could play something. Do you have any preference?"

"Mozart. He's my favorite."

"He's Lily's favorite too, and one of mine." Rose played one of Mozart's sonatas.

She continued, as Cameron gave her his rapt attention, and played through more of her repertoire. She had played for over an hour before she noted the time.

"Mr. Price," she said. "I should really get back to—"

"Yes, of course."

He touched her arm lightly, sending chills to her core. Slowly he whisked one finger back and forth in a light caress. It was the first time he had touched her deliberately.

"Thank you for playing for me, my lady. I'll not ever forget it." He stood. "I'll see myself out."

★ ★ ★ ★

Rose sighed. What a wonderful afternoon, but the next time they had met, things had reverted to their normal stiffness and formality. Until the night of the wedding ball, Rose had no idea that Cameron harbored such intense feelings for her. If only she were a commoner, or he a member of the peerage...

"Good afternoon, my lady."

Rose nearly jumped up when the object of her daydream stood before her, leading a brown-and-white stallion.

"Mr. Price."

"I hope I didn't startle you."

"No, not at all. I was just...letting my horse rest and drink a bit."

"You're quite a way off from the main house."

"Yes, I guess I am. I was so enjoying my ride that I lost track of where I was going. I hope I can find my way back."

"It's not difficult. I can show you."

"That would be very k-kind of you." *For goodness' sake, stop stammering.* Rose walked over to admire Cameron's horse. "This is a beautiful stallion, Mr. Price. What is his name?"

"Apollo."

"He is very good quality, from what I can see." Rose ran her hands over Apollo's flanks. "I know a little about judging horseflesh."

"You're no doubt wondering how a man of my limited means could afford such a fine animal," Cameron said sardonically.

"No, of course not." Rose warmed, willing her voice not to crack. "Why do you always assume...? Oh, never mind."

"The explanation is simple, actually."

"I'm not interested in any explanations, Mr. Price."

"He belonged to my father," Cameron continued. "His mare gave birth to Apollo right before my father died. I decided to keep him and train him."

"He must have excellent bloodlines."

"I doubt it, my lady. Our old mare was nothing special."

"Well, he's a beautiful horse."

"Thank you. What is your mare's name?"

"Begonia. She's Lily's. My horses are in Hampshire."

"When are you returning to Hampshire?"

"I'm not," Rose replied, her heart thundering. "At least not until the end of summer."

Cameron stroked Apollo's mane. "My lady..."

"Yes?"

"I would like to apologize for—"

"No," Rose interrupted. "You don't need to apologize for anything. It was my fault. I just...well, I just shouldn't have put myself in such a position."

Cameron snorted. "What position? Being compromised by a mere tenant?"

"Here we go again." Rose sighed. "Why do you make such a fuss about our respective stations?"

"Because our stations are a fact of life."

"Nonsense." Rose mounted Begonia and secured her riding habit. "If you'll show me the way back now, I would be obliged."

Cameron mounted and maneuvered Apollo so that he and Rose were next to each other. "Whether you think it was my fault or not, I want you to know that I regret...what I said to you as you left."

"It's no matter." Rose turned her face away from his.

Cameron reached for her cheek and turned her to face him. "I regret a lot of things about my life, Rose," he said, "but none so much as hurting you."

His silver eyes penetrated her soul. "It was my fault, Cameron."

"No."

"Yes. I...didn't know that I would cause you...*pain* if we stopped."

Cameron chuckled. "I've been in worse pain, sweetheart. Although at the time it seemed insurmountable."

Rose's skin tingled at the endearment. "If we had it to do over again, I would..."

"You would have left before we danced?"

"No." She looked away.

"Then what?"

"I would..." Her heartbeat was rapid and her skin cold and prickly. She spoke quickly. "I wouldn't have stopped you."

He caressed her cheek and stared into her eyes.

"I got frightened. I'm sorry."

"You don't need to be sorry." He lowered his face to hers and kissed her lips lightly. "I'll show you how to get back now."

"No." Rose touched Cameron's jaw. He hadn't shaved, and his black night beard was rough under her touch. She pulled his head to her and kissed him, parting her lips and exploring him with her tongue. She sucked on his luscious lower lip, nuzzled the top one. Kissing him was pure heaven. As their tongues coupled and twirled together, she moaned softly.

"Come here," Cameron said.

He lifted her from her sidesaddle and onto his saddle, facing him. Sitting astride, her riding habit was rumpled about her waist and rode up her legs. She was snug against Cameron's hard chest, as little room existed on his saddle for two people. He embraced her and sought her mouth again, kissing her with a passion that she had only known in her fantasies. He covered her face with tiny moist kisses.

"Oh, Rose," he said, "I dream of nothing but you."

"Yes, I know," she whispered, "because all I dream about is you."

Cameron's heart thumped against her chest. Her breasts swelled and her nipples tightened.

He kissed her ear and her neck, raking his hands through her tumbling locks that had come loose during her ride. "I can barely breathe when I'm with you. You make my heart race." He nibbled on her neck. "If only I could have you."

She shuddered against him. "You can, Cameron."

He pulled away from her. "What about Xavier, Rose?"

"I...I don't want him the way I want you."

"But he's a perfect match for you."

"Yes, and I'm...fond of him, but I don't desire him."

"You desire me?"

"Yes, oh yes." Rose sighed, kissing his face and neck, lacing her fingers through his coal-black hair. "I...think about you all the time. I have since we first met." She giggled. "Oh, this is embarrassing."

"Don't be embarrassed. I think about you all the time too." He caressed her back in soothing circles. "But we can never be together."

"Why not?"

"You know why, sweetheart."

"Yes." Rose sighed. "I guess I do." Tears formed in the corners of her eyes. "Please, Cameron, won't you kiss me again?"

"It's better if we stop."

Rose sighed and swung her leg over Apollo's saddle, dismounting expertly. She mounted Begonia as a tear fell down her cheek.

"Don't cry, sweet."

"I...I can't help it. I want to be with you. It's tearing me up inside."

"I know," he groaned. "But it would hurt more to make love and then leave each other, wouldn't it?"

"If it's going to hurt anyway, what does it matter?"

Before Cameron could answer, another rider galloped toward them. It was Cameron's younger sister Patricia.

"Cam!" she shouted. "Thank God I found you. You need to come home quickly!"

"What is it Tricia?" he asked.

Patricia caught her breath. "It's Kat. She's taken sick."

"What in bloody hell happened?" Cameron demanded.

"She came in from playing and wouldn't take any lunch. She's burning up, Cam. She's asking for you."

"I'm sorry," he said to Rose. "I have to go."

"I'll come with you," Rose said.

"There's no need."

"Don't be silly. I love that little girl." Cameron's seven-year-old sister, Katrina, had stolen Rose's heart the day they met.

"Do come on then, both of you." Tricia urged her horse into a gallop.

When they reached the Prices' cottage, a large woman

met them before they came near the house. "Doc is with her now, Cam. She's asking for you."

"Go ahead, Cameron," Rose said. "I'll take care of your horse."

Cameron's steely eyes were sunken and worried. "That's kind of you, but I couldn't impose on you. It's not gentlemanly."

"It was my idea," Rose said. "Now go on." Rose shooed Cameron and Tricia into the house. "Go see Kat. I'm perfectly capable of taking care of three horses."

★ ★ ★ ★

"She's nice, Cam," Tricia said as Rose led the horses to the stable.

"Nice, yes," Cameron replied.

Mrs. Price was sitting in a chair in Katrina's room while Dr. Hinkman examined her.

"Mum, what happened?" Cameron asked.

"She came in burning up," Mrs. Price said.

"Cam?" Kat's little voice croaked.

"Yes, Kitty-Kat, I'm here."

"I don't feel too good."

"I know. The doctor is going to help you."

Rose came in and stood in the doorway of Kat's room.

"Lady Rose," Mrs. Price said. "What are you doing here?"

"I met Mr. Price while I was out riding. A nice young man who works here, said his name was Arnold, offered to see to the horses so I could come see how Kat is doing. How is she?"

"We don't know yet," Mrs. Price said.

"I don't like the look of it." The doctor shook his head. "It could be scarlet fever."

"No!" Mrs. Price clasped her hands to her face.

"We won't know for sure until the rash comes," Hinkman said, "but in the meantime, I'm going to have to quarantine all of you."

"Quarantine? Why?" Mrs. Price asked.

"Because you've all been exposed. We don't want an epidemic on our hands."

"I should get back to Laurel Ridge," Rose said.

"I'm sorry, my lady," the doctor said, "but you'll have to stay here. I can't take the chance that you'll expose everyone on the estate to scarlet fever."

"Oh my..."

"Rose, I'm sorry," Cameron said, ignoring the stern look from his mother upon using Rose's Christian name. "If I'd known, I would have stayed away from you today."

"Goodness, it's certainly not your fault. But where will I stay? I have no provisions, or anything."

"You can stay in the hired man's cabin out back. Arnold lives a mile away and walks here every day, so he doesn't use it," Mrs. Price said.

Rose? In a hired man's cabin? Cameron shook his head. "That wouldn't be appropriate, Mum."

"I'm sorry, Cam. It's all we have."

"Don't be silly, Mr. Price. I'll be fine. I'll just...send a message to the house and have a servant bring me my personals."

Rose's face paled. Cameron wasn't sure if it was because she was worried about Kat, or worried about getting scarlet fever herself, or because she would have to live as a peasant.

"Fine. I'll show her to the cabin," he said.

Cameron led Rose to the back door of the cottage. "I'm

really sorry about this, Rose."

"It's not your fault, Cameron. I just hope Kat will be all right."

"Yes, me too."

"She's strong," Rose said. "My brother had scarlet fever when he was not but seven. He made a full recovery."

"Thank God I have the commission money from the duke." Cameron wiped sweat from his brow. "She'll have the best medicine. I'm sending a message to Bath to that doctor the duke uses. What is his name?"

"Blake. Dr. Michael Blake."

"Yes, I want him to see Kat."

"I'm sure he'll be happy to come out."

Cameron warmed with embarrassment. How could he expect Rose to stay in such a tiny cabin? "This is it," he said, opening the door. It was sparse, but clean. A double bed stood on two wooden planks, and a slipper tub graced the corner. A small fireplace, two chairs, and a tiny table completed the decor. The windows were curtained with threadbare cotton. "Hardly fit for a daughter of an earl, is it?"

Rose smiled and touched his cheek. "I'll be fine." She rose on her toes to kiss his lips.

"This is why you and I can't be together, Rose. You shouldn't have to live like this. You deserve better."

"I'll decide what I deserve. In the meantime, you're stuck with me." She kissed him again. "I...I would like for you to come to me tonight."

Cameron held her close, his cock pulsating. "Are you sure?"

"Yes, I'm very sure. Perhaps this was fate." She shook her head. "Then again, I don't like to think that Kat got sick just so you and I could be together."

"No, I don't want to think that."

"Let's just take it as it comes," Rose said. "I'll help you and your mother care for Kat. I know how to treat a fever. And you and I will spend some time together. Now, I have need of some parchment and a quill. I'll send a note to Aunt Iris telling her what has happened and ask her to send me some personals."

★ ★ ★ ★

A servant arrived with Rose's personals and a note from Auntie Iris. As bid by Rose, the servant placed the items one hundred feet from the house, and Cameron fetched them after he had left and brought them to Rose in the cabin. When she was settled, she went to the main house and played the old upright pianoforte in the sitting room. It was a bit out of tune, and the sound twanged, as though the instrument belonged in a tavern, but Rose hoped the music might soothe Kat. Later, Rose sat with the little girl while Mrs. Price fixed a hearty beef stew for dinner. She cooled Kat with a cloth dipped in ice water and held her wrapped in blankets when she trembled with fever chills. Mrs. Price came in and relieved her, telling her to go to the table for supper.

The stew and brown bread were delicious, though completely different from the kind of meals Rose was accustomed to. Five courses were the usual on normal evenings, and at least eight for special occasions. Yet Rose found the stew satisfying and her hunger adequately sated. After dinner, she sat with Kat for another hour and read to her from Mr. Dickens's *Oliver Twist*, which Aunt Iris had sent in her valise. Tricia came in to relieve her when the sun went down, and she headed out the back door to the cabin.

Cameron knocked on her door soon after.

She greeted him with a smile. "I didn't expect you so soon."

"Actually, I'm not here for the night yet," he said. "I wanted to see if you needed me to bring you some water for your bath."

"Oh, would you, Cameron? That would be heavenly."

"Of course. I'll be back in a few minutes."

Cameron brought the water, lit a fire, and heated it. "Tell me about when your brother had scarlet fever."

"I wasn't born yet," Rose said. "In fact, Mummy was pregnant with me at the time, and Lily was just a babe, so the two of them were sent home to my grandparents."

"Surely they've told you the story."

"Yes, of course. Although there isn't much to tell, Cameron. He was quite sick for about a week, but the fever broke and he recovered. In fact, he thrived. He was a strong and able child, just like Kat. You've seen him, haven't you?"

"Yes, at the wedding ball."

"He's taller than average, about your size. No residual effect from the illness at all." She moved behind him and massaged his shoulders. "I know how hard it is when a loved one is ill. When Lily fell over a month ago, and we didn't know if she would make it, I was distraught."

"Kat has always been special to me," he said. "My father died a few weeks after she was born, and I was twenty, so I've basically been her father. I'm not sure I could love a child from my own loins any more than I love her."

"I understand," Rose said, "and I love her too. She's so full of life." She sat down on Cameron's lap, wrapping her arms around his neck. "She's going to come through this. I just know it."

Cameron kissed her chin. "I hope so, sweet."

Rose laced her fingers through Cameron's silky black hair. "Did your mother have trouble bearing children?"

"Why do you ask?"

"There's such a difference in all your ages," Rose said. "My mother lost two babes after she had Thomas. She had pretty much resigned herself to only having one child, and then Lily and I came along, less than a year apart."

"I recall one lost between Tricia and Kat," Cameron replied. "There may have been some between me and Tricia. I don't know."

"You're what, twenty-eight?"

"Twenty-seven."

"How old is Tricia?"

"Fifteen."

"She's a beauty," Rose said. "She's a female version of you, the same way Lily and Thomas are. You're going to have to watch the boys around her."

"I already do, believe me. How old are you, Rose?"

"Twenty."

He caressed her cheek. "A fair maiden of twenty." He stole a kiss. "You're the most beautiful woman I've ever laid eyes on."

Rose smiled, her heart pounding. "You're a flatterer, Mr. Price."

"But you are. You're light where I'm dark. Soft where I'm... *not* soft." He squeezed her breast. "It's extremely...bewitching. You're an angel. No one is as beautiful as you are."

"I look just like my mother, except that my eyes are a darker blue. Lily and Thomas look like our father."

"Your mother is a very pretty woman, but you..." He ran his fingers up and down her arms, making her tremble. "You are absolutely captivating." He reached behind her neck and pulled her head toward him, capturing her lips with his. When he released her, he said, "I almost feel like I can deal with all of this, having you here."

"You can deal with it," Rose said. "Kat will recover, and I will do whatever I can for her and for you."

"You're an angel," Cameron said. "I don't deserve you."

"Perhaps I don't deserve you," Rose teased.

Cameron rolled his head back and erupted in laughter. "Now that's funny." He twirled his finger through a loose curl. "Only an angel as sweet as you could be that deluded."

"I'm not deluded." Rose smiled. "I'm not as angelic as you think I am."

"I'll never believe that." He stood up, lifting her, and kissed her as he held her in his arms. "I think your bath water is warm enough now, sweet." He put Rose down gently, took the water from the grate, and poured it into the slipper tub. "I'll leave you now."

"No. Stay. I want you to."

"You want me to stay while you bathe?"

"Why not?" She suddenly wanted it more than anything. "Then you can bathe here when I'm done."

He smiled. "As tempting as that sounds, I need to go back in and check on Kat. I'll come to you later."

"Promise?"

"Yes." He kissed her chastely on the forehead and left.

Rose bathed quickly, her legs cramping in the small tub. She washed her hair and toweled it dry as best she could. She brushed her teeth, creamed her body with scented lotion, put on her nightdress, and lay down seductively on the bed and waited.

And waited.

After two hours, she finally wept herself to sleep.

CHAPTER FOUR

"Rose, Rose."

Someone nudged her. For a moment, Rose didn't know where she was, until her eyes adjusted to the dark and she recognized Cameron's handsome face.

"Cam?"

"Yes, sweetheart, it's me."

"Why didn't you come to me?" she asked, fumbling for a match to light a candle on the night table.

"Here, let me." He lit the lamp. "I'm sorry. Kat took a turn for the worse. My mother was beside herself. I couldn't leave her."

"My God." Rose's belly churned. "Is she all right now?"

"Yes. She had a seizure, but she came out of it."

"Why didn't you come to get me?"

"There was nothing you could have done." He stroked her cheeks. "You were crying."

She swallowed. "I...I thought you didn't want me."

He laughed softly. "How could you think that?"

"Well, you didn't come, and I didn't know about Kat. I'm just so glad you're here now. Hold me, will you?"

He climbed onto the bed with her and took her into his arms. She nestled into his embrace and kissed his mouth passionately, frantically tugging at his shirt.

"Slowly, sweetheart," he said. "I'll love you all night long."

"Will you, Cam?"

"I like it when you call me Cam," he said. "It sounds almost like we're...."

"What?"

"I don't know. Married, I guess. But that can never be."

"Are you saying...that you..." Rose gulped as her heart thumped wildly.

"I'm saying that I love you, Rose. God help me, but I do."

"Oh, Cam..."

"I can't fight it any longer. The constant battle drains me. It's like trying not to eat or sleep." He smoothed her hair lovingly. "I've never said that to a woman before."

She caressed his cheek. "You've given me a precious gift," she said. "I don't—"

"Shh," he said. "You don't have to say it back, sweetheart. I just wanted you to know."

"I want to say it back. But I'm frightened. What if we can never be together? And what am I going to tell Evan?"

"Xavier? I tell you I love you and you mention Xavier?" Cameron shook his head and moved away from her.

"Don't pull away from me. Please. I didn't mean to anger you. I...do love you. I do." She pulled him to her. "My God, it felt good to say it. It felt *right.*"

"Yes, it did." He kissed her throat. "I'm not going to share you, Rose."

"You won't have to. We'll figure something out. But we don't have to work it all out tonight. Tonight is for us. Let's not worry about anyone else. I just want to be with you. It's all I've thought about for weeks."

Cameron slowly unbuttoned Rose's nightdress. He eased it over her shoulders and pulled it down and off of her body, until she was naked. "You're so lovely, sweet Rose. So very beautiful."

Rose shivered. "The candle, Cam."

"No. I want to see you."

"But—"

"I want to know every inch of you, and I want you to know every inch of me. The candlelight—it makes your skin glow."

He lowered his head and kissed her, coaxing her lips open with the soft caress of his tongue. He nibbled on her lips, kissed her deeply. He brushed his lips over her cheeks, to her ear, and gently caressed it, pushing his tongue into the shallow cove.

"Oh, Cam..." She quivered, and energy surged between her legs.

He nibbled her neck and chest. "So beautiful, Rose. Your nipples are as dark pink as your sweet lips."

His words made her shiver, her every nerve on edge. He licked her nipples and they tightened into hard buds. Then he nipped at them, harder and harder, until her insides nearly imploded. She arched off the bed, entwining her fingers through his hair and holding him to her as he pleasured her breasts.

"Do you like that?"

"Oh, yes. It's wonderful."

"Then I know you'll like what's coming next." Cameron left her breasts and kissed and licked her abdomen, tickling her navel. When he reached her triangle of honey curls, she squirmed. He was going to see her private parts! Quickly she placed a hand over herself.

"Don't, sweetheart," he said.

"But you don't want to look at that."

"Yes, I do. Every part of you is beautiful to me." He

winked. "Especially *that* part."

"Wait, Cam," she said. "Take off your clothes. I want to touch you."

"I suppose that's only fair." He winked again and undressed quickly.

Rose sighed at his muscular shoulders and arms. His chest was smooth and rippled, with a sprinkling of black hair covering it. His well-formed legs were also smattered with black hair. His giant arousal stood straight out from a nest of black curls. She widened her eyes.

"That's what you felt through my trousers the other night," he said wickedly.

"I had no idea," she said. "No wonder you were in pain."

He laughed softly. "It's not so bad, sweet."

"I promise you won't leave here in pain tonight." She stared in awe. "You're magnificent to look at."

"No more than you are, Rose. Now, where were we?" He lowered his head to her sex.

She couldn't help herself. She covered herself with her hand again.

"Don't hide from me," he coaxed. "Please, sweetheart, open for me. Let me look at your pussy." He gently toyed with her intimate folds, delicately tugging at them.

Rose squeezed her eyes shut, warming and turning her head into the pillow. *Pussy.* She'd heard the word. But still, it made her shiver. She felt wicked. Wicked and...*aroused.*

"Do you know what these are?" he asked, stroking her.

Rose didn't answer.

"Do you, sweet?" he asked again.

"No," Rose said, burrowing farther into the pillow.

"They're another set of lips, and you know what lips are

meant for, don't you?"

Again she didn't reply.

"They're meant to be kissed," he said, and he lightly touched his mouth to her.

A bolt of lightning shot through her. Surely he didn't mean to kiss her there. What man would want to do that? "Cameron—"

"Let me," he said. "I want to taste you. You'll enjoy this. I promise."

"But why would you want—"

"Because I love you, Rose. I love every part of you. From the top of your head to the tips of your toes, and every tiny bit in between, including your beautiful pussy. Let me give you pleasure."

Cameron slithered his tongue up and down over her opening. Rose sighed. It felt amazing, as if every nerve ending in her body were being stimulated. Cameron pushed her thighs forward until her intimate area was completely vulnerable to him. He kissed the insides of her thighs, leaving them moist. Then she shivered as he cast his hot breath upon the wetness. He moved back to her sex, licking in long languid strokes and pushing his tongue into her. She arched off the bed, moaning. He grabbed her across the belly and forced her down, making her lie still. His tongue moved upward, finding her swollen peak, swirling around it lightly, and then not so lightly.

"Oh, Cam, that's so...so..."

Soon he was sucking her, and when he filled her with a finger she arched again. This time he didn't hold her still. He moved with her, his finger moving in and out in a languorous rhythm, while his mouth teased her nub, making it throb beneath his tongue. Rose moved with him, running and running in her mind, until she reached the plateau. She shouted his name as she climaxed, her sex hugging his finger, convulsing, as he continued to lick her, nursing her through the crashing waves of joy, until the sweet rapture enveloped her and she went limp beneath him.

Slowly he moved toward her, kissing her abdomen, her breasts, her throat, her mouth. "Taste your juices," he said. "Taste how sweet you are."

Rose opened to him, swirled her tongue with his and tasted the tanginess of her own body. She kissed him hard, her desire overwhelming. She wanted to mark him. Brand him as hers.

The passionate kiss continued until Cameron broke away and inhaled sharply.

"My God, Rose. I've never been kissed like that." He panted against her neck. "I love you so much."

Rose rained tiny kisses against his moist neck. "What you...did to me was exquisite. I love you too."

"I licked your pussy, sweet." He chuckled against her neck.

"Cam..." Heat spread through her body.

"I do adore you, my Rose. You know you won't turn to stone if you say it."

"I know. It's just—"

He cupped her cheek. "I understand. And I'm so sorry that the next part might hurt a bit."

"I don't care."

"I do. I don't want to hurt you."

"Someone will have to do it eventually," Rose said. "I want it to be you, Cam. Only you."

"Touch me." He led her hand to his swollen shaft.

Rose grasped him. "It's so hard, Cam."

He laughed. "Of course it is. It's for you, my darling. Only for you."

"I don't know what to do."

"Just kiss me...and let me come inside you."

His mouth came down on hers, and she released his cock, using both of her hands to caress his muscular back and shoulders. His erection nudged against her.

"Are you sure this time?" he asked.

"Yes, Cam." Her body was on fire. "Yes. In fact, if you don't make love to me now, I think I may actually die!"

He stroked her lips lightly. "I assure you, you won't die." He smiled, and then turned serious. "You need to understand, Rose. When I come inside your body, that makes you mine."

"I want to be yours. I never wanted anything more—" She gasped as he stabbed her virginal flesh.

"I'm so sorry. I tried to hold on. I'll stop if you—"

"No, don't stop. I'm all right."

Slowly he descended into her, inch by inch. The stab changed to a burn. Still moving slowly. How large was he, anyway? And how deep was her...pussy? Finally he stopped moving.

"Are you in now?" she asked.

"Yes, sweet," he groaned. "I feel like you were made for me. How do you feel?"

"Well...full, I guess." She laughed a little. "Now what?"

"I'm going to move inside you. You tell me if you can't take it, all right?"

"Yes, Cam. Don't worry. I want to please you."

He pulled out of her, teasing her entrance, and plunged back in. The burning wasn't as bad this time, and his moans made her tingle. She was making him feel good, and that made *her* feel good. He repeated the motion several times, until the burning turned to longing. Then he circled his hips, moving inside of her, helping her get used to his invasion. His movements nudged her peak, sending shivers to her each time he collided with her. Soon she was climaxing again, grabbing his behind and pulling him into her.

"Oh, Cam, Cam," she moaned.

He pulled out and thrust back into her, his body trembling as his cock pulsated inside her. "God, Rose. My God." He collapsed on top of her and kissed her lips, her cheeks, her neck. "I'll never love another."

"Nor will I," she said, sighing softly.

"So, my sweet Rose." He turned them onto their sides, his cock still embedded in her. "What are we going to do now?" He threaded his fingers through her hair.

"I don't know," Rose said. "I wish I did, Cam."

"I've ruined you, sweetheart."

"I don't feel ruined."

"You are. And you've ruined me for anyone else. If you won't marry me, I'll die a monk."

Rose giggled. "You can't be serious."

"I am. I swear it. I'll take you to Gretna Green tonight, and you'll be mine by the end of the week."

"I'm yours already." She kissed his chin. "But we can't."

"Why not?"

"Well, for one thing, we're under quarantine. We can't leave. And there's Kat to consider. She might need us. And of course there's my family."

"No doubt they'd frown on me for a son-in-law."

"I won't lie to you. They won't be happy. Except for Lily.

She won't judge us. But I don't care. You're the one I want."

"And Xavier?"

"Well...that's a touchy situation. He's bringing his father to Laurel Ridge next weekend to meet me. I...I don't want to hurt him, Cam. He's been kind and generous with me, and he doesn't deserve what I'm going to do to him."

"Has he mentioned marriage to you?"

"No, not yet."

Cameron stroked her bare arms, making her shudder. "Rose, I should tell you... Oh, never mind." He got up from the bed.

"You're not leaving, are you?" Rose said.

"No, sweet. I'm just getting a warm cloth."

"What for?"

"To take care of you. There might be some blood." He wet a cloth in the lukewarm water in the basin and wrung it out. "Open your legs for me."

"I can't get used to you saying that," Rose giggled.

"Why?"

"It makes me feel so wicked."

He nudged her thighs apart. "It's not a wicked thing for the man who loves you to take care of you. Now, come on." He gently rubbed the cloth over Rose's intimate area.

The warm cloth soothed her. "Is there any blood?"

"Just a little. Does it hurt?"

"Not really. Not so much that I couldn't do it again." She smiled.

"No, sweet, you need to rest. Your body needs to heal a little."

"When can we do it again?"

He chuckled. "On the morrow, if you wish it."

"Oh, I wish it," she said, pulling him to her and kissing his lips. "Will you stay with me tonight?"

"I shouldn't. Kat might need me in the middle of the night."

"Please. I want to sleep in your arms."

"What on earth made me think I might be able to resist you?" He kissed her cheek. "All right, but I'm going to run to the house and check on Kat first."

"Mmmm. Don't forget to come back." Rose cuddled under the covers, closing her eyes.

"I won't."

When dawn broke, Rose woke up in Cameron's arms. He was snuggled against her, spoon fashion. She lifted his hand to her lips, kissed it, and whispered. "You came back."

He answered with a soft snore.

★ ★ ★ ★

Rose awoke to a soft knocking. She wiggled out from Cameron's arms, hastily pulled a dressing gown over her head, and padded to the door. "Yes?" she said through the door.

"My lady," came Mrs. Price's voice, "Dr. Blake is here. Have you seen Cam this morning?"

Rose's skin heated, even though Mrs. Price couldn't see her. "N-No, I haven't, Mrs. Price." She hated lying. Oh, what had she gotten herself into? "But I'd like to speak to the doctor. I know him quite well. I'll be in shortly."

"All right, my lady. Good morning."

Rose hurried back to the bed and nudged Cameron. "Cam," she said. "Cam, you need to wake up."

His eyes flashed open for an instant and he rubbed them

sleepily. He gave Rose a toothy grin, and then grabbed her and pulled her down for a kiss. "Good morning, sweet."

Rose gazed at his handsome face, his wide smile. She seldom saw him smile, and what a treat it was. His two front teeth overlapped slightly. This tiny imperfection in his otherwise flawless male beauty was irresistibly attractive. She loved running her tongue over the ridge that the overlapping tooth created. That she was the source of his cheerful grin filled her with joy.

Although tempted to stay in bed with him, Rose said, "Cam, we can't do this right now. Your mother was just at the door. She was looking for you. I...I told her that I hadn't seen you."

"You could have told her I was here," Cam said. "I have nothing to hide."

"No, I couldn't have. It's scandalous!" She kissed the tip of his nose, giggling. "But we need to get dressed. Dr. Blake is here to examine Kat, and we should speak with him. I'll get dressed and go in first, and you can come in a couple minutes later and make some excuse for where you've been."

"Of course we should, just as soon as I ravish you." Cameron pulled her down on the bed and rolled over on top of her, kissing her deeply.

He was naked, and his arousal poked her thigh through her dressing gown.

"Get off me, you rogue," she giggled, when he released her lips.

"No, I don't think I will," he whispered in her ear.

She ran her hands lightly up and down his muscular arms. "Oh, Cam. I do love you, and I do want you, but we must go see Dr. Blake."

Cameron rolled off of her. "You're wonderful, do you know that?"

"So are you." She tumbled off the bed and threw his trousers at him. "Now get dressed, love of my life."

"Yes, my lady." He saluted her. "Is this what I have to look forward to with you? Commands and drills?" He arched his eyebrows in a lazy grin.

"This isn't even the half of it." Rose threw his shirt at him, giving him a sensual glance. "But you'll survive."

"Maybe." He stood up and grabbed her, pinching her bottom. "But even if I don't, it's a hell of a way to go." He kissed her mouth quickly.

Rose dressed in a clean morning gown and left the cabin.

★ ★ ★ ★

Cameron took his time dressing. Kat was in good hands with Dr. Blake. He needed a shave, but his razor and lotion were in his chamber. He raked his hands through his hair and hoped he didn't look too much like a man who had just spent the night making love to the woman of his dreams.

Ugh. He'd have to send notice to Xavier and tell him he couldn't take the commission. He'd wanted to tell Rose about it last night, but he lost his nerve.

But no time to think about that now. Kat was waiting. When Rose had been gone about fifteen minutes, he ventured out the door.

"What in God's name are you doing, Cameron?"

His mother's voice startled him. He turned and saw that she had been waiting for him on the side of the cabin, out of Rose's view when she went to the house.

"Good morning, Mum. How's Kat this morning?"

"The same."

"Oh." Cameron's heart lurched in worry for his little sister. "Well, at least we have a decent doctor to look at her."

"Cam"—her voice was low and serious—"she's a lady of the peerage."

He cleared his throat. "I know who and what she is."

"You're just going to get yourself hurt. You know that, don't you?"

"What makes you think we're not just...fooling around?"

She scoffed. "Ladies like her don't fool around, Cam. You know that as well as I do." Then, "My God, you didn't force her, did you?"

He nearly snapped his neck at the accusation. "Do you really think I would do something like that?"

"I'm sorry." She shook her head. "Of course you wouldn't. I'm sorry."

Cameron raked his fingers through his sweaty hair. This was not the kind of subject he normally discussed with his mother. "Everything will work out."

"Are you daft? Either she'll break your heart, or you'll break hers."

"It's not that simple. I...I'm in love with her."

"Christ."

"She loves me too. She told me so."

"Sweet Jesus Christ."

"I'm going to marry her, Mum. I don't know how, but I'm going to. There's no one else for me."

"Holy Mother of God, sweet Jesus Christ, Cam." His mother shook her head at him and headed toward the house.

Cameron followed, entering the back way behind his

mother and walking into Kat and Tricia's room.

Kat appeared to be resting comfortably, her small hand in Rose's. Cameron cleared his throat.

"Ah, you must be Mr. Price." The doctor looked up. "Michael Blake. Good to meet you."

The doctor was a young—very young—man with reddish-blond hair and brown eyes. He didn't look any older than twenty-five years. Could he truly care for Kat?

Cam held out his hand. "Thank you for coming out, Doctor."

"Of course. Anything for a friend of Lady Rose. I've examined your sister, and I don't think she has scarlet fever."

"But Doc said—" Mrs. Price began.

"I'm sure your doctor is a fine man. Doctors disagree all the time. That's why it's called the practice of medicine. What is your doctor's name?"

"Hinkman," Mrs. Price said. "Sawyer Hinkman."

"Has he taken care of Kat before?"

"Of course," Mrs. Price said. "Doc takes care of all of us around here. He's been doing it for years."

"I've never heard of him. Do you know where he went to medical school?"

"No, I don't."

"It's possible that he didn't. He probably practices by experience, which works out most of the time. In this case, however, I think he made a mistake."

"Why don't you think it's scarlet fever?" Cameron asked.

"First of all, there's no rash yet. It usually occurs within a day, but can take two so I'm not making my determination on that fact alone." Dr. Blake rubbed his forehead. "Your sister's throat isn't red, and there has been no vomiting. She shows no signs of abdominal pain or distress. These are all common symptoms of scarlet fever."

"What is it then, Doctor?" Rose asked.

"I'm not sure, to be honest. I don't think it's small pox, because again, there's no rash."

"Let us have it," Cameron said.

"Your sister is not very responsive. I had to prick her foot with a needle before she gave me any reaction, yet she shows no signs of febrile delirium. The seizure your mother described concerns me also." Blake massaged the nape of his neck. "I'd like for her to be hospitalized in Bath."

"No!" Mrs. Price cried. "I won't have it. People go to hospitals to...to die!"

"I understand your concern, Mrs. Price," the doctor said, "but hospitals have come a long way in the last several years. The hospital in Bath is state of the art and specializes in the treatment of patients. Surgeries are performed there, and illnesses are cured."

"But—"

"You can of course continue to care for her at home," Blake said. "But when I can't make a firm diagnosis, I prefer my patients to be under the care of professionals who can respond to any unforeseen issues that may occur."

Cameron swallowed the lump that had formed in his throat. Hospitals cost money. A lot of money. But Kat's life was worth whatever it cost.

"Have you seen anything like this before?" he asked.

"Yes, I have."

"And..." Rose urged.

"Sometimes patients recover, and sometimes they don't."

Cameron caught his mother as she swayed into his arms.

"But she's a strong, healthy little girl, and she'll have the best chance in a hospital with professional care all day and night."

Cameron's gut felt hollow as his mother sobbed against him. "What would that kind of care cost, Blake?"

"Unfortunately, it's not inexpensive," Blake said. "The facility in Bath is state of the art, and fees run up to five pounds per day, and then there are doctor fees and nursing fees, as well as medication and supplies."

"Dear Lord," Mrs. Price said, weeping.

"And of course for a child of Kat's age, a parent should accompany her, and room and board for that will be another couple of pounds per week."

Cameron took a deep breath. "I see."

"If it will help, I will cut my fees, especially since you are friends of Lady Rose and the Duke and Duchess of Lybrook."

"That's not necessary," Cameron said.

"Cam—" Rose began.

"We've no need of charity, Doctor," Cameron said. "I'll see that payment is made."

"As you wish," Blake said. "And since I've ruled out scarlet fever and small pox, there's no need to continue the quarantine."

"How soon should we leave for Bath?" Cameron asked.

"The sooner the better. I'd be happy to transport her and your mother in my carriage, since I'm going back there anyway."

"We'd be obliged," Cameron said, "and we will of course pay you for the transport."

"That's really not necessary," Blake said. "I'm going anyway."

"I'll pay for it, damn it!"

Rose touched Cameron's arm, but he nudged her away.

"Mum, pack up a valise for you and Kat. I'm sure the doctor would like to leave right away."

"Cam," Mrs. Price said, "it's so much money."

"It's Kat's life, Mum. There's no price on that." He walked from the room, down the hall, and out the back door.

Rose followed him. "Cam, she's going to be all right." She took his hand. "She's a strong little girl, and she'll have the best care."

"Yes, yes," Cameron said. "Yes, I know."

"What can I do for you? Tell me. I'll do anything."

"Damn it, Rose, I don't need your charity either!" He wrenched his hand free of hers.

"I'm not offering charity. I just want to help. I love Kat, and I love you!" She pulled at his arm. "Please don't turn me away."

"I need to make some money, Rose. Some more money. And there's only one way for me to— Damn it all to hell!" He pulled her to him and embraced her, holding her as if a cyclone were trying to whirl her away from him.

He had to take Xavier's commission now. He didn't have a choice. With Xavier's money, he could pay for Kat's medical needs and still have enough left over to get his mother and sisters out of the cottage and into a townhouse in London. They deserved that much.

He would write a song for Xavier to give to Rose. For another man's proposal to the woman he loved.

He had to let Rose go.

CHAPTER FIVE

Dr. Blake left with Mrs. Price and Kat soon after, and Rose went to the cabin to gather her personals. The quarantine had been lifted and Kat didn't need her. She was worried about Kat and thankful she would be getting the best care available. She was also worried about Cameron. He was acting so strangely. But of course he was. Kat meant everything to him. Rose wished she could do more.

Rose was fastening her valise when Cameron opened the door to the cabin. She looked up. Dark circles marred his beautiful eyes, and agony rolled off of him in waves.

Her heart lurched. "Cam, I've been worried about you."

He strode toward her with purpose, as if he were stalking prey. "I want to love you, Rose. Now. Please." He grabbed her and kissed her hard.

"I—"

He stopped her with his kisses, and her muffled words disappeared in his passion. He moved to her neck, biting it, licking it, inhaling deeply. "Your scent. I'll never forget your strawberry scent."

"Cam, what on earth?"

"Please, sweetheart," he said, "just once more, so I can remember you."

"Remember me? What do you—"

His mouth was on hers again, drinking of her, feasting on her, taking from her. She gave willingly everything she had.

How she loved him! He was beside himself with worry, and she would do whatever she could for him.

Cameron walked toward the door without releasing Rose, locked it, lifted her in his arms, and set her gently on the bed. He climbed on top of her, still kissing her passionately while he fumbled with her bodice. He freed her aching breasts and buried his face between them.

"I'll never see beauty such as yours again in my life," he said. "I'll remember this day always, sweet. I'll remember that once, just once, an angel loved me."

"I'll always love you," Rose said. "You don't need to talk like that. Oh! That feels so good, Cam." Rose arched off the bed, struggling to be free of her dress.

Cameron ripped the rest of her clothes off with lightning speed, paused for just a moment to gaze at her, and then undressed and returned to the bed.

"Love me, Rose," he said. "Love me."

"I do, Cam," Rose breathed. "Tell me what you want. I'll do anything for you."

"Would you?"

"Yes, you know I would."

"Would you kiss me here?" He pointed to his mouth.

She pulled him to her and kissed him, letting her tongue invade his spicy sweetness.

"Here?" He pointed to the hollow of his throat.

She pushed him down on the bed and climbed atop him, kissing and licking the sensitive spot on his neck. He groaned her name.

"And here?" He pointed to his chest.

She ran her tongue through the fine black hair, licking his nipples as they hardened beneath her loving touch. He tasted of salt and musk and perfection. He tasted of the man she loved.

Cameron groaned. "What about here?" he said, gesturing to his raging erection.

Surprisingly, the idea didn't repulse her. In fact, she found she wanted nothing more. She loved every part of him, and she wanted to please him, so she lowered her head. She buried her face in his black curls, inhaling the musky scent of his sex. She ran her fingers through them, memorizing their texture and silkiness. Then she grasped his arousal and kissed the head of his cock. He gasped, and she smiled. She had given him pleasure. She twirled her tongue around it, and then tried to fit it in her mouth. He was so large, but what little she could do made him moan and writhe beneath her.

"That's the way, sweetheart. Love me."

"I do love you, Cam," she said, licking her way down and then back up. She kissed the sensitive skin between his thighs and smiled at his groan. Then she returned to his cock, spreading kisses over every inch of it, licking and stroking the head and sucking it into her mouth.

"Come here, Rose," he said, his voice filled with smoke. "Come love me this way."

She moved forward and kissed his lips as he gently positioned her over his erection.

"Tell me if it hurts, my darling." He eased her down upon his hardness.

"Oh!" The tip of his cock nudged her hardened clitoris. "No, Cam, it doesn't hurt. It feels— Oh!"

He was embedded completely inside of her body.

"You're so tight, sweetheart."

"Is that good?"

"God, yes." He lifted her hips. "Here, move on me, my love."

He lifted her and brought her back down, showing her the rhythm. When she had caught it, he moved one hand to her breast and toyed with her nipple, sending shock waves straight into her. With his other hand, he fingered her swollen peak. Slowly he massaged her as she made love to him.

She rode him up and down, her whole body blazing, circling her hips and finding a spot inside her that made her burn.

"Cam, Cam!" She moved faster, harder.

"That's it, sweet. Make it feel good. Show me how good my cock feels in your wet pussy."

His bold words sent fiery thrills through her, and she brought one hand to her other breast, pinching her nipple into a tight bud.

"Beautiful, Rose. So beautiful when you touch yourself like that."

His words exploded through her, and she reached the pinnacle she had come to know. She sobbed his name as his fingers kept working, forcing her to the crest again, and then again.

When she didn't think she could take one more climax, Cameron shoved his hips upward and groaned.

"Take me, Rose. Take all of me." He winced as if in pain, and then his features softened.

Rose collapsed on top of Cameron. He kissed her moist, swollen lips and cradled her to his chest.

"Sleep with me," he said.

She smiled and closed her eyes.

★ ★ ★ ★

Cameron awoke an hour later with Rose still nestled in his arms. He got up quietly, trying not to disturb her, dressed, and went back to the house. He found Tricia and told her to go to the next farm and stay with Mrs. Cooke until tomorrow because he would be gone all night on a special errand for the doctor. It was a lie, but he needed to get Tricia out of the house. He found a piece of parchment and a quill and sat down to write a note to Rose. He had to be harsh. He had to make her believe that he had never loved her. His stomach churned, but he swallowed back the nausea. His heart would heal. He hadn't a choice.

He should never have made love to her. His mother was right. He'd known it himself. He'd foolishly allowed himself to believe he could have something that innocent, that beautiful, that precious...

No, not Cameron Price. He hadn't been born for beauty. He would not make that mistake again.

A tear forming in his eye, he began to write.

Rose,

Tricia and I have gone to Bath to take care of our mother and Kat. Don't try to find me. I don't want you to. I told you I loved you so you would sleep with me.

Cameron

His tear fell on the parchment, smearing the ink. Damn it! He crumpled up the paper and threw it in the grate. He grabbed another, and then thought better of it. As much as it would hurt him, he needed to speak to Rose in person. She deserved that much. He hastily scribbled a note to be delivered to Laurel Ridge, requesting a carriage to fetch Rose and her belongings. He strolled out onto the main road and walked until he found a boy on horseback willing to deliver it for a couple of farthings. Then he went to the stable, groomed Begonia, and led her out to wait for the carriage.

When the carriage arrived, Cameron went to the cabin to fetch Rose. His throat constricted. She was so lovely, so angelic. And she loved him. He steeled himself for what lay ahead.

"Rose." He nudged her. "Rose, wake up."

She opened her eyes, yawning. "Cam?"

"You need to get up. A carriage is here to take you back to the estate. Come on, get packed up."

"Kiss me first." She reached for him.

How he ached to kiss her! But he stepped away from the bed. "No, you must leave."

"Cam?" Her blue eyes widened.

"Now, Rose. I...I'm tired of this."

"Tired of what? What are you talking about?" She sat up.

He swallowed, willing himself to be strong. "Tired of *you*, Rose."

"You can't be serious."

"I am serious. I...you and I...we don't belong together. We never did."

"Of course we do. You're not thinking straight, Cam. You're worried about Kat. I don't blame you." She stood and reached for him.

He used every ounce of strength he possessed not to rush into her arms. "That's not it. I mean...of course I'm worried about Kat. But, I...we...can't continue this...*tryst*."

"Tryst?" Her eyes glistened.

"Of course. That's all it was. A tryst. It could never be any more. We both know that."

"Cam, you're not making any sense at all. I...we just made love. You...you came to me. You needed me. I need you."

"Don't be ridiculous."

"I'm not being ridiculous." She sniffed. "Let me help you. I'll do anything I can for you and for Kat."

"For God's sake, I'm perfectly capable of taking care of my own family." He swallowed. "Now I want you to get out of here."

"All right, Cam," she said, turning. "If that's what you want, I'll leave. But I'll be at Laurel Ridge, and I want you to come if you need me."

"I won't. It's over, Rose."

"But—" Her eyes filled with tears. "You said you loved me!"

Cameron looked away from her. Her tears hurt him more than a thousand punches to his face. "I...I lied to you Rose."

"No, you didn't," she sobbed.

"Yes. I...lied to you so you would sleep with me." He shut his eyes, unable to look at her. He deserved to burn in hell for this.

"No. You love me. I felt how much you love me. You wanted to take me to Gretna Green." Still naked from their lovemaking, she grabbed him around the waist and buried her face in his strong shoulder. "I love you. You can't mean any of this. You can't!"

Filled with self-loathing, he wrenched her body away. "Cover yourself. Then leave. Your carriage is waiting out front."

"Cam, don't do this!"

He turned, walked toward the door, and opened it.

Without looking back at her, he said, without emotion, "Go back to Xavier, my lady. I don't want you."

Then he left, the sound of her crying still hammering in his head, even when he was beyond hearing distance. He stood in the stables for a half hour, watching from a small window, waiting until he saw Rose step into the carriage and drive away, Begonia trotting along behind.

Only then did he sit down in the hay and sob.

★ ★ ★ ★

When she returned to Laurel Ridge, Rose went straight to her chamber. Her eyes were swollen from crying, and her body ached with yearning for Cameron. Cameron, who was no longer hers. Who maybe never had been.

His cruelty had hurt, yet she still loved him, and she wanted to help him and Kat. She found her reticule and dug out the one hundred pounds she kept for emergencies. She hastily scribbled a note to Dr. Blake, asking him to please use the money for Kat's care and not to tell Mrs. Price or Cameron about it. She could trust Blake. He was Daniel's personal physician and he had taken excellent care of Lily after her fall. She called for a maid and asked her to give the envelope to Crawford and have it delivered to Dr. Michael Blake in Bath.

There. She had done all she could for Cameron. He was on his own now, as he wished to be. Rose curled up on her bed and cried some more.

★ ★ ★ ★

The next few days passed in a fog for Rose. Sophie and Alexandra tried to engage her, but she spent most of her time in her chamber, feigning illness. Finally, the morning Evan and his father were due to arrive, she forced herself to go down and join the others for breakfast in the ladies' sitting room.

"Rose, dear," Aunt Iris said, "it's so good to see you up and about. I trust you're feeling better?"

"Yes, much," Rose lied. "I didn't want to be ill for Lord Evan's visit."

"Yes, that would certainly break his heart," Lucinda Landon, the dowager duchess's sister, agreed. "He hasn't missed a weekend with you yet, has he?"

"No, not since the house party ended." Rose didn't want to talk about Evan. "Has anyone heard anything about young Katrina Price? I've been thinking about her."

"No, dear," Maggie, the dowager duchess, said, "but Crawford can send an inquiry if you'd like."

"Thank you, I'd appreciate that."

A servant brought Rose a plate of smoked salmon with tomatoes and capers, a scone with lemon curd, and a hardboiled egg. Rose mumbled her thanks and forced herself to eat. She needed strength to deal with meeting Evan's father.

"Oh!" She clasped a hand to her mouth. "I'm so sorry, Aunt Lucy, Aunt Maggie. With Kat's illness and then my own, I forgot to tell you. Lord Evan is bringing his father this weekend to meet me. I hope that won't be any trouble."

"Of course not, dear," Maggie replied. "We'd love to have the earl."

Aunt Iris went pale. "The Earl of Brighton is coming this weekend?"

"Yes, Auntie. I'm sorry I didn't tell you sooner."

"Oh, it's quite all right, Rose. Quite all right..."

"Is something the matter, Iris?" Lucy asked.

"No, no, of course not, Lucy." Aunt Iris fidgeted with a napkin. "Will they be arriving tonight, as usual, for dinner?"

"Yes, I assume so," Rose said. "Then leaving Sunday afternoon."

"Goodness," Aunt Iris said. "All right, then."

"Mother, what on earth is the matter?" Alexandra asked. "You're white as a ghost."

"I'm fine, dear. Just fine. I'm a little tired is all. I didn't sleep at all well last night."

"I'm sorry to hear that," Lucy said. "Is there anything wrong with your chamber?"

"No, no, it's fine."

"Well, if you have any more trouble, do come to me. I have a wonderful elixir that will guarantee a restful sleep."

"Thank you, Lucy. I will." Aunt Iris rose. "If you all will excuse me, I think I'll take a brisk walk. That may...er...wake me up a bit."

"I'll accompany you," Lucy said.

"You needn't bother."

"It's no bother. I enjoy a nice morning walk. If the rest of you will excuse me?"

★ ★ ★ ★

Iris stood on the front terrace, her reflection staring back at her in a small puddle. She pursed her lips. She was tall, like her daughter Alexandra, and had thick golden hair, streaked with only minimal silver. Though not as classically beautiful as her sister, Flora, the Countess of Ashford, she was attractive, with an oval face and high cheekbones, almond-shaped hazel eyes and a wide full-lipped mouth. Her nose had always bothered her. She thought it too large for her face. Thankfully her daughters' noses were smaller. They were both beautiful girls, and she had no doubt that they would make fine matches. She hadn't been so lucky.

Awkwardly shy when she was younger, she hadn't received an offer after four seasons, so at twenty-five, her parents, the Baron and Baroness White, had married her to Angus MacIntyre, the Earl of Longarry, a short and stout Scotsman, whose holdings were in jeopardy. He was attracted by Iris's substantial dowry. She was transported to Scotland for a quick ceremony attended only by her parents. Angus had been jovial, even affectionate...until Iris's parents returned to London. After that he had become abusive, especially when it took five years for her to give him a child, and then it was a girl, Sophie. Two years later Alexandra came along. The earl became a tyrant. He raped Iris weekly, demanding an heir, but one never came. He mistreated his children as well, blaming them for not being boys. Longarry had died of consumption two years previously, leaving Iris and the girls penniless. But penniless was so much better than living with Longarry. Iris thanked God every day that he was gone. And she thanked God for her sister and brother-in-law, the Earl and Countess of Ashford, who had supported her and the girls since his death.

Despite her hatred of him, Iris had been a good wife to the earl. She had taken care of his estate, what little was left of it, seen to his needs, and had never strayed from his bed. Except for once.

"Are you ready, Iris?"

Iris jumped at Lucy's voice, her thoughts muddling, as did her reflection when a bird dropped into the puddle.

"Yes, yes, let's go."

"Now, tell me," Lucy said, as they began walking down a stony path. "What is going on?"

"Oh, nothing, really."

"Iris, we may have lost touch over the years, but we were best friends once. Something is bothering you, and I'd wager a guess that it has something to do with our weekend visitors."

Iris sighed. She had kept the secret for nearly twenty years. "Oh, Lucy, it's... Oh I can't even say it."

"Of course you can, dear. I'll keep your confidence, if that is what you require."

"I definitely require confidence. And..."

"And what?"

"If you could possibly...not judge me too harshly."

"I won't. Goodness, Iris, what is it?"

"It's the Earl of Brighton," Iris said, swallowing to keep her voice from cracking. "I...had an affair with him."

Lucy's eyes widened. "How in the world?"

"It was about twenty years ago. Sophie was two and Ally was just a babe, and the girls and I had traveled to Hampshire for a house party at Flora's estate. Longarry stayed in Scotland to tend to business matters, and frankly, I was looking forward to escaping him for a month. Oh, it was so beautiful, Lucy, and Lily and Rose's nannies took care of my girls, so I had a lot of time to myself. Walking about the estate one day, I met David."

"The Earl of Brighton."

"Yes. You know how shy I always was, but somehow I could talk to him. We walked and laughed, and he introduced me to his children, who were romping about. Young Evan was six, Miranda was seven, and Jacob, his heir, was ten. I asked to meet his wife, but he said the countess had been feeling poorly and had chosen to go to Bath, to take to the waters for a month."

"Oh, Iris."

"As you can imagine, one thing led to another. We shared a bed for most of the house party. I had only recently recovered from having Ally, and I hadn't slept with Longarry in quite some time. He found my pregnant belly unattractive. Frankly I was glad for the respite. Being with David was...lovely. Just lovely."

"What of his wife?"

"It wasn't a love match. They had been promised to each other since birth. Still, he told me that he had never strayed from her until me."

"And you believed him?"

"I did, actually. Perhaps it was silly, but I believed him. He told me that he loved me."

"And did you love him?"

Iris warmed at the memory. "Yes, Lucy, I did. He was kind and compassionate. Tender and loving. Everything that Longarry wasn't. Plus he was handsome as the devil."

"Yes, that he was. He still is."

"Have you seen him recently?"

"About two years ago, at his wife's funeral. He hasn't ventured out much since then. Even before then, he wasn't much for house parties. I wonder why he attended the one where he met you?"

"Perhaps because his wife went to Bath. I don't know." Iris drew a deep breath, hoping to calm her nerves. "Lucy, I never told anyone about this, not even Flora. I was always afraid it would get back to Longarry, and then he would..."

"He would what, Iris?"

"He would...beat me, or rape me, or do something else

horrid."

"Iris!" Lucy stopped walking. "I had no idea. I'm so sorry."

"The girls and I persevered. I shielded them from as much of it as I could, although he wasn't kind to them. I know it's terrible, but I'm so glad he's gone."

"Of course you are. Who wouldn't be?" Lucy led her to a small bench.

Iris sat down, her body full of...what? She wasn't sure. She turned to her friend. "David and I, we really were in love. But we weren't free to be together. He was so passionate, Lucy, so loving. He—" Iris smiled slyly. "He made love so sweetly. He made me feel beautiful and desirable."

"You are, Iris. You are."

"I never thought I was. Flora was always the beautiful one, and she caught Ashford on her own, when she was not but eighteen. But David made me feel like I was everything to him. The way he looked at me... He was wonderful." Iris lowered her voice. "He did the most scandalous thing."

"What?"

"Well, I was nursing Ally at the time, and he...he drank my milk from me."

Lucy gasped.

"I know it's wicked," Iris continued. "He did things to me that I never imagined. It was heavenly."

"Did you tell him about how Longarry treated you?"

"Only small bits and pieces. I didn't tell him about the violence, but I did tell him that the earl wasn't kind, and that I didn't love him."

"What did he tell you about his wife?"

"Only that she was a fine woman, a good mother to his children, but that he didn't love her."

"Did she love him?"

"He didn't know. It wasn't something they talked about."

Lucy patted her hand. "What are you going to do?"

"I don't know. I've been both anticipating and dreading this moment since Rose took up with Lord Evan. I knew our paths would eventually cross again. Now that we're both widowed…" She shook her head. "No, it's been too long."

"Perhaps not. How did you end things?"

"We went our separate ways. We decided not to continue the affair. It would have been too difficult, with my living in Scotland. Plus, he had no desire to hurt his wife, and although I didn't mind hurting Longarry, I knew how he would react if he ever found out. So we parted as friends."

"And you haven't seen him since?"

"No."

"Well, Iris, take out your best dress, because you're going to see him tonight at dinner."

"Good Lord," Iris said, sighing softly. "Good Lord in heaven."

CHAPTER SIX

Kat is the same.

The message said no more. Cameron paced, reading the note in his mother's hand dated two days previously. Damn it! How was he supposed to exist this way, with this kind of news? He wanted to go to Bath. Better yet, go somewhere else. Saddle up Apollo and just ride. Ride away from this torturous existence that fate had dealt him.

But he couldn't. He had to stay here in his stupid little cottage on the Lybrook land. He had to look after Tricia. He had to write that goddamned song for Xavier to give to Rose.

His Rose.

No. No longer *his* Rose. He had let her go.

If only his heart could accept that sad truth.

But she still haunted him—the angel who never left his thoughts. Her beauty tormented him during all waking hours, and he couldn't even escape her at night, as his dreams were filled with her kisses, her lush body enveloping his, her lips telling him that she loved him. He was consumed by her for all time. He would never love another woman.

He couldn't shake the look on her angelic face, the sound of her velvet voice, the tremors of her body when he had turned her away. Revoked his love for her. He'd never told a bigger lie, and the pain on her delicate features was etched in his mind for all time.

But for Kat, he felt he wouldn't want to live at all.

Tricia was at the stove, putting something together for their dinner. Cameron had to eat, but he had no appetite.

Worry for Kat.

Loneliness for Rose.

Hatred for himself.

No happiness. No contentment. No peace.

"Cam, dinner's ready," Tricia said.

Cameron sighed. He would eat. He needed strength for Kat. And he needed his brain at full functioning power to write that damned composition for Xavier. He would start tonight.

★ ★ ★ ★

Crawford, the Lybrook butler, led the two men into the main parlor. "May I present the Earl of Brighton and Lord Evan Xavier," he said.

Iris gulped as Maggie rose to greet them.

"My lord," Maggie said to the earl, "it has been too long. We are so glad to have your presence here at Laurel Ridge."

"Thank you, Your Grace," Brighton said. "My son speaks highly of the hospitality you have shown him over the past month. May I congratulate you on the marriage of your son."

"Thank you, my lord. We are so sorry that you were unable to come to the wedding."

"Alas, I was out of the country, as I'm sure Evan told you. I had business in Spain that took a little over two months. The Brighton estate has substantial holdings there."

"It's good to have you home, my lord. You remember my sister, Miss Lucinda Landon?"

"Yes, it's good to see you, Miss Landon." The earl bent over to kiss Lucy's hand.

"And may I present the Countess of Longarry. She is a longtime friend of Lucy's and mine, and aunt to my new daughter-in-law."

Iris stood, but her legs wouldn't propel her forward. David had hardly changed in twenty years. His brown eyes, fringed in dark lashes, still had a way of penetrating her soul. His dark blond hair was now streaked with silver, and his face, pleasantly handsome like his son's, defied his age. Only a few laugh lines around his eyes revealed his sixty years. He strode toward her, so tall and broad, like Evan, and took her hand.

"My lady," he said, their eyes meeting.

"I-It's...good to see you, my lord," Iris stammered. "I trust your journey was pleasant?"

"Yes, thank you."

Alexandra cleared her throat.

"My lord," Iris said. "May I present my daughters, Lady Alexandra and Lady Sophie MacIntyre."

"Such charming young ladies," the earl said, taking each of their hands in turn. "Just babes when I saw you last."

"Have we met, my lord?" Alexandra asked.

"You were but a few months old, as I recall. I met you two and your mother at the Ashford estate some...twenty years ago, I'd say."

"Father," Evan interrupted, taking Rose's arm. "I'd like to present Lady Rose Jameson."

"It's an honor, my lord," Rose said.

"Another charming lady who I last saw as a babe," Brighton declared. "She is a beauty, Evan."

"Yes, I think so too," Evan replied.

Rose flushed. "I...have been looking forward to meeting you. I'm sure my sister and brother-in-law will be sorry that they missed your visit."

"On their honeymoon?" Brighton laughed. "I doubt they'll be the least bit sorry. I am looking forward to meeting the new duchess though. Perhaps all of you could come to my estate for the weekend after they return."

"That's a fine idea, Father," Evan agreed.

"We'll plan on it, then." Brighton took an aperitif from a maid and took a sip. "I'm looking forward to dinner. You and Lybrook, may he rest in peace, always served the finest meals here, Your Grace."

"We have had the same kitchen staff for over ten years," Maggie said. "I'm sure they have something elegant planned."

Crawford entered quietly. "Dinner is served, Your Grace."

"Wonderful, Crawford. If you would all follow me," Maggie said. "I hope you don't mind. Since we are such a small group, I thought the informal dining room would be nicer and more...intimate."

Iris warmed from head to toe. More intimate indeed. Maggie couldn't possibly know about her affair with David, could she? Lucy had promised to keep their conversation in confidence. When she found herself seated next to David, though, she cast Lucy a sideways glance. Lucy's lips curved ever so slightly upward. Yes, it had been purposefully arranged. David, always the consummate gentleman, held Iris's chair for her as she sat down nervously.

"Tell me, my lord," she said, "how are your other children?"

"They're well, my lady. Jacob, my heir, is betrothed to Lady Emily Wilkes, the daughter of the Earl of St. Clair, a fine young woman. And Miranda is married to Viscount Odegard. They have a small son, Peter."

"How nice." Now what to say? The silence was becoming stifling. She pleadingly looked at Lucy.

"Do you enjoy grandparenthood, my lord?" Lucy asked, giving Iris a subtle wink.

The earl laughed jovially. "Oh, yes, Peter is a spry little fellow. I wish I saw him more. My daughter and her husband prefer to spend most of their time in London, so we aren't together often. The countess would have doted on him. I only regret that she passed on before he was born."

The countess. Why did he have to mention her? "I was sorry to hear about your wife's passing," Iris said.

"It's been a little over two years now," the earl said. "How is your husband?"

"Longarry passed on about two years ago also."

"I'm sorry. I didn't know."

Iris eyed her plate and fidgeted with her napkin. Where was the first course? What to do with her hands? "That's perfectly fine. The girls and I have managed quite well."

"Of course. Where are you keeping yourself these days?"

"In Mayfair. We have a townhome there."

"You didn't stay in Scotland?"

"No. Longarry had no family to speak of, so there was no reason to. The girls and I decided to return to England. I spend much of my time with my sister, and now that Lucy and I have renewed our friendship, I hope to see more of her as well."

Finally! A footman served the first course. Iris raised a lobster canapé to her mouth and was suddenly very conscious of her chewing.

"Iris and I were best friends as girls," Lucy chimed in. "It's been wonderful getting to know each other again."

"Yes, I can see how it would be." David gazed at Iris with

his warm brown eyes. "It certainly would be."

Iris inhaled as a servant set a plate of tomato bisque before her. Was it the steam rising from the soup that made her feel hot all over? Or was it David's gaze? And why in hell did the chef prepare something red and runny? The way her hands were shaking, she wasn't sure the soup would make it to her mouth.

"Father," Evan said, "Rose is an excellent rider. I thought maybe the three of us could go riding on the morrow."

"Hmm?" The earl turned to his son.

"I thought the three of us could go riding tomorrow. You, Rose, and I."

"Yes, of course. I've heard you're quite the horsewoman," he said to Rose.

"I'm afraid your son flatters me, my lord."

"Nonsense," Evan said. "She's amazing on horseback. And at the pianoforte. You should play something for my father, Rose."

"Evan..."

"I'd love to hear you play, my dear," the earl said.

"Of course, I would be honored."

"Tell me, how is your father?"

"He's fine, my lord."

"Good, good. And your lovely mother?"

"Fine as well."

"Good." He turned back to Iris. "My lady?"

"Yes?" Iris fussed with her napkin, which was now a twisted knot in her lap. She still hadn't braved a spoonful of the soup.

"Would you—?"

They were interrupted by the chef, who came in wielding

a large carving knife over a roast baron of beef.

"That looks marvelous, Pierre," Maggie said.

"*Merci, Madame.*" The chef bowed and began carving.

Minutes passed like hours. Iris barely tasted her roast beef. Or her potato soufflé and vegetable casserole. Even the fruit and cheese slid down her throat like dry crackers. She washed it all down with claret and began to feel a bit light-headed. She was secretly relieved when Evan and his father retired to the smoking room for their cigars and port.

Sophie, Alexandra, and Rose took their coffee on the front terrace, but Iris stayed in the main parlor. She was lost in thought when Lucy entered.

"Are you faring well, Iris?" Lucy asked.

"Yes, I'm fine." Iris rubbed her temple. "Goodness, I shouldn't have drunk so much wine."

"Nonsense, you had only two glasses, the same as the rest of us."

"Yes, but if you noticed, I didn't eat very much. I couldn't seem to choke anything down. I felt like... Lucy, he was looking at me. I couldn't chew or anything. I was deathly afraid I'd do something ridiculous, like spill that dreaded tomato bisque down the front of my gown."

"Iris..."

"This is so silly. I'm fifty-two years old, for goodness' sake, and I'm acting like an infatuated school girl!"

"You were fine. No one noticed a thing."

"Lord. Lucy, did you tell Maggie about the earl and me?"

"Of course not. I gave you my word."

"Thank goodness."

"Although I think Maggie would be understanding."

"Yes, I'm sure she would. And I do mean to tell her...

eventually. Flora too. But right now I can't even think straight."

"You need some air, dear. Why don't you go out onto the back terrace? It's a beautiful evening. I'll have Eunice bring our coffees out there."

"Yes, that would be lovely. I will."

Iris left the main parlor and walked down the long hallway to the stairway leading to the ballroom. She stopped in the ladies' retiring room and assessed her appearance, thankful that her dusty pink dinner gown wasn't dripping tomato or claret. Quickly she descended the grand staircase and strode through the vacant ballroom, out onto the back terrace. The sun had almost completely set, and the half moon shone brightly in the night sky. Within a half hour, the fiery stars would light up the clear sky. She took a deep breath, relishing the fresh night air, her hands on the railing, her body leaning into the soft breeze of the evening.

"You haven't changed a bit, Iris."

She turned, gasped, and stood only a hair's breadth away from David Xavier, the Earl of Brighton.

★ ★ ★ ★

Rose was sitting alone on the front terrace when Evan appeared.

"Where are your cousins?" he asked.

"Sophie got a chill, and Ally went upstairs to write a letter to Mr. Landon."

"Good," he said. "Not that I mind their company, but I'm glad to spend some time with you alone. Would you care to walk a bit?"

Rose sighed. This was her destiny. This nice, honorable

man, who clearly adored her. She was fond of him, but she didn't love him. Would never love him. She loved another. Would always love another. But Evan, not Cameron, was her future.

"Of course." She stood and took his arm.

Together they walked toward the stables and turned down a small winding path.

"Could we stop at the kennels?" Rose asked. "I'd like to see Brandy. I promised Lily I would take good care of her." Brandy was a St. John's Dog puppy, a gift to Lily from the duke.

"Yes, that's fine," Evan said.

But he stopped, turned Rose to face him, and lightly brushed his lips down upon hers.

Evan's kiss.

It was sweet and gentle. Enjoyable, but not astounding. Pleasant, but not life changing. Rose wanted more. She flung her arms around Evan's neck and drew her to him, taking his mouth with hers. Perhaps it wasn't Cameron that made their kisses so special. Maybe she could kiss like that with any man. She intended to find out.

She plunged her tongue into Evan's mouth and slid it over his smooth teeth, his soft gums, the warmth of his inside cheeks. He responded, soft moans escaping from the back of his throat. She had never kissed him like this before. He clearly liked it.

Rose sucked lightly on his lower lip and then took it between her teeth and nipped it gently. She traced his full lips slowly, seductively, and covered his chin with tiny moist kisses.

"Rose," Evan rasped. "What has gotten into you?"

"Kiss my ear, Evan," she said.

He moved his lips to the outer rim of her ear and traced it lightly with his tongue, nibbled on the top, the lobe.

"Put your tongue in my ear."

He obliged, thrusting into her ear canal with more force than she wanted.

"No, not like that," she said. "Lightly, softly."

He licked the inside of her ear, moving his tongue into each little crevice. Rose squirmed. It was pleasant, but not quite right. Evan moved to her neck, nibbling and kissing her, trailing down to the hollow of her throat.

Rose wanted more. She grabbed his hand and ran to the side of the kennels, bracing her back against the hard outside wall. Inside the dogs barked and whined, but she ignored the noise. She was determined to find what she had lost. Surely she could have those feelings with another man. It didn't have to be Cameron. Anyone could fill the emptiness.

"Touch me." She led Evan's hand to her breast.

"Rose..."

"Don't you want to touch me?"

"Of course, but...I didn't think you wanted..."

"Then touch me, damn it!" She took his hand and forced it under the neckline of her gown, beneath her corset and chemise, onto her bare breast.

Evan gasped. He fumbled, but her corset was too tight. He couldn't move his hand.

"Here, undo me," she said, turning.

He began unfastening the back of her gown. "Are you sure you want to do this?"

"Yes, yes. I want you to touch me."

She drew a deep breath as he loosened her corset strings and eased her gown over her shoulders. She turned to face him. The moonlight cast a silver glow upon his handsome face, and his eyes were ablaze with fire. He was no pagan god, but a fallen angel, come to take her. Slowly she pulled her corset down, baring her breasts to his gaze.

"Kiss my nipples, Evan."

"My God, Rose." Evan gulped. "You're lovely. Your skin is like white marble in the moonlight, your nipples... I haven't the strength to deny you." Slowly he lowered his mouth, stroking her nipple with his soft tongue.

She moaned. "Yes, yes, that's it."

His mouth felt...good. Not the soul-inspiring sensation she felt when Cameron touched her, but still, it felt *good*.

He gently circled her rosy areola and then sucked the taut nipple into his mouth. He moved to the other one, tugging on it softly as he caressed the first breast with his fingers and pinched the nipple lightly.

Rose entwined her fingers in his blond hair. "Evan."

He didn't respond.

"Evan." A little louder.

He released her nipple with a pop and looked up. "Yes?"

"I want you to..."

"What?" he rasped.

"I want you to"—her hair tumbled out of its chignon, falling around her naked breasts in honey curls—"make me"—her voice husky, her skin warm and radiant—"*come*."

Evan stepped back, his eyes wide. "Pardon?"

"Pardon?" Rose shook her head. "You heard me."

"How do you even know...?"

"I have a married sister. Goodness. I know just about... *everything*."

"But you're a lady."

"A lady who wants to—"

"No, no." Evan clutched his forehead. "Don't say it again, Rose. Good God."

"Evan, surely you know how to—"

"Yes, of course. But not with you. Not until... Just not with you. It isn't right."

Rose raised her eyebrows. "But you've been with other women?"

"Yes."

"Then why not with me?"

"You're...*different.*"

"How so? I have two eyes, two ears, a mouth." She smiled and jiggled her breasts just a little. "Two breasts, and this lovely secret place where I get really—"

He quieted her with a kiss. "Rose, you mustn't talk like that."

She lowered her hand to the bulge in his trousers. "You want me."

"My God!" He brushed her hand away. "What in the world?"

She reached forward again, but he stopped her.

"What's the problem? I'm just like every other woman you've been with."

"No, you're special."

How ridiculous. How was she to be sure she could feel magic with him if he wouldn't allow her to experiment? "How so?"

"You're a lady of the peerage. I can't...take advantage of you that way."

"But you can take advantage of some other woman?" Ire rose within her. First Cameron had been obsessed with her

116

station, and now Evan. "That's a bit hypocritical, don't you think?"

"No, there are women, and there are...*ladies.*"

Rose scoffed. "Nonsense. Women are women, no matter to whom they're born. None of us had a say in it, you know. I didn't ask to be born to the Earl and Countess of Ashford. If I had been born a commoner, you would give me what I want, wouldn't you?"

"Rose..."

She quickly pulled her corset up and turned around. "Do me up, please."

"I didn't mean to upset you."

"If I had been born a commoner—" She stopped. If she had been born a commoner, she would be Cameron's woman. Cameron's wife. The wife of the man she loved.

Or maybe not. Cameron had rejected her, after all.

"You weren't born a commoner, and neither was I." Evan fastened the last button and turned her to face him. "You're lovely, and I would be lying if I said I didn't want you, but it isn't right for us to do this."

"Of course it's not," she said. "You've just made me realize what I've known all along. A person can't change who or what he is. Not for all the gold in the world." She sighed. "I want to go to bed."

"You don't mean you want me to—"

"Heavens, no. I wouldn't dream of asking you to come to my chamber. Your high morals certainly wouldn't allow that." She smoothed her dress. "But tell me, Evan. If I looked the same, had the same mind, the same brain, the same body, but instead of a lady of the peerage I was a servant or a peasant girl, and I wanted you to bed me, would you?"

"Rose, I'm...not going to answer that."

Rose snorted. "You just did. Good night, Evan." She turned and walked away from the kennels, back toward the main house.

★ ★ ★ ★

"Thank you, my lord," Iris said quietly, her heart raging beneath her breasts.

David laughed softly. "Iris, call me David. Please."

"That's hardly proper. We haven't seen each other in twenty—"

David brushed a stray curl behind her ear.

"—years."

"I'm sixty years old, Iris, and a widower. I hardly care about the proprieties at this stage in my life."

"I was truly sorry to hear about the countess," Iris said. "I know you...cared for her."

"Yes, I did. Ours was a good marriage. We were content."

"I know."

"And you, my Iris?"

My Iris. Her belly fluttered.

"You were never content, were you?"

She looked at the ground. "I'm afraid I wasn't."

"You never told me much about Longarry," David said, touching Iris's arm lightly. "Only that he wasn't always kind. But I did some asking around...after. I found out some things that...disturbed me."

"Rumor and innuendo travel more quickly than the rail, my lord."

"David. Please."

She closed her eyes and let out a breath. "David."

"Why didn't you tell me he was mistreating you?"

Iris looked at her feet. "What would have been the point?"

"I could have helped you."

"How? And how did you find anything out? I never told anyone. Not even Flora."

"Flora had no reason to pry. I did."

"Whatever reason did you have?"

"I was in love with you, Iris."

Warmth rose to her cheeks. "Well, even if you were, you weren't going to leave the countess, and Longarry would have never let me go."

"No," he said. "You're right. I wouldn't have left Maureen. But I could have...*helped* you."

"No, you couldn't have. I'm telling you, he wouldn't have let me go."

"I could have made it worth his while financially."

"David, just how much do you know?"

"Enough. And I'm sorry, Iris."

"For what?"

"For not helping you."

"You couldn't have."

"I hired a private detective to track you down and find out your situation. Maureen found out about it."

"So you...?"

"So I...did nothing. I've always regretted it, but I felt I owed some loyalty to Maureen. I'm so sorry."

Iris's nerves danced under her skin. "What exactly did you find out, David?"

"That Longarry was in near financial ruin, and that he was known to be a tyrant and he did not treat you and the children kindly."

"And?"

"That's it, my Iris."

"Oh." *Thank goodness.*

"What more is there?"

"David, I don't want to talk about this right now."

David raked his fingers through his long silvery-blond hair. "It was bad, wasn't it?"

Iris fidgeted with the sash on her dinner gown. "We survived."

David tilted her chin upward, forcing her to meet his gaze. "Tell me."

"Maybe later. I don't want to talk about Longarry. In fact, I spend most of my life trying to forget that he ever existed."

"Iris—"

"And it wasn't all bad. He gave me my girls. They're both so beautiful, much more so than I ever was."

"I might debate that." David smiled. "They are lovely, but no lovelier than you."

"You are kind."

"I am only truthful, my dear." David touched his hand to her cheek and slowly brought his face to hers.

Iris's heart jumped. He was going to kiss her. Lord, it had been so long. When his lips brushed against hers, she felt a surge in her womb that she'd thought long dead. Slowly he caressed her with his mouth, and she opened her lips, welcoming the soft velvet of his tongue. He kissed her cheeks, her neck, her ears.

He whispered, "You're the only woman I ever loved. Do you know that?"

Iris couldn't breathe. Her pulse raced madly, and her skin

was fiery hot. "I can't think, David. I can't—"

"I'd like to take you to your chamber," he said, caressing her arms and rubbing the nape of her neck.

"I don't think that would be wise." Iris melted farther into his embrace.

"I don't think I care," he said.

"Neither do I," Iris breathed.

CHAPTER SEVEN

Cameron sat under the giant oak tree behind the hired man's cabin, strumming his guitar and picking out a tune. A spring breeze blew, catching his long hair and whipping it side to side, despite the protection of the tree. The grass swayed, and the flowers danced. His mother's roses were budding. Pink roses, the color of his beloved's lips. The bushes swayed back and forth, and a bud burst open before his eyes, bringing forth a perfect coral bloom. The flower moved in the wind, seeming to hum a melody as it glissaded slowly, methodically. Cameron picked out the notes on his guitar, strumming slowly, soon playing along with the flower's song. A heady gust of wind plucked the bloom from the bush, its petals floating upward, spinning and swirling, and then it wasn't a flower anymore, but his Rose dancing. Her feet were bare, and her body was clad only in the sheerest coral silk that moved with the wind as she glided gracefully through the air. She was singing. Singing for him. Her true love. The melodies and harmonies blended together, infusing joy and peace into Cam's heart. This was happiness. Bliss. A song made of his love for Rose. She danced before him, smiling, seducing. She reached out and touched her slender fingers to his cheek, ever so lightly, and then teasingly moved away from him, making him want her even more. It was all in the tune—her beauty, her love for him and his for her, the teasing, the seduction, the complete and pure peace when their bodies joined. She danced and glided, moved away. She was a bloom again, and the wind tore the petals from the stem, scattering them, and she was gone.

He woke up in a cold sweat. The tune. Rose. It was the middle of the night, but he pulled on a pair of trousers, lit a lamp, and scurried out to the pianoforte in the main room. Grabbing a quill and paper, he sat down and began picking out notes. If he hurried, he could get it all down before the memory of his dream left him.

★ ★ ★ ★

Rose bathed and dressed quickly the next morning. She wasn't looking forward to seeing Evan. She would apologize for her wanton behavior, beg his forgiveness, and move forward. She'd learned a valuable lesson. He wasn't Cameron. She couldn't recapture the feelings that Cameron evoked in her. Only one man existed for her, and she would never have him.

But that wasn't Evan's fault. He was who he was. She was thankful he had stopped her. She didn't want to come for anyone but Cameron. Unfortunately, that meant she may never experience that earth-shattering feeling again.

She descended and went into the main parlor for breakfast. Evan was already there, as were Sophie and Ally.

"Good morning," Rose said nervously.

"Rose, good morning," Ally said. "You're up early."

"Yes, I couldn't sleep any longer." She turned to Evan. "My lord, might I have a word with you? In private?"

"Yes, of course." He stood up and escorted her out into the hallway.

"Evan," she said, "I want to apologize for my...behavior last night. I don't know what got into me."

"There's no need to apologize."

"Yes, there is. I guess—" What excuse could she give? "I guess my curiosity got the best of me. Lily and I...well, we've had conversations..."

"You don't need to say any more. I understand."

"Do you?"

"Of course I do. I want you too. I've wanted you since I first laid eyes on you. But it's not...proper."

She exhaled. He thought she desired him. Well, why wouldn't he? She had thrown herself at him like a strumpet. "Yes, of course. I know that, Evan."

"I'm very fond of you, Rose. I don't want to ruin what we have together. I think...I'd like to..."

"What is it, Evan?"

"I care for you more than I've cared for any other woman."

"I'm flattered."

"So I want to do this right, do you understand?"

"Yes, I understand."

"Good. Now, when would you like to go riding today?"

Rose sighed. "Whenever you would like. Just fetch me when you're ready. Would you care to join me for breakfast?"

"Thank you, but I've had enough. I will see you later."

"Yes. Later."

★ ★ ★ ★

Iris woke up in David's arms, feeling, for the first time, *secure*. Twenty years ago, when he had loved her, it had been wonderful. An escape. But now, Longarry was gone, and he would never find out. She was in no danger. Had she ever felt so safe before in her entire life? No. Never.

He had loved her tenderly, and she had been amazed at how her body had responded. Feelings she thought long dead had resurfaced, sending her into an ecstasy that she had nearly forgotten. She smiled and leaned over and kissed David's lips. His eyes fluttered open.

"Good morning, my Iris."

"Good morning, David."

He cuddled her close. "I didn't realize how much I missed making love to you."

"You haven't forgotten any of the tricks." She warmed at her own words, but why stand on ceremony now? They were in bed together, for heaven's sake.

"I have a few more up my sleeve, you know." He lowered his head and nipped her breast.

"Do you?"

"Yes, my love. I shall show you." He pulled her on top of him and slid her body down onto his erection. "Now, my Iris, you will ride with me this morning."

When they had both sated their hunger and collapsed in exhaustion, David rubbed her back soothingly.

"Iris," he said.

"Yes?"

"I don't want to lose you again."

"You won't."

"Won't I?"

"Of course not. Neither one of us is bound. We can continue our affair for as long as we like."

"You want an affair with me?"

"Well...yes." Her nerves jumped. What if he didn't? "Don't you?"

"No," he said flatly.

Iris's heart sank. He meant to leave her after this weekend. "All right, David. Forgive me. I just thought—"

"I want to marry you."

Iris gasped. "You...what?"

"You heard me. I love you, Iris. Marry me. Be my countess."

Her whole body sizzled. "David, isn't this a little bit sudden?"

"Not really. It's been twenty years in the making."

"Oh, David."

"Is that a yes?"

How she wanted to pounce on him and accept. But, "Well, there's just so much to consider. My girls, for one. They're the most important things in my life, and I couldn't make this decision without... And I have nothing to offer you, David. Nothing. Longarry left us penniless. If it weren't for Flora and Crispin, we would be out on the streets."

"What about your parents?"

"My mother died ten years ago, and my father lives alone in London. Neither Flora nor I see him. I'll never forgive him for marrying me off to Longarry."

"So your sister knows the whole situation?"

"Yes, she does now. She knew I wasn't happy, but she didn't know the whole truth until Longarry died."

"When will you tell me the whole truth, my Iris?"

"David... Later, all right?"

He stroked her cheek tenderly. "All right. But it doesn't matter anyway. I still want you to be my wife."

"But the girls. Crispin gave them dowries. I don't know how I will ever repay him for that."

"I'll give them dowries. I'll take care of all of you now."

"But what of your own children?"

"My children will not suffer, I promise you. We are well off. Jacob and Evan both receive substantial annual allowances, and Miranda married well and is no longer my responsibility. I have plenty, darling, and I want to share it with you."

Iris sniffed, her eyes misting. "But I have nothing, David."

"How can you say that? You have yourself. You're all I've dreamed of for twenty years."

"I'm afraid I come with a lot of...baggage."

"I'm not afraid of baggage, my Iris. The only fear I have is losing you again."

She smiled weakly, her heart pounding. "Oh, David. I do love you."

"Then you'll be my wife?"

"Yes. Yes, yes, yes!" She kissed his face, his neck, his chest. "I never thought I'd know true happiness."

"Nor did I, my love. But we both will. For the rest of our lives."

Iris leaped out of bed. "I want to bathe and dress. I want to go downstairs and tell everyone our news."

David chuckled softly. "Whatever you wish."

★ ★ ★ ★

Cameron busily scraped his quill on parchment, putting the last notation on his ballad for Rose. He titled it *Wandering Rose*, in memory of how she had danced before him in her sheer pink veiling in his dream. Dawn had broken several hours before, and he heard Tricia stirring in her chamber. He had been up for hours, working through the tune on the pianoforte and scribbling notes and chords. The work was nearly complete.

It was both the easiest and the most difficult piece he'd ever written.

"Do you want some tea, Cam?" Tricia asked, padding out into the sitting room in her nightdress.

"Yes, thank you."

"What are you doing?"

"Working on a composition. I'm sorry if I disturbed you last night."

"I heard the pianoforte now and then, but you didn't disturb me. I haven't been sleeping all that well anyway."

"Neither have I."

"Cam, do you think we could ride into Bath and see Kat today?"

He smiled at his sister. "You know, I had a very productive night. I think there is time to go see Kat today."

Tricia gave him a quick hug. "That's wonderful. I do miss her. I know she's in good hands, but it's frightening, not knowing what is wrong with her."

"Yes, I know."

"Cam..."

"Hmm?"

"How are we going to...? That is, where will the money come from for Kat's care?"

Cameron took a breath before answering. "Don't worry about it. I have it under control."

"How?"

"I got another commission, and I just completed it." He set down the parchment. "I need to go to Bath anyway to get some new quills and parchment so I can make my final copy." He sighed. "This is my best work ever," he said, more to himself than to his sister.

"Who commissioned the work?" Tricia asked.

An invisible knife stabbed him in the gut. "Just some stuffy aristocrat. He wants to use my music to propose to his future wife."

Tricia brought him his tea. "Cam?"

"Hmm?"

"I was wondering... What happened between you and Lady Rose?"

Cameron took a sip of his tea and cleared his throat. Just the topic he didn't want to discuss. "What do you mean?"

"I'm not a child, Cameron. I saw the way things were between you."

"You're imagining things."

"I don't think so."

"She's a lady of the peerage. She has no interest in me, nor I in her. Now leave it, will you?"

"Cam," Tricia said, "that night she stayed here, when we thought Kat had scarlet fever, I got up in the middle of the night to use the convenience, and then I checked on Kat. Mum had fallen asleep next to her, and Kat was awake. She asked for you, so I went to your chamber, but you weren't there. So I went back to Kat, but she had fallen asleep."

"Trish..."

"I didn't think much about it, but since Lady Rose left, you've seemed so...*lost*."

"I'm just worried about Kat, the same as you."

"Why have you never married, Cam?"

Marry? How could he marry when he bore the responsibility for her, Kat, and their mother? He'd never even considered it until Rose. And now...well, he'd never marry. If he couldn't have the woman he loved, he didn't want any substitute. "None of your business."

"There are scads of pretty maidens who adore you, but you've never given any of them a look. But the way you looked at Lady Rose..."

"Tricia, I'm only going to say this one more time. There is nothing between Rose—er, Lady Rose—and me. And you're only fifteen years old! This isn't any of your concern."

She smiled. "You know, many maidens marry at fifteen."

"You won't, however." *Not while I live.*

"Perhaps I should. There's no shortage of men vying for my favors, and then there would be one less mouth to feed around here."

"You are far too young."

"Perhaps I could find a wealthy young lord who would take care of all of us. Lady Rose's brother, for instance. He is dashing." Tricia closed her eyes.

"Good God, the man is my age!" Cameron shook his head. "And when the hell did you ever meet him, anyway?"

"A few days before the duke's wedding. I was out riding and I met the duke and Lady Lily. The duke's horse is the most beautiful black stallion. Anyway, Lady Rose and Lord Jameson, that's his name, were with them, and Lady Lily remembered me and introduced us."

"How do you know he's not already married?"

"Lady Lily mentioned that he wasn't."

Cameron rolled his eyes. "You're too young to marry, Tricia. I won't have you tied down during the dawn of your youth. And you may as well accept the fact that you won't marry an aristocrat. None of us will. It's not our place."

"What if I think we're better than"—she motioned around the room—"this."

"It doesn't matter."

"It does. Cameron, you're as talented as any contemporary composer. More so even, because you've had no formal training. If you'd had the advantages that are available to the peers, or even to the more wealthy—"

"But I haven't. This is my life. It's where I belong."

"No, it's not. And it's not where I belong, either. I want to learn. I'm smart. Did you know that, Cam?"

"Of course."

"And so is Kat. I taught her the multiplication tables. She memorized them in two days. And she can do complex equations in her head. She's only seven!"

"I'm afraid that's our curse, Tricia."

"It's a curse to be bright?"

"When you're limited as to what you can accomplish due to your station in life, yes, it is a curse to be bright."

Tricia shook her head. "I'll never believe that."

"Well, if you're so inclined to use your intelligence, tell me, why are you so eager to marry yourself off at such a tender age?"

"I'm not really. I just thought it would make things easier for you."

"That's silly."

"No, it's not. You were going to go to London and write music, do you remember?"

"Yes."

"But then Papa died, and you had to stay here and take care of us. You could have been famous by now."

Would this harrowing conversation never end? "It wasn't in the cards."

"But it still could be. If you and Lady Rose got together."

"That will never happen."

"But if it did, she could help you. Introduce you to the right people."

"I have no intention of being a kept man. Why am I talking to you about this anyway?" He scoffed. "You're my sister, and you're too young to be having such thoughts."

Tricia closed her eyes. "And then you could introduce me to Lord Jameson again, and he would take one look at me and fall madly in love—"

"This conversation is over, Tricia." Cameron finished his tea and loudly set his cup down on an end table. "I'm not your father, but this is the best advice I can give you. Accept your station in life. Don't try to change it. It only leads to heartbreak." He cleared his throat. "Now if you'll excuse me, I'm going to have a bath, and then we'll go see Kat."

★ ★ ★ ★

"Iris, what on earth?" Lucy said.

Iris had dragged her into the main parlor. Sophie and Alexandra sat together on the divan, while Rose sat opposite them in a wingback chair, Evan standing behind her. The dowager duchess was perched on a settee, drinking a cup of tea.

The Earl of Brighton rose and took Iris's arm.

"I'm sorry to keep you waiting, David. I couldn't find Lucy. She was hiding in the kitchen, helping Cook prepare our luncheon."

"I often help in the kitchen. I enjoy it."

"Lucy is a marvelous cook," Maggie said.

"All those years of friendship, so long ago, and I had no

idea," Iris said. "Now I'll know where to find you when you sneak off."

"Goodness, then, what is going on?" Lucy asked.

"Yes, Mother, why have you called us all in here?" Alexandra smoothed her skirt.

"David—that is, Lord Brighton and I... We have some news."

A smile curved onto Lucy's pretty lips. "Iris, you don't mean..."

David cleared his throat. "This lovely lady has agreed to become my wife, and I couldn't be happier."

"Father?" Evan walked forward. "Are you serious?"

"Never more serious, Evan. Iris and I are going to be married."

"But isn't this a bit...sudden?"

"Your mother has been gone for over two years."

"But you and Lady Longarry just met."

"Yes, my goodness, Mother," Ally agreed. "What has gotten into you?"

"I know this must seem odd," David said, "but Iris and I have known each other for some time. We are very happy to have renewed our acquaintance."

"You don't mean that you..." Evan frowned.

"Frankly, it's none of your business how we met, and I'm not going to go into detail. Suffice it to say that we are in love with each other, and since we are both currently unattached, we have decided to spend the rest of our years in happiness together."

"Well," Sophie said, rising and giving her mother a quick hug, "I for one am very happy for you, Mother."

Iris shrugged. Sophie's tone didn't quite indicate

happiness, but Iris appreciated the attempt. "Thank you, Sophie dear. I assure you that we will all be very happy with this arrangement."

"Yes, yes," David said. "The three of you will come and live on the Brighton estate. It's not quite as large as this one, but it's beautiful. I think you'll find it to your liking."

"Our own estate?" Alexandra gasped. "How completely lovely!"

"Not exactly *your* estate," Evan interjected.

"Of course it will be their estate, Evan," David said. "Iris will be my countess, and the girls are part of the package. I'm taking full responsibility for them, as well."

"Father, what about Jacob and me?"

"What is this about, Evan? You're my son, and Jacob is my heir. You'll want for naught. You never have, have you?"

"Of course not. I'm sorry, Father. It...will just take some time to get used to it all."

"Well, get used to it quickly. We're getting married tomorrow."

"David!" Iris exclaimed.

"I've waited twenty years for you. I'm not waiting any longer."

"But, David, I'd like for Crispin and Flora to be here. And Lily and the duke won't be back until the solstice."

"Iris—"

"Please, David. I had a hasty wedding the first time to a man I didn't even know. This time I want my family and friends with me."

"Yes, Maggie and I can make you a beautiful wedding here at Laurel Ridge," Lucy said.

"That's a marvelous idea, Lucy," the dowager duchess

agreed.

Iris shook her head. "I couldn't possibly impose."

"Nonsense," Maggie said. "We've been friends since we were babes. Lucy and I would love to do this for you."

"You're both so good to me." She turned to her fiancé. "Please, David. I do so want a real wedding."

David smiled, taking Iris's hand and kissing her upturned palm. "Whatever you wish, my Iris."

Rose stood and hugged Iris. "I'm so happy for you, Auntie," she said. Then, turning to David, "and you too, my lord."

"Uncle David, my dear."

"Oh, goodness. I suppose you're right."

Evan rose and cleared his throat. "Congratulations, Father, my lady." He strode quietly out of the room.

"David..." Iris worried her lower lip.

"He'll be fine," David said. "Evan was the youngest and was very close to his mother, so I imagine it will take some time for him to get used to this idea. But he's a sensible lad. He will come around."

"I'll talk to him," Rose said.

"No, my dear, leave him for an hour or so," David said. "Then you can go to him."

"If you think best"—she smiled—"Uncle David."

"This is all too exciting," Alexandra said. "Mother, we must find you the perfect dress. We should summon Lily's modiste right away. Aunt Lucy, Aunt Maggie, may I help you plan?"

"Of course," Lucy said.

"We should have a string quartet. That would be lovely," Ally said. "And Rose, maybe you could get Mr. Price to write a song for Mama."

"His little sister is still in the hospital, Ally. I think he probably has other responsibilities at the moment."

"I suppose you're right. You'll just have to make do with Mozart, Mama. Perhaps you could be married on the solstice itself! No, then we'd miss the celebration. When are Lily and the duke returning?"

"Daniel didn't give me an exact date, but he said they'd be home for the solstice," Maggie replied.

"Good. Then we'll all go to the celebration, and the wedding can be the day after that. How does that sound?"

"Goodness, Ally. Let Mama catch her breath a minute," Sophie said.

Iris smiled, her heart warm. "It's all right, Sophie. I'm glad she's excited."

"Oh, I am. Sophie, Rose, you both must help me plan. Oh, and of course, you too, Mother, and Aunt Maggie and Aunt Lucy."

"We'll all help," Rose said. "Isn't this grand? Another wedding so soon!"

"I'm afraid this one won't be quite the affair that Lily's was," Iris pointed out.

"If it's a grand affair you want, my dear, it's a grand affair you shall have," David said.

"No, no. All I want is a real wedding, with my family and friends. Not some huge affair."

"But, Iris—"

"I'm serious, David. I want Flora and Crispin, of course, and Thomas. Lily and the duke, your children, and all of us. And of course, any other family and friends that you want to include. That's it."

"If you're sure."

"I'm positive. It's a second marriage for both of us. A grand affair wouldn't be appropriate. And I've no desire to hobnob with a bunch of people I hardly know."

"I think an intimate gathering sounds wonderful, Iris," Lucy said. "Maggie and I and the girls will have loads of fun planning it, won't we?"

"I'm chock-full of ideas, Auntie Lucy," Ally gushed. "Do let's start planning!"

"All right, dear," Lucy laughed.

★ ★ ★ ★

Cameron and Tricia stopped in a small shop in Bath to pick up the quills and parchment that he needed, and then they rode to the hospital. A young nurse showed them to Kat's room. Kat was sitting up in bed, and her mother was feeding her broth.

"Cam!" Kat shouted.

"My sweet Kitty-Kat," he said, "you're better aren't you!"

"Much."

"Mother?" Tricia asked hesitantly.

"I sent word this morning," Mrs. Price said, her face beaming. "Of course I knew it wouldn't reach you until tomorrow or the next day. I had no idea you were coming."

"Tricia wanted to come, and I finished work on my new commission, so we had some time. What happened?"

"Kat had a terrible day yesterday. Her fever escalated to nearly one hundred and six degrees, and it wouldn't come down. The doctors and nurses were beside themselves."

"Oh dear," Tricia said.

"Then she had another seizure."

"Yes, I was shaking and drooling and they had to tie me down!" Kat laughed.

"Mum?" Cameron said.

"She's right, I'm afraid. It was awful." She looked to Kat. "Goodness, Kat, it's not funny!"

"Sorry, Mum, but it is. I wish I could have seen myself."

Cam smiled at his impish little sister. "Kitty-Kat, you will be the death of all of us, do you know that?"

"Tell them the rest, Mum," Kat said.

"Dr. Blake said it was the worst seizure he had ever seen. They had to give her several different injections before she came out of it. And the doctor said"—Mrs. Price wiped her eyes—"had we not been here, in the hospital, Kat would surely have died."

Tricia gasped.

Kat continued laughing. "Yes, I almost died, Cam!"

"That's not the least bit funny, Kat," Cameron admonished. "Thank goodness you brought her here, Mum."

"Yes, I've thanked God constantly. But Cam, the bill has gone so high. It's over one hundred fifty pounds already because of all the medication and the special doctors who have been in to look at Kat, and Dr. Blake said that she needs to stay for a few more days to be observed."

"Don't worry about the bill, Mum. I can take care of it. But why does she need to stay? Isn't she better?"

"Yes. The fever has broken, and obviously she's responsive now. But since they don't know exactly what caused her illness in the first place, they want to make sure she doesn't relapse. Evidently there are conditions that can recur, especially conditions that involve seizures."

"Oh." Cameron's heart lurched. "Well, then you'll stay of

course. How many more days?"

"Three or four."

"That's no problem. We only want the best for our Kitty-Kat." Cameron sat down on the bed next to his little sister, gathered her in his arms, and kissed her cheek. "Trish and I sure have missed you."

"I've missed you too, Cam. I'm so glad you came. I'd like to have more visitors. Could you bring Lady Lily and Lady Rose to visit me?"

Cameron jolted at Rose's name. "Kat, Lady Lily is the duchess now. She's on her wedding trip. You'll be home by the time she returns to the estate."

"What about Lady Rose?"

Mrs. Price cleared her throat. "Cameron..."

"Mum, Kat, I'm going to go downstairs to the office and take care of the bill. Stay here, Tricia. I won't be long."

"But, Cam..." Kat said.

"I'll be back in an instant, Kitty-Kat."

"But when will you bring Lady Rose?"

"Hush, Kat," Mrs. Price said. "Lady Rose is a busy lady of the peerage. She doesn't have time to visit you."

"She will if Cameron asks her to."

"I'll be back." Cam walked out the door before he could hear any more of this dreaded conversation. He went down to the first floor and asked for guidance to the bookkeeping office. He entered and found a young man sitting behind a mahogany desk stacked with papers. Cameron cleared his throat.

"Yes?" the man said.

"I'm here to take care of a bill."

"Of course. What is the name?"

"Katrina Price."

"All right, give me a minute." The young man regarded Cameron. "Are you the child's father?"

"No, our father is deceased. I'm her brother."

"Oh." He shuffled several papers. "Yes, here it is. Your bill currently comes to fifty-six pounds."

"I'm sorry, you must be mistaken," Cameron said. "I just spoke to my mother, and she said the bill was over one hundred and fifty pounds."

"You did say Katrina Price?"

"Yes."

"That's the name on this bill. Fifty-six pounds."

"What does that include?"

"Room and board for Katrina and your mother, Dr. Blake's fees, fees for several specialists, nursing fees, medication, laundry, etcetera. It's all written out here if you'd like to have a look."

"Yes, please." Cameron took the paper. "Wait a minute." He handed the bill back to the man. "This shows a credit of one hundred pounds. Why is that?"

The young man adjusted his spectacles. "It appears that you made a payment two days ago of one hundred pounds. Pretty straightforward."

"But I haven't made any payments."

"Perhaps your mother—"

"I only gave her thirty pounds." What was going on? "Perhaps there's been some mistake. Is it possible that you credited the wrong account?"

"Of course not. I never make mistakes like that."

"There's always a first time, sir."

"I'll look into it, but I doubt it." The young man snorted. "In the meantime, I can only take the fifty-six pounds from you."

"Of course." Cameron counted out notes and paid the man. "Here you are."

"Thank you. I'll contact you if I find an error."

"I would appreciate it. Good day, sir."

"Good day, Mr. Price."

Cameron headed back up to Kat's room. She was still her gay self, laughing and chatting.

"You're back, Cam!"

"You didn't think I was going anywhere, did you?"

"How long can you stay?"

"Tricia and I need to head back soon. It's a long trip on horseback, and I want to get home before sundown."

"Can you come again tomorrow?"

"Kat," Mrs. Price said, "it's too hard of a trip for them to come again. We'll be home in a few days."

"But I thought you'd bring Lady Rose the next time."

"Dear Lord." Mrs. Price crossed herself.

"Mum," Cameron said, thankful to be able to change the subject, "the bookkeeper said someone made a payment of one hundred pounds on our bill a few days ago. Do you know what that is about?"

"No. There must be some mistake."

"Yes, I figured as much. The bookkeeper is looking into it." He counted out notes from his billfold. "Here is one hundred pounds. Keep it. They'll no doubt come back with the error sometime tomorrow, and I don't want them to have to wait for their money. In fact"—he counted out more bills—"here's another thirty. That should cover the next few days plus your transport home. If you could take care of it before you leave, that will save us having to send the payment."

"But does that leave you and Tricia with any money?"

"Yes, I have a few pounds left, and I've already paid Arnold through the end of next month. We'll be fine. Besides, I finished another commission and I'll be getting paid the balance soon."

"All right, if you say so, Cam."

"Tell me, will Dr. Blake be by yet today?"

"He was here just before you and Tricia came. He probably won't be back until this evening."

"I would have liked to talk to him." Cameron stood. "Well, I guess you've told us everything he said, haven't you?"

"Yes, Cam."

"All right then." He leaned down and kissed Kat on the forehead. "I'm so glad you're well, Kitty-Kat. Trish and I will both sleep better tonight."

"Yes, that's for sure," Tricia added, squeezing the little girl's hand.

"We'll see you in a few days then," Mrs. Price said. "Thank you for coming. It meant a lot to both of us."

"To us as well," Cameron said. "Come on, Tricia."

★ ★ ★ ★

Cameron and Tricia arrived home at sundown and supped on tea and sandwiches. Tricia retired to her chamber to read, while Cameron stayed up far into the night, finalizing his composition and neatly transferring it to parchment. He knew Xavier was at Laurel Ridge visiting Rose for the weekend, so he sent a message to him early the next morning that the commission was complete.

Cameron sighed. It was official. He had sold Rose, his

soul mate and only love, for two hundred pounds.

He cursed himself before falling into bed Sunday morning.

CHAPTER EIGHT

Rose didn't get a chance to speak with Evan alone regarding his father's impending marriage. They never went riding with his father over the weekend, nor did she play the piano for him. Evan was out of sorts for the remainder of his visit. Although Rose tried to engage him several times, he would not speak to her about what was bothering him.

"He's a sensible lad," Lord Brighton had said to her again. "We'll be back next weekend, and I'm sure he'll be ready to talk about it then."

When the two men left Laurel Ridge on Sunday afternoon, driving away in the Brighton carriage, Rose's heart ached a bit for Evan. She did care deeply for him, even if she could never love him, and she hated to see him suffering. He had come to her in the conservatory and kissed her goodbye before he left, squeezing her and telling her he would see her soon. She had stroked his cheek and told him that she was here for him if he needed her.

The next day, Lucy and Maggie readied to visit the Lybrook tenants and see to their needs. The servants packed up food and other staples and loaded it into several wagons. Aunt Iris decided to go along, since she would soon be responsible for the Brighton tenants. She had never had any responsibility to the Longarry tenants, what few of them there were, because the Longarrys had barely had enough to see to their own needs, let alone others'. Sophie and Ally decided to ride along as well, and although Rose would have relished a day alone on the estate, her cousins begged her to come. She dreaded running into Cameron, but she was interested in hearing any news on Kat. She hadn't heard from Dr. Blake in a few days, and she still worried about the little girl.

Rose admired the way Maggie and Lucy handled the tenants. They were both kind and humble, with an affectionate way of giving that made it seem that the tenants were doing them a favor by taking their extra goods. Rose smiled. Soon Lily would be making these rounds as the Duchess of Lybrook. Most of the tenants were kind and decent folk, clean and well fed. The Lybrooks clearly took care of their own. Responsibilities like this were not in Rose's future. Evan, as a second son, wouldn't have an estate of his own. The responsibilities for the Brighton tenants would fall to his brother's wife after Uncle David passed on.

When they arrived at the Price cottage, Tricia was sweeping the front veranda. She smiled as her gaze met Rose's. "Lady Rose, it's so nice to see you!"

"Good afternoon, Tricia," Rose said, running to the younger girl as the rest of the women descended from the carriage. "I've been so concerned about Kat. The last I heard there was no change. Tell me, is there any news?"

Tricia laughed. "It's wonderful, my lady. Cam and I went to see her two days ago, and her fever had broken!"

Rose breathed a sigh of relief. "Oh, thank goodness. I've been fraught with worry. I do love that little girl."

"I know. Would you please come in and have a cup of tea? I know Cam would like to see you."

No, he wouldn't. Rose breathed deeply and forced a smile. "I'm afraid we don't have time to stay, but I want to introduce you to my aunt and cousins."

Rose made the necessary introductions and Tricia curtsied politely. Maggie asked about Kat, and Tricia filled them all in.

"That's wonderful news," Lucy said. "We've all been concerned about the poor little thing."

"When will she be coming home?" Rose asked.

"Tomorrow or the next day, most likely," Tricia said. "The doctor wanted to keep her a few days for observation since they never figured out exactly what caused her illness. They want to make sure she doesn't have a relapse."

"That's good thinking," Maggie said. "Tell me, my dear, is there anything our family can do for you? I know hospitalization is very expensive."

"Thank you, but Cam was able to take care of it. He got a commission for another song, you know."

"Really?" Rose tried to hide her unbounded elation. "That's wonderful."

"Yes, and he was quite pleased with the results. He said it was his best work ever."

"Who commissioned it?"

"I'm not sure. All he said was that it was a peer."

"That's fine, just fine," Rose said. "I'm happy for him." And she meant it.

"Please won't you all come in for some tea?" Tricia asked again.

"Could we, Aunt Maggie?" Ally asked. "I'm absolutely parched."

"I suppose there's time," Maggie said. Then, to Tricia, "Is your brother at home?"

"He's around here somewhere."

"You all go ahead in," Rose said. "I need to get a package out of the carriage that I brought for Tricia."

She quickly hurried back to the carriage to fetch the box of novels she had brought for the younger girl, and she hastily dug out a ten pound note from her reticule and placed it in one of the books. As she descended the carriage, she stood for a moment. The small cottage beckoned her. This was a home. Cameron's home. A tear fell gently down her cheek. She would have lived here happily—without servants, without seven-course meals, without modern plumbing—if only she could have been with Cameron. If only he had really loved her.

★ ★ ★ ★

Cameron watched his beloved from the stables. Her blond hair was braided and twisted on top of her head in a severe style, so unlike the styles she normally wore. But today they were visiting tenants—a laborious day for a lady of the peerage. Her tan morning gown hugged her lush body, and she carried a box of what appeared to be books. Slowly he stepped out of the stable, unable to take his eyes off of her. *Start walking, Rose*, he said silently to himself. But still she stood, taking in the scenery. He should go back into the stables to avoid being seen. But he couldn't make his feet move.

Rose turned, and her mouth dropped open. She set down her box of books and walked toward him slowly. He resisted the urge to flee. His heart thundered.

"Mr. Price," she said, when she was about six feet away from him.

"My lady."

"I...I'm so glad to hear about Kat. Tricia told me that she's going to be all right. I've been so worried about her."

"Yes, she's going to be fine."

Rose sighed. "Well, I'll leave you to your...whatever it is you're doing." She turned.

"She asked for you," Cameron said, and then cursed himself silently. He was doing a lot of that lately. He had made the comment only so Rose would stay just a moment longer.

Rose turned back toward him. "Did she?"

"Yes, she wanted you to visit her."

"Why didn't you summon me?"

"I didn't think you would have the time to—"

"How could you even begin to think I would refuse her?" Rose shook her head, fire burning in her blue eyes. "I love that child."

"It wasn't appropriate for her to ask you to visit."

"I can't believe this. You actually thought I wouldn't come." Rose tucked a stray strand of hair behind her ear. "I would have done anything she wanted. I still will. I would never abandon her just because her big brother tossed me out like a...a...scrap of refuse!" Tears welled in her eyes.

"Rose..." Cameron's heart lodged in his throat.

"I love that little girl. Unlike some people, I don't profess my love only to refute it the next moment. I love her, and I will always love her. Just like I'll always—" She kicked the dirt under her feet. "I shall return in three days, Mr. Price, when Kat is back home. If you don't wish to see me, I suggest you make yourself scarce." She turned and began walking back to the house, and then abruptly looked over her shoulder. "Tricia has invited us to tea, so you'd best stay in the stables a bit longer." She flounced toward the house, picked up her box of books, and went inside.

Seeing her was exquisite torture. He wanted to be near her, even if he couldn't touch her. He walked out of the stables and ran toward the cold stream behind the hired man's cabin. He jumped into the cool water.

★ ★ ★ ★

Rose entered the cottage and found the others in the sitting room sipping their tea. "I'm sorry to keep you waiting," she said. "I brought these books for you, Tricia. I noticed how you devoured my Dickens novel when I was here last."

Tricia took the box. "Oh, what treasures! Thank you, my lady!"

"You are quite welcome, dear. Some of these are duplicates from my own library. I do wish you would keep them. Then there are a few others I thought you might enjoy that you can return at your leisure."

"How lovely!"

"Come," Rose said. "Let's take them to your chamber and I'll show you the ones you can keep. Will the rest of you excuse us for a few moments?"

"Of course, my dear," Maggie said.

Rose followed Tricia to her chamber, pulled out the five books for Tricia to keep, and opened one, showing her the ten pound note. "Don't tell your brother," Rose said, "but I want you to take this for Kat."

"Oh, I couldn't, my lady."

"Rubbish. I want to help. He won't let me, so I'm trusting that you will. It's not much, but please, promise you'll come to me if you need anything. Anything at all."

"Why are you doing this?" Tricia asked.

"Because I love Kat," Rose said.

"And...is Kat all you love?"

"Well, of course I care for you too, Tricia."

Tricia smiled. "I didn't mean me, my lady."

Rose warmed. "I'm afraid I'm a bit confused."

"You love Cam, don't you?"

Was she truly so transparent? "Tricia, where did you get that idea?"

"Because the two of you... I'm not a child, my lady. I recognize two people in love when I see them."

"Your brother is not in love with me." The words cut at her insides.

"Of course he is. Any fool could see it."

"I'm afraid you're mistaken."

"I don't think so. He lights up whenever you're around."

"I'm around now. Where is he?"

"Well...I don't know. Perhaps he went on an errand."

"Without telling you?"

"He could have."

"I highly doubt that, Tricia."

"Oh, my lady, please tell me. Do you love Cam?"

"My feelings for Mr. Price are irrelevant. We are from two different worlds."

"Please. He's been so unhappy. Tell him that you love him."

"Oh, Tricia," Rose took the younger girl's hand. "If you were older, we might have been best friends." She sighed. "I'm going to tell you something in confidence. You mustn't tell Cameron that I told you. Do you promise?"

"Yes, of course."

"I do love him, and he knows, Tricia. But he doesn't want

me. He sent me away."

Tricia's eyes widened. "I can't believe that, my lady."

"It's the truth. I...would have done anything to be with him."

Tricia shook her head. "What a nincompoop."

"I beg your pardon?"

"Not you, my lady. I love my brother dearly, but if he isn't the stupidest man in the world!"

Rose couldn't help chuckling. "He can't help it if he doesn't love me."

"Oh, but he does. That is what's stupid about the whole thing. I'll have to do something about this."

"Tricia, you gave me your word," Rose said.

"Of course, I would never break your confidence, my lady. I'll think of something. Will you come back to see us soon?"

"Yes, I'm coming back in three days to see Kat."

"Perfect," Tricia said, her eyes sparkling with mischief. "Just perfect."

She looked so happy. Rose didn't have the heart to tell her not to bother. Tricia would know the truth soon enough.

Cameron didn't love Rose, and he never had.

CHAPTER NINE

Toward the end of the week, Rose gathered a bag of sugar candy and some more books together and summoned Lily's carriage to take her to the Price cottage for her visit with Kat. She was secretly glad that Ally and Sophie were busy with Aunt Iris and Lily's modiste, Madame LeRou, choosing gowns for the wedding. Rose wanted to go alone. She had a servant hitch Begonia to the back of the carriage. Perhaps she would take Kat riding, if the little girl felt up to it. She didn't fear running into Cameron. He would no doubt be off somewhere else.

Tricia met her outside when the carriage arrived. "My lady," she said, running to greet her, "Kat is so excited to see you! But I fear I have some unfortunate news."

"Is anything wrong?"

"No, no, of course not. The unfortunate news is that... well, Cam left this morning. He'll be gone on errands all day."

"Because I was coming, no doubt."

"Yes, I'm afraid so. He's stubborn as a mule, that one."

Rose forced a smile, hoping it looked sincere. "My dear, I told you the truth the other day. He doesn't want to see me. But that won't keep me from visiting you and Kat."

"Yes, my lady."

"Tell me, are you enjoying your new books?"

"Oh yes. I've already devoured two of them."

Rose laughed. "You read like Lily. She can lose herself for hours in a book. Come on." She linked her arm with the younger girl's. "Let's go see that adorable little sister of yours."

Kat's eyes danced when Rose entered the cottage. "Lady Rose!" she shouted, running into her arms.

"Dear little Kat," Rose said, "it's so good to see you running about."

"I almost died!"

"Oh my."

"Kat, don't frighten Lady Rose," her mother admonished, coming in from the kitchen. "Good afternoon, Lady Rose."

"Good afternoon, Mrs. Price. I'm so very glad that everything is well with Kat."

"As we all are, my lady."

"Tell me, were the doctors ever able to ascertain the cause of her condition?"

"I'm afraid not. But once the fever broke, she had no more symptoms, so after a few days they let us come home."

"Do they consider her cured?"

"Yes, at this point they do. But I'll be walking on pins and needles until I'm comfortable that she won't become ill again."

"I understand. But look at her. It's marvelous to see her back to her old self."

"Yes, it is."

"Is there anything I can do for you, Mrs. Price? You are tenants on my sister's land, and I know the family would like to help in any way they can."

"No, Cameron would never forgive me if I took any charity, my lady."

"Goodness, I'm not offering charity. Neighbors help each other, Mrs. Price."

"We've no need of your help at this time." Mrs. Price's tone was curt.

"All right. But I hope you won't hesitate to come to us if that changes."

"Of course."

"Now"—she turned to Kat—"my precious, what would you like to do today?"

"I have it all planned," Kat said. "First, I want to listen to you play the pianoforte. Then, we'll read a story. Then, I want to go out and play."

"Kat, Lady Rose is a lady of the peerage. She doesn't play," Mrs. Price said.

"Of course I do! I'd love to play with you, Kat. We'll do whatever you like. She is strong enough to play, is she not, Mrs. Price?"

"I'd rather she not run around, my lady."

"Mum!" Kat whined.

"Don't you worry, Kat. I have another idea," Rose said. "I brought Lily's mare with me, and I can take you riding. Would you like that?"

"Oh, could I, Mum?"

"I suppose so. She would ride with you, my lady?"

"Yes."

"Can Tricia come too?" Kat asked.

"Of course. I was planning to invite her."

"Just don't go too far," Mrs. Price warned.

"We'll let Tricia lead the way," Rose said.

"Perfect," Kat said.

"Good. Now, what would you like to hear me play first?" Rose sat down at the pianoforte.

"Anything at all," Kat said. "You play wonderfully."

"All right. What is this, I wonder?" Rose fingered some parchment sitting on the bench. She put it in order and began to play. It was a ballad. "Did Mr. Price write this?" she asked.

"Yes, my lady," Tricia said. "Those are some of the notes for the commission he was working on when Kat was in the hospital."

"Really? These are only drafts?" Her fingers danced over the keys. "It's lovely isn't it?"

"Yes," Tricia said. "He said it was his best work."

"Right. You told me that, didn't you?" Rose continued playing.

The music was tender and loving and brought a tear to her eye. The notes evoked images of Cam's tender lovemaking, of him bringing water for her bath, taking care of her virginal body. Abruptly she stopped playing.

"Is anything wrong?" Tricia asked.

"No. Let's just have something a little more lively, shall we?"

Rose played some rowdy folk songs, and they all sang together. Even Mrs. Price joined in. After about an hour, Mrs. Price made some tea and they all partook.

"Now, little Kat. What story would you like to hear?" Rose asked.

"Cam gave me a new book when I got home from the hospital. Could you read that one?"

"Of course. Bring it to me."

Rose read while Kat sat on her lap. The story was not long, and when Rose had spoken the last word, she held Kat on her lap for a few more moments, stroking the little girl's dark hair. "Are you ready to go riding, my dear?" she asked.

"Yes, let's."

"All right. Let's go get Begonia ready. Tricia, are you coming?"

"Yes, I'll saddle Mary."

Rose laughed. "You named your mare Mary?"

"It seemed...appropriate," Tricia said, giggling.

"It's adorable, actually. Is she the one you were riding the day that Kat got sick?"

"Yes."

"Oh, she is a beauty."

When the horses were ready, and Rose had Kat snuggled against her on her sidesaddle, they took a long ride around the Lybrook land with Tricia leading the way. The trees were lush and green, their newly sprouted leaves swaying gently in the afternoon breeze. Wildflowers were beginning to bloom, and the pinks and yellows decorated the lush vegetation. Squirrels and rabbits abounded. Kat laughed and pointed every time she saw another one running away from them.

"Lady Rose, they're afraid of us. Why? We wouldn't hurt them."

"Yes, but they don't know that, dear."

"But I love all animals. I would never hurt one. How can I let them know that?"

"They won't understand, I'm afraid. They're from a different world. They'll never understand that you mean them no harm."

"That's so sad," Kat said. "I want only to be with them."

"I know exactly what you mean, Kat," Rose said softly. "Believe me, I know."

★ ★ ★ ★

Cameron returned from his errands to find the Lybrook carriage still parked in front of his cottage. "Damn," he said out loud.

He stabled Apollo. "Damn again." Mary was gone. He stole quietly into the house.

"Where did they go, Mum?" he asked.

"They're out riding." Mrs. Price set down the quilt block she was stitching. "When are you going to tell me what is going on?"

"What do you mean?"

"I mean with you and Lady Rose. The last I heard, you loved her and you were going to marry her, and now you can't seem to stand the sight of her."

"She...she doesn't want me, Mum," Cameron lied. "Can you blame her?"

"You said she loved you."

"Evidently I was mistaken."

"You mean she didn't say that she loved you?"

"I guess I read too much into her language." He'd burn in hell for this.

"What exactly did she tell you, Cameron?"

"What does it matter? You were right. She and I have no future together."

"My poor boy." His mother patted the sofa. "Did she break your heart?"

No, I broke hers. "No, I'm fine. If you'll excuse me, I'm... going out. I don't want to be here when they return."

Cameron walked out back to the hired man's cabin. He would hide out there until Rose was safely off the premises.

What a mistake.

He hadn't been there since that fateful day when he had made love to Rose and then sent her away. The blankets were still rumpled. His mother hadn't cleaned the cabin because she hadn't been here. No one had.

Cameron sat down on the bed, grabbed the pillow, and hugged it to his body. It still smelled like Rose, that intoxicating blend of strawberries, cream, and woman. He could almost imagine holding her in his arms. He tossed the blankets off the bed and lay down upon it, remembering the warmth of her lovely body snuggled against him in sleep. The musky remnants of their lovemaking drifted to his nose. The aroma had been trapped under the blankets for nearly two weeks.

Why? Why had it come to this? He should have left her alone in the first place.

But would he change any of it? Would it have been better never to have loved her at all? To pine for her from afar, never having known the sweetness of her body joined to his?

No, it never should have happened. He had taken her virginity and given her nothing in return. He had ruined a lovely maiden and tossed her aside, hurting her beyond measure. He was a scoundrel of the highest order.

He would never marry. No one would ever replace Rose in his heart.

He sat cross-legged on the bed and buried his head in his hands.

★ ★ ★ ★

The girls returned from their ride, and Rose sent Kat and Tricia inside while she tended to the horses. She put Begonia in an empty stall next to Mary and headed toward the cottage. The hired man's cabin stood in the distance. Without thinking, she turned and headed toward it. The door was slightly ajar, and she quietly opened it. Cam sat on the bed, his head in his hands. He hadn't heard her come in.

"You didn't have to lie to me, you know."

Cameron looked up, his eyes sunken and wet. "What?" he asked hoarsely.

"You didn't have to tell me you loved me," she said. "I would have gone to bed with you anyway." The truth of her words stung. She strode forward slowly and regarded his beautiful face, eyes moist and nose running. "What is the matter? Did you hear something from the doctor?" She sat down next to him and tentatively touched his arm.

Nothing.

"Cameron, why don't you answer me?"

"Leave me," he said.

"No, if it's about Kat, I want to know."

"Kat's fine."

"Thank goodness." Unable to stop herself, she stroked the black silk of his hair. "What is it then?"

"I'm fine."

"Cameron, you're not fine. Anyone with a brain can see that."

"I...I..." He turned and gazed into her eyes. "You would offer me comfort after the way I've treated you?"

"You seem to think me some sort of shrew. I don't know what I did to deserve that. But I would offer anyone comfort who needed me."

He remained silent. After a few minutes, she rose, went to the basin, and returned with a wet cloth. "This water's a bit old," she said, "but I think it will do the trick." She gently wiped the tears and grime from his face, and then she took his hands in hers and wiped them as well. "What on earth have you been doing today, rolling in the dirt?"

Again he didn't answer. She got up, rinsed the cloth, came back, and ran it over his face again, pushing his hair behind his ears and wiping his neck. Then she touched the moist cloth to the part of his chest bared by his shirt, slowly caressing him, wiping away the dust and sweat. "There, that's better." She set the cloth on the night table. "Oops, I missed a spot." She grabbed the cloth again and wiped a smudge from his chin. He touched his hand to hers, moving with her as she continued to wipe around his jawline.

"I'm sorry, Rose," he said.

"Sorry for what?"

"Sorry for treating you...badly."

"I meant what I said. You didn't have to lie to me."

"What I did to you was unforgivable. I took your virtue, and I offered you nothing."

"Don't be silly. You didn't take anything. I gave it to you, and I wouldn't change a minute of it, Cameron." Again the words stung her, despite their truth.

"Cam. Call me Cam."

"I don't think that's appropriate, given the—"

"Please." He took the cloth from her, tossed it on the floor, and gently fanned his fingers over her cheek.

He was going to kiss her. She saw it, felt it, wanted it. "Don't do this," she said, her eyes misting. "Please don't."

"Just one." He lowered his lips to hers.

As their mouths glided together, a sob caught in Rose's throat. She tried to pull away, but he put his arms around her, crushing her to him, as he coaxed her lips apart with his silken tongue. She closed her eyes and let her heart take over her mind, joining in the kiss and searching him, tasting him, relishing the spicy sweetness of his mouth. She ran her tongue over his teeth, his lips, caught his lower lip in her teeth and bit it gently. He moaned, shuddering against her body, nibbling on her neck, her throat, her ears.

"Rose," he breathed softly. "My Rose."

His language startled her. She broke away forcefully. "Don't do this to me. It's not fair. I'm not *your* Rose."

A tear trickled slowly down her cheek. Cameron wiped it away with the softest touch of his finger.

"I'm so sorry."

"You didn't want me, remember? I offered myself to you completely, without condition, and you rejected me."

"Rose..."

"I gave you my virtue, Cameron, and more importantly, I gave you my love. I don't regret it, but I won't let you hurt me again."

She ran from the cabin, her eyes blinded by her tears, until she crashed into a wall.

Rose wiped her eyes with her fingers. The wall was Cameron's mother. "Mrs. Price. I'm sorry. I don't know what is the matter with me. I didn't see you."

"Cam is in the cabin, isn't he?" Mrs. Price said.

"What?"

"You were with him, weren't you?"

"I...yes, he's there."

"My lady," Mrs. Price said softly, but harshly, "I know that you are the duchess's sister, and we are living on Lybrook land, but I have to ask you not to return to our home."

"Pardon?"

"I know Kat is fond of you, and you of her, but your presence here... It is harmful to Cameron. He is hurting, and I can't allow it to continue."

"*He* is hurting?"

"Yes. He fancies himself in love with you. He'll get over it, but not if you keep coming around here, rubbing his nose in it."

"But Mrs. Price, I never—"

"I'm sorry, but that is my final word on the matter. I want you to go back to the estate now. I'll make excuses for you to Kat and Tricia."

"I can't—"

"That is *all*, my lady. Now I must see to my son." Mrs. Price walked away briskly.

★ ★ ★ ★

Cam looked up when his mother entered the cabin. She sat down next to him on the bed and stroked his hair.

"She's gone now, Cameron, and she's not coming back."

Cameron sniffed, his heart so broken he feared it could never heal. "You sent her away?"

"Yes. I won't let her hurt you anymore."

"This is silly, Mum." Maybe she would believe his falsehood. "I'm fine."

"You're not fine, Cameron. I'm your mother. You don't need to try to be strong for me."

He opened his mouth to speak, but she gestured him to be quiet.

"It's unfair, what you've been forced to do for us because your father died. You're a musician, Cam, and a fine one. If only you could have had the proper training. But that wasn't possible. Even so, you could have made it on your own if your father hadn't died."

"I don't blame any of this on him, or on you, Mum." And he didn't. He loved his family. How could he resent them?

"I know you don't. You're a good boy, Cam, and a fine man. Any woman would be lucky to have you. But Rose isn't worthy of you."

He let out a broken laugh. "That's where you're wrong. It's I who am not worthy of her. She is...amazing. She's not like some of the nobility. She sees people for who they are, not who they were born to."

Mrs. Price shook her head. "If she truly cared for you, she wouldn't have rejected you. How can you defend her after what she's done to you?"

"We did it to each other," Cam lied. "Neither of us is more to blame than the other."

"I don't see it that way."

"Well, that's the truth of it."

"It's not the truth of it, Cam. If she really loved you, she would have..." Mrs. Price closed her eyes.

"She would have what?"

"Cam." She opened her eyes and took one of his hands in her own. "There's something I need to tell you. Perhaps I should have told you long ago."

"What is it?"

"God forgive me for keeping this from you." She let out a breath. "I've always told you that my parents—your grandparents—were dead."

"Yes."

"Well, they may be, for all I know. But they may not be. The truth is, they abandoned me."

Cam widened his eyes. "What? Why?"

"Because I married your father."

"I don't understand."

"My father was a baronet, Sir Rexford Lyttleton, a

member of the gentry. I was Miss Clementine Lyttleton, and your father was a groom in our stables."

Cameron jerked forward. His mother's eyes held honesty.

"He came to work for my father when I was but ten and he was eleven. He was the bastard son of a local woman who died of cholera. Colton didn't know who his father was, only that he was a young earl. Your grandmother had been a housemaid in his father's employ. When he found out that she was pregnant by his heir, he tossed her into the streets. Her name was Joy, and she was not but sixteen."

Cameron shook his head, his mind a mass of swirling jumbles. "So you're telling me that I'm the grandson of a baronet, and the grandson of an earl?"

"Yes, that is exactly what I'm telling you."

Cameron tried to wrap his mind around this new reality. "And my great-grandfather tossed out a maid for getting pregnant by his son, and my grandfather tossed out his own daughter for falling in love with a servant?"

"Yes." She nodded.

"This from our nobility and gentry." Cam shook his head again. "The tyrants. Go on."

"My father took Colton in after his mother died and brought him to our small estate in Hampshire. He became a stable boy and eventually worked his way up to groom. He was amazing with horses. He was so intelligent. He seemed to be able to communicate with them."

Cameron's head continued to whirl. None of this made sense. His father had been a kind and loving parent, but intelligent was not a word Cameron would have used to describe him.

"I followed him around shamelessly," Mrs. Price

continued. "He was something when he was young. He looked a lot like you, Cam, except that you have my black hair. His was a dark brown. Your eyes are his, though. You probably remember them more as a dark grey, but when he was young, they were as silvery blue as yours. Your talent for music comes from him too. He used to play the guitar and the harmonica simultaneously in the loft of the stables in the evenings. He wrote his own songs. I used to sneak out of my room at night to listen to him play."

"Mum, Papa never played music. He never took any interest in mine."

She frowned. "There's a reason for that."

"What would that be?"

"I'll get to it. Anyway, Colton finally noticed me when I turned sixteen. We started sneaking around, meeting each other in clandestine places, stealing kisses." Her eyes lit up. "I adored him. I would have followed him anywhere."

"It seems that you did."

"Yes, I did. I never abandoned him, even after..."

"After what?"

"Well, when I was seventeen, I became pregnant with you."

"Before you were married?"

"Yes. I'm not proud of it, but it happened, and you were the result, so I've never been sorry. When my father found out, he threw us both out, and then he paid a gang of thugs to beat and bloody Colton." Mrs. Price took a few deep breaths. "Your father was never the same after that beating. I nursed him back to health as best I could, but I had no money to get him the medical help he so desperately needed. The other servants were sympathetic to our plight and let us hide in their quarters until Colton could travel. One of the thugs had hit your father in the head with a club, and it must have done something to his brain. That wonderful silver sparkle that your eyes have? Your father never had it again after that night. He never made music again. In fact, he couldn't do even the simplest ciphering anymore, and he could barely read. But he remembered me, and still he loved me and I him. He was what he was because of his love for me, so I couldn't abandon him. I didn't want to. But there was no way for him to make a decent living doing anything that required intelligence. When he was well enough to travel, the servants gave us enough money to leave Hampshire and travel here. Your father was strong and muscular, like you are, and was willing and able to work hard. We traveled along until the opportunity to work the Lybrook land presented itself." She sighed. "We've been here ever since."

"So we were never meant for this life, were we?"

"No, Cam. But the point of my story is—"

"Trish and I were talking the other day," Cameron interrupted. "She and Kat are so smart, Mum. In the back of my mind, I always knew we were different."

"Yes, the three of you are quite gifted. If only you could have had a proper education."

Cameron's mind raced. "It's too late for me, and probably for Trish too, but not for Kat."

"But how?"

"Let's leave here. We should have done it long ago. I'll go to Bath the first of the week and look for work. If there's nothing to be had there, we'll go to London."

"But the money."

"I have plenty. I finished that other commission,

remember? Assuming we don't have any more unforeseen medical costs, it will be enough for several months or more."

She touched his arm. "I haven't yet told you the point of the story."

"The point is that we were never meant for this life. And now that I know that, we're leaving."

"Cameron, that's fine. You've done your time here, and if you think you can make a better life for us elsewhere, we'll go, but that's not why I told you all of this."

"All right, Mum. What is the point?"

"I never abandoned your father, Cam. I never rejected him, even though he was below my station. Even when his brain was damaged and he couldn't do anything other than hard labor. I stayed with him and bore his children, made a home for him, because I loved him."

"Yes, that was noble of you."

"This is why Lady Rose isn't worthy of you. She wasn't willing to give everything up for you."

Cameron shook his head. "You don't know the whole story."

"I know enough. Now let's not mention her again."

"That's fine with me," Cameron said. God alone only knew how the mere mention of Rose made his heart suffer with an incurable yearning. She was no doubt betrothed to Xavier by now anyway. He had to forget her. "If I can find work in Bath next week, I'll rent a townhouse for us. If not, we'll go to London by rail."

"Goodness."

"And I can still take private commissions. I'll make a name for myself. I'll make you proud. You and Papa both."

"Your papa was always proud of you, Cam. You were

the light of his life. He never wanted you to know about his beating. He was afraid it would make him weak in your eyes. I told him over and over that you wouldn't feel that way, that you would be glad to know your musical gifts came from him, but he wouldn't be swayed. He made me promise on his deathbed that you children would never know the truth. Dear Lord, I hope I don't burn in hell for this betrayal."

"You did the right thing, Mum."

"That remains to be seen. If only there were more money. Oh!" Mrs. Price gasped. "Money! I nearly forgot. I still have the hundred pounds you gave me to pay the hospital bill."

"Didn't they find the error?"

"The bookkeeper said he did a thorough accounting, and he couldn't find an error."

"Who made the payment then?"

"He didn't know. Evidently it came in while he was on his lunch break. It was in an unmarked envelope, with a note attached saying it was to be used for Kat's care."

"I don't like the sound of this."

"It's a bit odd, but Cam, can't we just accept it?"

"It's charity."

"I don't know that it is. Maybe it's just our time. And Dear Lord, it's been a long time coming."

"Mum—"

"Don't tell me that an extra hundred pounds won't come in handy while you're looking for the perfect situation for your incredible talents."

"Of course, but—"

"Then let's just let it go this one time. We've never taken this kind of help before. We don't even know where the money came from, so we can't return it. Let's just say it was a gift from

God this one time."

Cameron smiled at his mother. "All right, Mum. Just this one time." He gave her a quick hug.

CHAPTER TEN

Cameron's first day in Bath was a disappointment. No one was hiring for anything, especially not an untrained composer who could play the pianoforte and the guitar. The next day, on a whim, he entered the Regal Theatre of Bath, a new playhouse that had been only recently completed. Since Bath had been linked to London by rail in 1841, the Theatre Royal, which had been built in 1805, had been bolstered. One of its most successful actors, Zachary Newland, had branched out on his own and constructed the new theatre, putting together a company and hoping to draw the crowds in from London and Bristol.

Cam had read about the Regal. Though similar to the Royal in size, the Regal sported a cozier atmosphere. Newland wanted to produce quality plays and musicales within his own company, as well as debut national productions that would eventually end up in one of London's noted theatres. It was near the end of the working day when Cameron knocked on the door of Newland's office.

The tall auburn-haired man opened the door. "May I be of assistance?"

Cameron cleared his throat. "Zachary Newland?"

"Yes?"

"Good afternoon." Cam held out his hand. "I am looking for work."

"Are you an actor?"

"No. A composer, actually."

"Hmm. Published?"

"Yes. Two pieces published in London. A folk tune and a waltz."

"No experience in composing for the theatre, then?"

"I'm afraid not. But I feel certain that I could do it."

"Where did you study?"

Cameron sighed. This was always the question he dreaded. "I'm purely self-taught."

"Oh." Newland pulled his timepiece from his pocket, looked at it, and frowned. "I'm on my way out, but if you'd like to leave me a calling card, perhaps I'll get back to you. However, I'm afraid I can't offer you much promise."

"Of course, I understand." Cameron reached in his pocket and pulled out a card with his name and address written on it and handed it to the gentleman. "Here you are. Thank you for your time." He turned and headed toward the door.

"Wait." Newland came up behind him. "You're Cameron Price?"

"Yes."

"That name sounds familiar to me. You say you've been published?"

"Yes."

"Perhaps I am familiar with your work."

"It's possible, though neither was widely distributed. I was young and unfortunately didn't really know how to market my music. I chose a small publishing house and wasn't paid much."

"You don't say." Newland scratched his head, regarding Cameron as though he were trying to solve a riddle. Suddenly his eyes widened. "Wait here, will you?" Newland briskly walked into another room and came back holding a piece of music. "Did you write this?"

Cameron took the parchment. It was a copy of *Lily's Waltz*. "Yes, I did. But I'm not sure how you came upon it. It was a private commission for the Duke of Lybrook."

Newland chuckled. "The duke sent it to me, along with a sizable donation to the theatre. His father was a great patron of the arts and was one of the Theatre Royal's greatest benefactors."

"I see. Why would Lybrook send you my waltz?"

"He suggested that I might find it interesting."

"And did you?" Cameron dared to hope.

"As a matter of fact, I did. It's a beautiful piece. You are quite talented. I never would have guessed that you received no formal training."

"Thank you, Mr. Newland."

"Tell me, would you be interested in serving as the house composer for the Regal Theatre?"

Cameron nearly jumped out of his skin. "Yes, definitely." Then, "But...would you have given me a second look if the duke hadn't sent you my piece?"

Newland laughed heartily. "Absolutely not."

Cameron frowned. "I'm afraid I can't take your charity, Mr. Newland. Good day." He turned to leave the theatre.

Newland came up behind him and blocked his exit. "Don't be a fool, Price. I'm offering you a chance that you wouldn't otherwise have."

"Of course I'm grateful. But in the back of your mind, you no doubt hope that by hiring me, you will continue to receive Lybrook's support."

"Don't be ridiculous." Newland chuckled. "That's not

in the *back* of my mind at all. It's in the front of my mind."
Newland slapped Cam heartily on the back.

Cameron opened his mouth to speak, but Newland
hushed him.

"Look, Price, I understand that you have your pride, and
I respect that, but it's nearly impossible for any student of the
arts to succeed without a patron backing him. I myself was
discovered by the Marchioness of Denbigh. She saw me in an
obscure little theatre outside of London fifteen years ago. I
was nineteen, and I hadn't had any formal training either, but
she thought I had promise, so she paid for my transport here to
Bath and set me up at the Royal. The rest is history."

"I really don't think—"

"And surely you've heard of Thomas Attwood."

"The composer? Of course."

"The Prince of Wales himself took note of him and sent
him abroad for training at his expense. Attwood eventually
became a student of Mozart and later returned to England
and enjoyed a hugely successful career."

"I understand, but—"

"I could name dozens more composers, actors, artists,
who only made names for themselves because they garnered
the favor of some wealthy patron. Besides, I have heard your
work"—he pointed to the waltz—"and I know you have talent.
It's not as though I'm hiring you blindly."

"No, I suppose not."

"I'm giving you a chance, is all. Lady Denbigh may have
discovered me and set me up at the Royal, but would I have
become the name I am today if I didn't have the talent to back
it up? If it makes you feel any better, rest assured that I'll send
you packing if your work is mediocre, regardless of the duke's

generosity."

Cameron couldn't help laughing. "You make a valid point."

"So what do you say? Would you like to give it a try?"

Cameron smiled. "Yes," he said, "I would."

"Excellent. We're a new theatre, as you know, and I'm just now putting our first production together. Opening night is scheduled for the solstice. We're doing, appropriately enough, *A Midsummer Night's Dream.*"

"What type of music are you looking for?"

"Original composition for preludes and postludes, scenery changes. Sometimes I'll want a piece for a particular scene."

"The solstice is only two weeks away."

"Yes, I know. Will that be a problem?"

"It depends. For a full orchestration I would probably need more time."

"We don't have an orchestra yet. I'll need arrangements for the pianoforte and a string quartet."

"I think I can accommodate that," Cameron said, hoping he wasn't overextending himself. "But tell me, with opening night only a few weeks away, what were you going to do if I hadn't walked in here?"

Newland let out a chortle. "What I always do, Price. Act. I would have acted like I knew what the hell I was doing. My pianist would have played some classical themes, changing them a little here and there."

"You could still do that."

"Yes, but original music would be much better. It will lend notes of authority and elegance to our first production."

"I see."

"I'll tell you what, Price. Let's see how you do for the next two weeks. We'll treat it as a private commission. I'll pay you... fifty pounds. Is that fair?"

"Yes, extremely."

"If it works out, we'll make the position full time, at three hundred fifty pounds per year. Will that work for you?"

Cameron tried to hide his jubilation, without much success, he feared. He felt ten feet tall. "That will be acceptable."

"I can give you an office here, or you can work at home. Whichever you prefer."

"I've never worked out of an office before."

"Then you can work at home."

"I think I'd like to try an office, actually." An office in the theatre. He couldn't stop smiling.

"That's fine. You can do both for all I care, as long as you get the job done."

"What about private commissions?"

"What you do on your own time is your business. As long as my work gets done, I don't care how many private commissions you take. Shall we shake on it?"

Cameron shook Newland's hand heartily. "I can't thank you enough, Mr. Newland."

"Just Newland is fine."

"All right. I appreciate your confidence in me."

"I'll see you tomorrow morning, around ten, and we'll go over what I need for the new production. I assume you've read *Midsummer*?"

"Yes, but it was years ago."

"Here." Newland handed him a copy of the play. "Read through this tonight so you're ready to discuss our musical needs in the morning."

"I will. I guess I'll see you tomorrow at ten, then."

"Wonderful. I'll see you out."

"Thank you. Oh, by the way, I'm looking for a townhome to rent in the area. Are you aware of any that are available?"

"For just yourself?"

"No, actually. For myself, my mother, and my two sisters. My mother is widowed and they are my responsibility."

"Yes, yes. I may have just the place, Price. I own a townhome not far from here. It has four bedrooms plus servants' quarters. I think you will find it quite pleasant. I can take you there now if you like."

"What are you asking for rent?"

"Five pounds per month."

"That sounds reasonable. Yes, if you have time, I'd be obliged to see it now."

The townhome was perfect, and Cameron paid Newland for two months' rent. Although it was nearly six o'clock, he stopped at a transport company and arranged to have his household moved later in the week. Then he mounted Apollo and began the long ride home. It was ten o'clock when he reached the stable, and he still had to read through the Shakespeare play and get up early to be at the theatre by ten. He wouldn't continue this commute. This would be the last night he spent in the cottage.

His mother was waiting up for him. "Better luck today?"

Cameron scooped his mother into his arms and twirled her around. "Much better, Mum," he said. "We are leaving this place. Pack up. A transport will be here in two days to move you and the girls to our new townhome in Bath."

"What?"

"You heard me. I got a job. I'm going to be the composer for the new Regal Theatre."

"Cam, what on earth...?"

"And I rented a townhome for us. It has four bedrooms, plus two parlors and a formal dining room. A schoolroom for the girls. Wait until you see the kitchen. And servants' quarters too."

"Can we really afford all this?"

"And indoor plumbing, Mum!"

"You need to answer my question, Cam."

"Yes, yes, we can. We have two hundred pounds. And I'll be making three hundred fifty pounds per year as the house composer for the theatre, plus I'll still be able to take private commissions."

"Oh, Cam, our time really has come!"

"You bet it has. You should have told me about Papa years ago."

"I know. You're absolutely right. It was foolish of me to keep such a silly promise."

"It's no matter. Things are looking up. Once you get moved in, I want you to hire a maid and a governess for the girls, and a cook—"

"I'll do the cooking, Cameron."

"Don't be silly."

"I'm not. We're not going to be spendthrifts, for goodness' sake."

"We have the money."

"Well, yes, thanks to a few private commissions. But we can't be sure things will continue to go our way."

"It's thanks to one of those commissions that I got this job. The duke sent a copy of my waltz to the owner of the

Regal, and he liked it. He recognized my name when I went in today, and he hired me. Of course, it sticks in my craw a bit that I didn't get the position on my own, but, well, suffice it to say that my new employer made some valid points."

His mother smiled. "If you're comfortable with the situation, Cam, so am I."

"I am. If it means getting you and Trish and Kat out of here, I am. I only wish I had done it years ago."

"I know. I should have told you the truth long ago."

"Don't berate yourself. I should have believed in myself more. It shouldn't have mattered what my background was. But I'm not going to berate myself either. It's time to move forward, Mum. We are finally moving forward!" He twirled her around again.

"Goodness, Cam, you're making me dizzy!"

He kissed her cheek. "Go to bed, Mum. You have a big day tomorrow, packing and all. You'll need to send a note to the estate telling them we're vacating the land. And Arnold. You'll have to let him go. Tell him to keep the money I paid him through next month as severance."

"Can't you take care of Arnold, Cam? I hate giving people bad news."

"I can't. I have to be back in Bath by ten tomorrow to begin my job."

"My, you'll have to get up with the sun. You'd better get to bed."

"I can't. I have to read this." He showed her the Shakespeare play. "It's the Regal's first production. They're opening on the solstice, and they need original music."

"That's little more than two weeks."

"Yes, but I told Mr. Newland I could do it, and I damn

well will." He smiled. Energy pulsed through him. He might well be up all night.

"Cam..."

"Don't worry. I'm not going to blow this opportunity."

"I know you won't."

"Could you do me a favor and pack a valise for me? I won't be back tomorrow. I can't continue this commute. I want you and the girls settled in Bath by the end of the week."

"Yes, of course. My, it's all so much to think about."

"Don't think too much. Just pack my valise and get to bed. I need to read through this play, and then I'm going to get as much sleep as I can before I need to get up and go back to Bath." He looked around the cottage. "It's hard to believe this will be my last night here."

"Yes. I imagine it is. You've been here your whole life."

"Wait until you see the townhome. I know it will please you."

"I'm sure it will. Would you like some tea?"

"No, thank you. It won't take me more than an hour or two to read through this, and then I'm going straight to bed."

★ ★ ★ ★

Cameron's morning meeting with Newland went well. Determined not to get writer's block, Cam sat in his new office, behind a solid cherry desk, comfortably ensconced in a lush leather chair. Newland had moved an old upright pianoforte into the room for Cameron's use, and he had brought his guitar in as well. Soon he was picking out notes and chords. Within a few hours he felt he had a good start, so he took a break for luncheon and walked around the city for a while. On a whim, he entered a furniture gallery and used ten of his precious pounds to purchase a new bedroom suite for his townhome. He couldn't sleep on the floor tonight, after all. It was a lavish mahogany four poster, with two night tables, a highboy and a lowboy, and satin sheets and spreads. He made arrangements to have it delivered before he returned to the townhome for the night. After he had enjoyed a meal of roast chicken at a local eatery, he made his way back to the theatre to resume work. About an hour later, Newland entered his office.

"Price, we're going to do a complete run through of the show. It might help you to have a look."

"That would be fine. I've gotten a pretty good start, I think. Seeing how you've put together the production will show me if I'm on the right track."

"Come on, then."

Cameron followed Newland into the auditorium and took a seat in the front row next to Milton Trenton, the director. They shook hands briefly and then sat back to watch the play. Trenton took copious notes on the performance, and Cameron was distracted at first by his scrawling, but soon got lost in the fantasy world of Shakespeare's enchanted forest. Newland played the part of Puck, and although he was tall and handsome with auburn hair and brown eyes, his acting ability was so great that Cameron had no problem imagining him as the impish Robin Goodfellow. It was a treat for Cam, who had never been to the theatre before. This was just a run through, not even a dress rehearsal, but the performance drew him in.

He was going to love this job.

He applauded enthusiastically after Newland's final monologue, and then left the auditorium and went back to his office. His work needed a few minor changes based on what he had seen, so he sat down and began writing, plucking notes on his guitar as he went along.

Several hours later, Newland poked his head in the door. "Still here?"

"Yes," Cameron replied. "What time is it, anyway?"

"Nearly seven. How did it go today?"

"Well, I think. Would you like to hear what I have so far?"

"Tomorrow, Price. I'm exhausted. Can I give you a lift home?"

"I should really stay and work through some more of this."

"Nonsense. It's your first day. Come on. I assume you're staying at the townhome tonight?"

"Yes. My mother and sisters will be here by the end of the week."

"Have you brought in provisions yet?"

"I ordered furniture for the master suite today, but other than that, no. There hasn't been time."

"So the kitchen is empty then?"

"I'm afraid so. I ate out for lunch."

"Then you can sup with me. My chef is excellent."

"I couldn't impose."

"It's no imposition, Price. In fact, my sister is visiting. I'm sure you'll enjoy her company."

Lord. He was trying to play matchmaker. Yet Newland was his employer and it wouldn't do to turn down his invitation.

"I'd be obliged, Newland. Are you far from here?"

"About a half hour in my carriage. Only a few blocks from your new place. You'll be able to walk home from there."

"All right. Shall we, then?"

Newland's townhome was about three times the size of what Cameron had rented. "How long have you been here?"

Cameron asked.

"About five years. Before that I lived in the house you're renting. I stayed there many years after I could have afforded to move. I felt it necessary to watch my money carefully. I grew up poor, you see, and that's a mentality that doesn't go away overnight."

"I understand what you mean," Cameron said. "Has the other home been vacant for long?"

"About a month. The family renting it moved to Bristol."

"I'm lucky it was available then."

"Yes, sometimes timing is everything," Newland agreed, handing his hat to his butler. "Ah, here comes Evelyn now. My dear, I'd like you to meet Mr. Cameron Price. He's the new composer I was telling you about. Price, my sister, Miss Evelyn Newland."

"It's a pleasure, Miss Newland," Cameron said, bowing.

"The pleasure is mine, sir." Evelyn beamed. She was attractive, with auburn hair and dark brown eyes.

Although her stature was average, Cameron found himself thinking that she was too short. He was comparing her to Rose, of course, who was tall. It was his eternal damnation to compare every woman he met from now on to Rose, and he would no doubt find them all lacking. Perhaps he was meant to remain a bachelor forever.

"The chef has prepared his specialty tonight, *coq au vin*," Evelyn continued. "I'm sure you'll find it to your liking, Mr. Price."

Cameron cleared his throat. *Coq au vin?* He guessed that was French. "I'm sure it will be excellent," he said, hoping it wasn't brains or stomach. The French were fond of eating strange things.

It turned out to be chicken cooked in red wine, and it was indeed delicious. It was served with buttered green beans, creamed vegetable marrow, and new potatoes with parsley. A fruit and cheese tray followed, and coconut cake for dessert. The Newlands were lively company, and Cameron smiled and laughed more than he had in a long time. When the last dessert plate was taken from the table, Newland stood.

"Would you care for a port, Price?"

"Yes, of course." He rose.

"If you two gentlemen will excuse me." Evelyn stood and left the dining room.

"She's pleasant," Cameron said.

"Yes, Evie's a great girl. Come, we'll take our port in the smoking room."

Newland led Cam to a lush room adorned in distinctly masculine decor.

"Do you hunt?" Cameron asked, noting the head of a stag mounted on the wall above the hearth.

"Heavens, no," Newland said. "Where would I find the time? That's just decoration. Hunting is a sport for the nobility."

Cameron nodded. He should have known that. Determined not to make an idiot of himself again, he took a cigar when Newland offered his humidor, even though he had never smoked one in his life. He followed Newland's lead, biting off the tip and taking small puffs as Newland lit it for him. The smoke tasted bitter in his mouth. He was wondering why men had any desire to suck on these tobacco sausages, when a bit of the smoke touched the back of his throat, sending him into a spasm of wheezy coughing.

"I say, Price, are you quite all right?" Newland asked.

"Yes, of course," Cameron lied.

"This is your first cigar, isn't it?"

"No, of course not," Cameron said. Then, "Well, yes, it is."

Newland erupted in laughter. "I couldn't stand it the first time either. You'll get used to it. You'll have to, if you're to hobnob with the theatre crowd."

"What do you mean, 'the theatre crowd?'" Cameron asked.

"The theatre won't run itself, you know. I expect my productions to be successful, but good reviews and ticket sales aren't enough to keep it going. We depend on our patrons."

"I see." Cameron nodded. "After all, you hired me to make Lybrook happy."

"Yes, in part. I also hired you because you have talent."

"What exactly are my responsibilities as far as the theatre crowd goes?"

"Your responsibilities are to write excellent, unforgettable music for our productions, Price."

"And...?"

"That's it. Although I will expect you to attend the soirees that I give for our patrons. I imagine many of them will want to make your acquaintance."

"And are many of them women?"

"Some," Newland said. Then, "Ah, I see what you're asking." He chuckled. "No, you won't be expected to barter your sexual favors for the good of the theatre. Although, when you meet some of the ladies who support us, you may not have a problem with it."

Cameron smiled. "I hope I didn't offend you, Newland."

"Not at all. My first patron, Lady Denbigh, never asked anything like that of me. Believe it or not, her intentions were purely altruistic." He laughed. "Just as well, since she was in her early sixties at the time, and I was nineteen. Too much even for a randy lad like myself to consider."

Cameron chuckled. "I see."

"Not that I've been a saint, mind you, but in all honesty I haven't made it a habit to—shall we say—service rich ladies to get donations for my theatre." Newland let out a chortle. "I usually service them for different reasons entirely."

The two men continued laughing together. The port was smooth, and the cigar began to taste much better by the time Cameron was finished. If this was the high life, he was ready for it.

★ ★ ★ ★

"Pardon me, sir, but Mr. Larson is here to see you."

"Christ." Dorrance Adams extricated his cock from the whore he was fucking and turned toward his servant's voice. "Could this have possibly waited a few minutes? And did you consider knocking?" He buried his erection in his trousers and grunted.

"I beg pardon, sir. I knocked but you didn't answer. And you told me to always fetch you straightaway for anything Mr. Larson deemed important. And he says this is important. *Quite* important."

"Fine, fine." He shooed the woman away. "I'll be down in a moment." He straightened his trousers, his cock still hard and unsated. He willed it down. Or tried to, anyway.

Within minutes he met Larson, a constable who'd been on his payroll for decades, in his sitting room.

"What in God's name is it, Larson?"

"I'm sorry, Adams, but I knew this would interest you."

Adams sat and motioned for Larson to as well. "Get on with it, then."

"I got word from one of my informants that a man was looking for work in Bath all day yesterday. He left his calling card in numerous places." Larson handed a card to Adams.

"Why on earth would I—" Adams jerked forward, his eyes wide. *Cameron Price.* Then he shook his head, regaining his composure. "It's a common enough surname. This is of no consequence."

"That was my first thought as well, but the young man fits the description of the bastard and his father. Dark hair, silver-grey eyes."

"Impossible. The bastard was killed decades ago."

Larson cleared his throat. "Yes. There's no way he could have survived that beating."

"Then what is this about?"

"He might have fathered a child. I don't know. I'll find out all I can. But I thought you'd want to know." Larson nodded and left the room.

"God damn it," Adams said under his breath. "God damn it all to hell."

CHAPTER ELEVEN

Near the end of the week, Rose summoned Lily's coach and rode out to the Prices' cottage, determined to find out the truth. She had stayed away for a week, but she couldn't get the words of Cameron's mother out of her mind. She had intended to honor the older woman's wish for her to stay away, but damn it, she needed to know. Did Cameron love her? Mrs. Price had indicated he did. Yet Cam himself denied it.

But he had kissed her the previous week, a kiss filled with love and passion. Rose expected Evan to propose to her any day now. Before she could decide how to respond, she had to know the truth of Cam's feelings.

Her heart thumped as the carriage stopped in front of Cameron's cottage. Bracing herself to be strong, she descended with the help of Lily's coachman. She breathed deeply and readied herself for a fight with Cameron's mother, who had told her in no uncertain terms that she was never to return here. Rose knocked hesitantly on the door.

No response. She knocked more forcefully.

Again no answer. The door was slightly ajar so she opened it and went in. "Mrs. Price?" she called. "Cameron?"

She walked out of the small entryway and into the sitting area. She breathed in sharply, shocked. The house was vacant. The tattered chairs in the corner were gone. The worn brocade sofa was gone. The twangy pianoforte, gone. Quickly she ran from room to room. Everything was gone. She ran out the back door to the hired man's cabin. The slipper tub was gone. The nightstand and the table and chairs were gone. But the bed, where she and Cameron had made love, remained, the covers still rumpled.

She walked to it and sat down, brought the quilt to her face and inhaled. Cameron's spicy aroma still permeated the fabric. Slowly she lay down upon the bed, enfolding herself in Cam's scent. He hadn't taken the bed. He had left it.

He had left her.

She wept quietly into the pillow.

Several minutes later she rose from the bed, folding the quilt neatly. She would take it, as a token to remember her time with Cameron. He hadn't wanted it or the bed. Apparently she had meant nothing to him after all. His mother had been mistaken. A huge sigh escaped Rose's throat as she wiped her eyes and nose on the folded comforter and threw it back on the bed.

She would leave it. The time had come to say goodbye to Cam and what they had shared. She would get on with her life.

She would accept Evan's proposal when it came.

★ ★ ★ ★

When Rose returned to Laurel Ridge, she was surprised to see Evan's carriage. Although it was Friday, he and his father weren't due to arrive until later that afternoon. She stepped out of the carriage and hurried into the mansion. She knew her eyes were red and swollen and her cheeks stained with tears. She nearly ran to the staircase, hoping to avoid Evan, but ran straight into Lucy.

"Goodness, dear, why are you in such a hurry?" Lucy

widened her eyes. "What is the matter?"

"I'm sorry, Aunt Lucy, I should have been looking where I was going," Rose replied, and then burst into tears.

"Darling girl, come with me." Lucy led her up to the third floor, to her suite of rooms in the north wing. She rang for a tea tray, sat Rose down on a rich brown velvet sofa, and took her hand.

"Now, what on earth is going on?"

Rose's sobs came in large gulps. "I...need to talk to someone," she wept. "Usually it's Lily I talk to, but she's not here. And now... Oh, I don't know what to do!"

"Goodness."

Lucy rose and came back with a large handkerchief and a moist cloth. She gently wiped Rose's face, which only made Rose cry harder as she remembered wiping Cameron's face.

"There, there now. You can talk to me. Or if you'd rather, I'll get your aunt or one of your cousins."

"No, that's not necessary," Rose said. "In fact, I think you might be the perfect person to talk to."

"I'll help in any way I can." Lucy swept the handkerchief over Rose's nose again.

A knock on the door brought the tea tray.

"You take it sweet, don't you?"

"Yes, just slightly." Rose sniffled.

Lucy prepared the tea. "Here you are." As she prepared another cup for herself, she said, "What in the world has you so upset?"

"I'm not sure where to begin," Rose said.

"At the beginning, of course."

"I...I've fallen in love, Aunt Lucy."

"With Lord Evan?"

"No. It's not Evan. I only wish it were. Life would be so much simpler that way."

Lucy smiled. "Love is rarely simple. Believe me, I know."

Rose cleared her throat and blew her nose noisily into the handkerchief. "I...I don't want to pry, but Auntie Iris once told me that you were in love once, with a Scottish sailor."

"He was Irish, actually. And yes, I was deeply in love with him."

"How did you meet him?"

"I was not but seventeen. He was on shore leave and was visiting his aunt and uncle, who happened to live in the townhome next door to ours in London. Oh, he was splendid. He had a shock of thick red hair and a chiseled face that sculptors would envy. We took to each other right away. He had a month of leave, and we spent nearly every day together."

"That sounds lovely."

"Oh, it was. Of course, my parents weren't thrilled with the match. Our family wasn't part of the nobility, you know. My father was a self-made man, a successful businessman with interests here and abroad. He had helped manage the estates of many aristocrats and his advice was quite sought after. He had high hopes that his daughters would marry into the peerage. And of course, Maggie did."

"What exactly happened to your— What was his name?"

"Nolan. Nolan O'Brien." Aunt Lucy smiled. "He and I became betrothed, much to my father's chagrin. Nolan went back to sea, and he and I wrote each other every day." Lucy rose, walked into a different room, and returned with a cluster of letters bound with red ribbon. The parchment was withered and browned with age. "I kept every letter he ever wrote me. I still read them sometimes." She sighed. "Anyway, several months later, I had just turned eighteen, I got word that he had been lost at sea." A tear glistened in the corner of Lucy's eye.

"How sad. I'm so sorry, Aunt Lucy."

"Well, it was nearly thirty-five years ago."

"Why didn't you ever marry? Surely a woman as beautiful as you must have had other offers."

"I had a few in my day. About a month after Nolan died, Maggie became betrothed to the duke. They were married a week later, and I had no wish to stay at my father's house, knowing how he had felt about Nolan, so Maggie was kind enough to bring me here. The first few years, when Maggie's boys were young, she and the duke hosted many galas and house parties. I met a young earl who was quite taken with me, and I with him. And though I thought to marry him, in the end, I couldn't. My feelings for him just didn't match what I had felt for Nolan. Several years later, I was courted by a widowed viscount. He was also a very nice gentleman and I cared for him deeply, but I didn't love him." Lucy closed her eyes. "I suppose it was silly, looking back. I could have had a happy life with either one of them, and I truly would have loved to have had children."

"Why didn't you try?"

"I just wasn't willing to settle for less than what I felt for Nolan."

"I understand," Rose said. "I really do."

"I've had a full life," Lucy said. "Maggie and the duke treated me as one of the family, and I had a great relationship with Daniel and Morgan. They were almost like my own children."

Rose smiled at the lovely woman sitting next to her. At fifty-two, Lucinda Landon was still beautiful, with pale blond hair slowly turning to white and sparkling green eyes. She had a nurturing nature that was unequaled. For an instant, Rose imagined herself thirty years from now, in Lucy's place, living with Lily and Daniel as spinster Auntie Rose, forever pining for her one true love.

Of course, one giant difference glared between the two situations. Nolan hadn't wanted to leave Lucy. He had died. Cameron left Rose intentionally. She would never have a bundle of love letters to give her comfort.

"Goodness." Lucy embraced her. "Do you want to tell me what is going on?"

"Yes, yes," Rose wept. "I need to tell someone." She blew her nose again. "You must keep my confidence though."

"Of course. You know I will."

"Well," Rose began, sniffling, "you know Mr. Price, the man who composed *Lily's Waltz?*"

"Yes, of course. He seemed quite charming and attractive."

"He is. Or was. I don't know. But he's a commoner. Completely unsuitable for me. While we worked together on the waltz for Lily, he made it quite clear that I was above his station, a snotty pampered lady of the peerage. But we were attracted to each other. I found out how he felt the night of the wedding ball. He, well, he had been drinking, and he wanted to dance with me. It was the most wonderful feeling to be in his arms."

"Go on."

"He and I...that is...I thought... Oh, I can't bear this!"

Lucy tightened her hold on Rose and stroked her back. "There, there. It's going to be all right."

"I...I love him. And I thought he loved me. At least, he said he did. But he lied to me, Aunt Lucy. He lied to me so I would... so I would..."

"Oh dear, you don't have to say any more, sweetheart."

Rose let out a giant sob. "That's what he called me. Sweetheart."

"I'm sorry. I didn't know."

"I gave him everything. I gave him my body and my love. I gave him my soul. I would have lived with him anywhere. In squalor. I didn't care that he was a commoner. A tenant. I would have learned to cook and clean. I would have taken care of him. I would have..." Rose trembled against Lucy.

"My goodness, you poor little thing," Lucy consoled. "I can't believe Cameron would treat you this way. I've known that boy since he was a babe. His father was a fine man, a hard worker, and his mother is intelligent and strong. They were good parents. I never would have believed that he could... Well, even *I* have misjudged a person in my day. He's not worth this anguish, Rose."

"Oh, but he is. He's brilliant, really. His music touches me so deeply. I feel like it flows from his soul straight to my fingers when I play it. It's amazing, the talent that he has. I would have followed him anywhere, done anything to be with him."

"I know. I know."

"Aunt Lucy, did you and Nolan ever...you know?"

Lucy smiled. "I've never told anyone this, not even Maggie. But yes, we did. Twice."

"Did you ever regret it?"

"Not ever."

"I don't regret it either. It was my choice, and I loved him. I wanted him." She sobbed again. "I miss him so. When will it stop hurting?"

"It will fade, dear. It always does."

"It's just that...I could have sworn he was sincere. The things he said to me, the way he... Well, obviously I was just too naive and simple-minded to see through him, I guess."

"None of this is your fault."

"I know. I don't blame myself. I don't blame him either, really. I...still love him."

"I know."

"I just love him with all of my heart. I gave him everything and he—" Rose clutched at her stomach as a wave of nausea enveloped her. "Oh dear, I think I'm going to be sick."

Lucy hurried to fetch a basin, and Rose retched into it. Lucy smoothed her hair and wiped her mouth with a damp cloth.

"You poor thing." She took the basin away and then returned. "Is that better?"

"Yes, I don't know what's wrong with me."

"You're distraught, dear. Anyone can see that. Emotions turn physical every now and then. Calm yourself down. It will be all right."

Rose nodded. "But then there's Evan. He's been kind and gentle, and he cares for me and I for him. I'm fairly certain he's planning to propose marriage to me. But I don't love him. And I'm not sure if he loves me."

"Many successful marriages are based on virtues other than love, dear."

"I know. But you weren't willing to settle for that."

"No. But many do, without regrets."

"Yes, I know." Then, "Cameron doesn't love me. He left me, actually. His family is gone from the land. I went to see him today. His mother, well, she intimated that he was in love with me, so I went to find out the truth. They were gone. I have no idea where they went. Even knowing how he treated me, the thought of never seeing him again is nearly unbearable."

"I know."

"But Evan... I don't know what to do! And he's here, Aunt Lucy. I saw his carriage when I came back."

"Yes, he arrived early. Lord Brighton isn't due until dinnertime."

"So now I'll have to see Evan and pretend like nothing is wrong, and... I thought I had made up my mind to accept him, but now, after hearing about you and Nolan, I just don't know."

Lucy rocked Rose in her arms. "Don't you worry about Evan right now. I'll take care of you. You can lie in here for a while and rest, and then I'll have my maid come and fix your hair. You don't have to see Evan until you're feeling up to it."

"I'm not sure I'll feel up to it this century."

"You will. The pain fades after a while. I promise you that it does. Come now." She stood, helped Rose to her feet, led her into her bedchamber, and loosened her gown and corset. "Lie down for a while, dear. I'll send my maid in two hours to attend you."

★ ★ ★ ★

Later, after Rose had napped and changed clothes, she descended to the main parlor and found Evan waiting for her.

"Good afternoon, Rose."

"Evan, I didn't expect you so early. I'm sorry I wasn't here to greet you. Is your father here as well?"

"No. He had some business to attend to. He will be here in time for dinner, though."

"Are you feeling better about his marriage?"

"I'm dealing with it," Evan said. "But that's not what I came here to talk about. Could you come with me for a moment?"

"Of course."

Evan led her to the conservatory where a dozen red roses greeted her.

"How lovely," she gushed.

"That's only the beginning. Come here." He showed her to the grand piano. "I want you to play something for me."

She sat down on the cushioned bench and regarded the music set before her. It looked slightly familiar. As she began to play, the pleasant tune came back to her. It was the song she had played on Cameron's twangy pianoforte, from the notes she had seen. The final version was brilliant, and on the grand piano was nothing less than exquisite. Rose's fingers danced over the ivory keys, and her eyes misted.

This song was for her. Images of her and Cameron making love floated up from the keys, so clearly that she felt sure Evan could see them as well. Her cheeks warmed.

"This is a beautiful tune, Evan."

"It's called *Wandering Rose*. I had it written for you."

Rose closed her eyes and willed back the tears. Cameron had written the song for her.

Well, no, he hadn't. He had accepted money to write it for Evan to give to her.

Yet the music spoke to her, as if Cameron had entered her mind and taken the tune from her very soul. She opened her eyes. She was only imagining it. Cameron had been able to write a compelling waltz for Lily, one that spoke to Lily and her beloved, Daniel, without being in love with his subject.

This was no different. She swallowed, steeling herself.

"It's lovely, Evan," she said. "I do thank you for the gift."

"Come with me."

Evan took her hand and pulled her up from the piano bench and over to the satin couch, urging her to sit. He knelt before her. Rose sighed. She knew what was coming next.

"Rose," he said, "we've known each other for over two months now, and I care very much for you. I would consider it an honor if you would become my wife." He took a diamond ring out of his pocket and placed it on the fourth finger of her left hand.

"Evan, I'm honored, I truly am," Rose said, eyeing the ring he placed on her finger. It was a beautiful flawless diamond, at least three carats, she guessed.

"Then your answer is yes?"

"I...well...I'm v-very fond of you," she stammered, "but, I need to know. Are you...in love with me?"

Evan rose from his knees and sat down next to her on the couch, taking her right hand in his. He played gently with her fingers. "I care very deeply for you, Rose. As to love? I don't want to lie to you. I honestly do not know if I'm in love with you. I may well be. I care for you more than I've ever cared for another."

Rose sighed. "If you were in love with me, you would know."

"Are you in love with me?"

"No, Evan. Although I wish I were. I truly do."

"Then how can you say I would know if I loved you?"

Because I'm in love with someone else. "My sister told me," she lied. "It's not something one can put into words, apparently, but you'll know when it happens. You've no doubt never been in love."

"No, I suppose I haven't." He toyed with her hand. "But I do hold you in high esteem. And I'm attracted to you, and I want you. Many marriages have been built on less than that."

"Yes, I know."

"So I offer you my proposal. I think we could have a good marriage, Rose. We could be content. You would want for naught, I promise you, and I will devote myself to you and to our children."

She smiled. He was a good man, and she didn't want to hurt him. "I think we could have a good marriage too. And I believe you to be an honorable man, and I find you attractive and intelligent, and I enjoy your company."

"Then why don't we give it a try?"

"I had thought to do that. But, Evan, I've decided that... I think we both deserve better."

"Better meaning...?"

She squeezed his hand. "We deserve *love*, Evan."

He massaged her palm with his thumb. "We may never find that."

"True, we may not. But what if one of us did? What if, five years from now, you found your soul mate, but you were unable to be with her because you were committed to me? I know you are honorable, Evan, and you would never leave me."

"No, of course I wouldn't."

"But you would want to."

"No, I—"

"Look at your own parents' marriage."

Evan looked away. "My parents had a good marriage."

"Yes, but...how much do you know about the history between your father and my aunt?"

"They met years ago and became...friends."

"They met twenty years ago, Evan, and they didn't become friends. They fell in love. Yet they couldn't be together because they were both already committed to other people whom they didn't love."

"My mother was a wonderful woman, Rose. She was a good wife to my father."

"From what I've heard, she sounds like an amazing person," Rose agreed, "and I don't doubt that she was, to produce a son as fine as you." She smiled, patting his hand lightly. "But your father wasn't in love with her. Surely you knew that."

"Yes." Evan sighed. "I suppose I did."

"So when he met Aunt Iris all those years ago and fell in love, he wasn't free to be with her, nor she with him. That's sad, don't you think?"

"Well, they're together now."

"Yes, after twenty years!" Rose chuckled softly. "Do you really want to wait twenty years for your true love?"

"You and I could grow to love each other in time," Evan said. "That happens."

"Yes, it does. I believe it did so with Maggie and the duke. And it could, with us. I hold you in high regard and I enjoy our time together and I enjoy our...kisses. But if that is the case, shouldn't we wait until we fall in love to get married?"

"It's time I got married, Rose."

"Heavens, you're only twenty-six. My brother is twenty-eight and unmarried, and the duke is thirty-two and only now just got married. You don't need to be in any hurry."

"My father thinks I should marry."

"Really? I should think your father would understand

your need to wait until you fall in love."

"All right." He let out a breathy laugh. "My father hasn't said anything. I made that up."

"Why?"

"I don't know. I care for you more than any other woman I've known. Maybe it's not true love, but it's something."

"It is. It's a very nice something. But we are both young. Neither of us needs to be in any hurry."

"Perhaps you're right."

Rose withdrew the ring from her finger, placed it in his palm, closed his fingers over it, and clasped his hand in hers. "Let's wait. We can still see each other if you would like, or we could take a break and see if that perfect someone comes along for either of us."

"You're a wise woman, Rose." He kissed her cheek. "I wish we *were* in love."

"Oh, Evan, so do I." She brushed her lips lightly against his, in what she knew in her heart was their last kiss. "You will make some lucky woman very happy someday."

"And I envy the man who wins your love, my dear." He stood, helping her to her feet. "I have enjoyed our time together."

"As have I," Rose said earnestly. "I will always value your friendship, my lord."

"May I escort you into the parlor for an aperitif?"

"Of course. I'd be delighted."

"I'll speak to my father later," Evan said as they walked. "I'll tell him you and I have decided to...wait a bit before rushing into marriage."

"Thank you. I hope I haven't put you in an awkward position."

"No. I feel...*good* about things, actually."

"I'm glad. Truly glad." Rose smiled into his handsome face. "I couldn't bear it if I had caused you pain."

He smiled. "You haven't. I will miss you though."

"I'll miss you too," Rose said, and she meant it with all her heart.

They found Sophie and Alexandra in the parlor.

"May I inquire as to Lady Longarry's whereabouts?" Evan asked.

"Why?" Alexandra said. "So you can be rude to her?"

"Ally!" Sophie touched her sister's arm. "My lord, she's on the back terrace."

"Thank you, my lady." Evan excused himself.

"Rose, dear," Alexandra said, "you look a little pale. Are you feeling well?"

"It's just been a trying day," Rose said, "and I had a bout of nausea earlier. It's just nerves."

"Nerves? About what?" Sophie asked.

Rose took a deep breath. The girls didn't know about Cameron, and she didn't want to tell them. At least not yet. But she did need to tell them about Evan. "Lord Evan and I have decided to stop seeing each other."

"That cad!" Alexandra said hotly. "The way he reacted to mother's engagement, and now this. What on earth did he do to you?"

"He did nothing, Ally," Rose said. "It was a mutual decision."

"Dearest Rose, don't try to be strong. And please don't defend him."

"I'm not. Really," Rose said. "It honestly was a mutual decision. We're simply not in love with each other."

"He's a fool," Ally said.

"No more so than I," Rose replied. "We decided that we're both young yet, and we don't want to tie ourselves down when we might find love with another. Look at his father and your mother. They fell in love twenty years ago but couldn't be together because they both were committed to others."

"And he understood that?" Sophie asked.

"Yes. And he agreed."

"Then maybe he'll treat Mother with a tad more respect now," Alexandra said. "Although I won't hold my breath."

"Ally, he's going to be our brother. You shouldn't speak of him with such contempt."

"*Step*brother, Sophie. There's no blood between us, and I personally think he's a rude and obnoxious beast. A mountainous beast. Quite easy on the eyes though..."

"No, he's not a beast," Rose said. "He's a very honorable man. He was kind and generous with me. I'm going to miss him, actually."

"If you like him so much, I don't understand your decision," Alexandra said. "I know he's only a second son, but money doesn't seem to matter much to you. He's outrageously handsome, even if he is a beast, and you like him. What more do you want in a marriage prospect?"

"I want love, Ally." Rose sighed.

"Rose, just because Lily found a love match doesn't mean it's in the cards for the rest of us. It rarely happens, you know."

"But what about your mother and Lord Brighton?"

"A geriatric love match." Ally rolled her eyes. "How charming."

"Ally!" Sophie shook her head. "Mother and Lord Brighton are in the prime of life."

"Prime of life? Holy hell, Sophie." Alexandra erupted in giggles. "I can't even picture the two of them—"

"Goodness, Ally," Rose said, and then she too began giggling. "That's not something we should picture about anyone."

"It's fairly easy to picture Lily and the duke."

"Really, Alexandra," Sophie said.

"I'm sorry, but the duke is purely scrumptious. And even I shall admit, so is our dear stepbrother-to-be, even if he is a haughty beast." Alexandra smiled. "One only has to imagine—"

"Ally," Sophie said again.

"Don't you think Lord Brighton is attractive?" Rose asked Alexandra. "He reminds me a lot of Evan, actually. He's a very dashing older gentleman."

"I'm sure he was a gem in his day, Rose," Alexandra said. "But he's sixty!"

"We'll all be there someday, dear," Rose said. "He's still attractive, and Aunt Iris is still a very pretty woman."

"She certainly is," Sophie agreed. "It took me a few days to get used to the idea, but now I can truthfully say I am thrilled for both of them."

"Of course I am as well," Alexandra said. "Especially since it means we will be living on our own estate. Even if Evan will be there. He may be impossible, but at least it won't be painful to look at him. He is *splendid*."

★ ★ ★ ★

Iris turned toward the footsteps coming toward her.

"My lady," Evan said, approaching, "might I have a word?"

"Of course." She led him to a corner. "What is it?"

"I wish to apologize to you for my behavior on the last weekend, after you and my father announced your betrothal."

She smiled. "Goodness, you don't need to apologize."

"Please, my lady. I wasn't aware of the...*depth* of my father's feelings for you. I was very close to my mother, you see, and...well, I know she and my father were content, but I suppose it was obvious that they were never..." Evan looked at his feet. "I'm sorry, my lady."

"Please, I wish you would call me Iris."

"Of course...Iris."

"Evan," she began, "I have no intention of taking your mother's place. I could never do that in your heart, or even in your father's. But I love him very much and will spend the rest of my life trying to make him happy."

"You already make him happy," Evan said. "Even a fool such as I can see that. I just wish he and my mother could have had...what the two of you seem to share. She was a wonderful person. She deserved to be loved."

"I'm sure she did, and your father did care for her deeply. He never would have hurt her."

"I know that."

"And she gave him you. He adores you and your brother and sister. Sometimes he talks of nothing but the three of you."

"Then I hope he won't be disappointed that..."

"That what, dear?"

"Lady Rose and I have decided to...discontinue our relationship."

"Goodness. Why?"

"We aren't in love with each other."

"I see. Why do you think that would disappoint your

father?"

"Because Rose is...well she's Ashford's daughter, for one."

"Evan, your father wants nothing but your happiness. If you and Rose aren't in love, don't you think he will understand better than anyone why you choose not to marry her?"

"Rose thought he would."

"Of course he will." Iris smiled.

"If you'll forgive me for being bold, my la—er, Iris, I can see now why my father adores you. I can't promise to be completely comfortable with this situation, but I do wish happiness for both of you."

Iris took his arm. "That is all any could ever ask of you, dear. I think I'd like a short stroll before dinner, and David should arrive any moment. Would you mind escorting your future stepmother to the front terrace to await him?"

"It would be my pleasure."

CHAPTER TWELVE

Cameron had been working for Zach Newland for a week and had completed the music necessary for opening night. He had finished the final copy for the pianoforte, and he sat in the auditorium as the cast and crew readied for a dress rehearsal with music for the first time. Opening night was only a week away, and Cam still had his work cut out for him. After today, he would rework any parts of the score that didn't fit well, and he still needed to do a final copy for the strings. He yawned. He had been working past midnight and rising at dawn, but he was determined to please Newland. He would not waste this opportunity, even if he had to go the entire next week without sleeping a wink.

It had all been worth it when he had moved his family to the townhome. Kat's eyes had nearly popped out of their sockets when she beheld her own room and the bath chamber that she was to share with Tricia. Cam had gone out the next day during his lunch break and bought new bedroom suites for the three of them, furniture for the main parlor, and a new upright pianoforte to replace their old one. He also bought himself some new clothes. After all, he couldn't be the house composer of the Regal wearing farmers' clothes. Then, feeling guilty, he had given his mother ten more pounds to purchase new clothes for herself and the girls. He was down to one hundred pounds in savings, but rent was paid for two months, and soon he would receive his fifty pounds in commission for his two weeks' work. Newland seemed pleased, so Cam had every reason to believe that he would stay on as composer and begin drawing regular pay.

He had left home that morning with strict orders to his mother that a maid and a governess be in place by day's end. He had conceded and had allowed his mother to take care of the cooking, but had secretly decided to hire a cook after opening night. His mother had worked hard all of her life, and he wanted her to relax and enjoy her remaining years.

Cameron watched the rehearsal with rapt attention, scribbling notes regarding minor changes in the music. All in all, he was pleased with his efforts, although his heart thumped nervously when Newland approached him at the end of the dry run.

"So, Price," Newland said, "how do you think it went?"

"I'm pleased, although I'm going to make a few changes in the melody during the second act."

"I think it suits well. I agree with your assessment of the changes in the second act, and I'd also like you to perk it up a bit during my final monologue. It's supposed to be a bit more light and airy, I think."

Cam wrote some quick notes. "I'll get right on that. I'd like to have these changes made by the morrow, and I'm going to work late tonight to finish the final score for the strings."

"Not tonight, Price. I'm sorry I didn't mention this earlier, but I require your attendance at a gala at my home this evening. Several wealthy patrons will be there, and I would like for them to meet you."

Cameron's stomach flopped. So much work... He had no time for a party. "I would really like to complete my work. It's only a week until opening night, and the sooner I have the score finalized, the sooner we can practice the whole production."

"You're nearly done now, and I congratulate you on an excellent job. Clearly I made the right decision to hire you."

"Thank you. I'm glad you're pleased. If I could just finish—"

"I need you tonight, Price. There are several bigwigs that I'm still courting for contributions. Having another good-looking young man there will be...helpful."

"I thought you made it clear that I wouldn't be expected to offer services of that nature."

"Yes, I did. But I also made it clear that I would require your presence at my soirees."

Cameron sighed. "Yes, I suppose you did."

"You understand then. Go home. Bathe and change. I'll see you at my townhome at nine sharp."

After apologizing to his mother for skipping out for the evening, Cameron nervously walked the three blocks to Zachary Newland's large terrace home, rehearsing in his mind what he would say when he was inevitably asked where he received his music education. Newland didn't seem concerned about the issue. At least he hadn't mentioned it. It unnerved Cameron, however.

He had asked his mother to trim his hair before he left. His once unfashionably long locks now fell in gleaming black layers just touching his shoulders. He dressed in formal evening attire and looked the part of accomplished theatre composer. If only he could pull it off. If he didn't impress the theatre's patrons, he could probably kiss his job goodbye.

Newland's butler greeted Cameron and announced him, and Evelyn Newland rushed toward him, taking his arm.

"Mr. Price," she said enthusiastically, "Zach and I are so

glad you could make it this evening. I do hope we're not keeping you from your work. Zach says you are quite dedicated."

"Not at all, Miss Newland. I am happy to be here."

"Evie, please," she said. "That's what everyone calls me."

"Of course...Evie."

"Do come with me. There are so many people who are dying to meet you."

There were? Evie led him into the main parlor where guests were gathered together drinking aperitifs and grazing from trays passed around by servants. "Pamela, darling!" Evie led Cameron to an attractive redhead. "This is the man I've been telling you about. Zach's new composer, Cameron Price. Mr. Price, my dearest friend in the world, Miss Pamela Rhodes."

Cameron bowed politely, taking Pamela's hand. "It's a pleasure," he said.

"Oh my," Pamela said, batting her eyes. "You were right, Evie. He is something."

"I can pick them, can't I?" Evie said.

Cameron's cravat tightened around his neck like a noose. These two women were sizing him up like a side of beef. He was relieved when Zach Newland came by a few seconds later.

"Price," he said. "Come with me. There are some folks I'd like you to meet."

Thank God. Cameron followed Newland to a corner of the room where several men and women were gathered. "Here he is, the man of the hour," Newland said to the group. "The Regal's new house composer, Mr. Cameron Price. Price, may I present the Earl and Countess of Myerson, and Viscount and Viscountess Homington."

"I'm charmed," Cameron said.

He was drawn into conversation about composing, and blessedly no one asked him about his credentials. Newland brought several more guests by to meet him, and by the time dinner was served, he had learned—and forgotten—the names of more people than he had known in his lifetime. At dinner, he was seated next to Evelyn Newland and the Countess of Myerson. He did his best to see to both of their needs. Thankfully, he didn't have to worry about keeping the conversation going, as both women seemed determined to monopolize his attention. Trying to speak with both of them at the same time became tiring. He was thankful when it was time to retire to the smoking room with the other men. Too soon, however, company was mixed again as coffee and dessert were served casually in the main parlor. As the hour turned late, guests began leaving, but the actors and other staff of the Regal stayed, so Cameron did as well. He breathed a sigh of relief when the last guest had been shown the door.

Newland approached him as he was saying goodbye to a group of props men. "Price, thank you for coming."

"Not at all, Newland. It was a pleasant evening."

"I'm glad you thought so. You made quite an impression on Lady Myerson."

"She was engaging. I enjoyed her company as well."

"Good, good. She has asked you to dine at her residence tomorrow evening."

"She has?"

"Yes."

"I'm afraid I don't understand, Newland. If she wanted to invite me for dinner, why didn't she ask me?"

"Oh, that's just how things are done in this set sometimes, Price. Surely it wouldn't be too much to accept the invitation?"

"I suppose not. She and the earl were pleasant."

"Yes, yes. Good then. They'll expect you at eight tomorrow evening. Here is her calling card."

"All right."

"See you tomorrow at the theatre, Price."

"Of course. Good evening."

Cameron walked home briskly, the June air pleasant. He fell into bed exhausted, not relishing the idea of another late night on the morrow.

★ ★ ★ ★

The next day Cameron worked doggedly in his office, determined to complete the final scores before leaving to change clothes for his dinner with Lord and Lady Myerson. He completed them in the nick of time, rushed home, changed, and found, to his surprise, that the earl and countess had sent a carriage to fetch him.

Kat jumped up and down as she watched from the front window. "It's a coach just like Lady Rose's!"

Cameron smiled at his little sister, although jerking inwardly at Rose's name. "We'll have a coach like that before long, Kitty-Kat," he promised. "Then I can take you and Tricia and Mum around town in style."

"Will we, Cam?"

"You bet."

"That will be such fun! Maybe we can drive back and visit Lady Rose and Lady Lily sometime."

"Maybe."

"Why do you have to leave again tonight?" Kat's small hand tugged on Cameron's.

"It's just part of my new job."

"But I miss you."

"I miss you too. It won't be every night. I promise. Now you hurry along and get ready for bed. Don't give Mum any trouble tonight."

"All right. Good night, Cam."

"Good night, Kitty-Kat."

The coach ride to the Myerson home didn't take long, and Cameron was escorted in and announced. Lady Myerson rushed to greet him.

"Mr. Price," she said. "It is such a pleasure to have you here."

Cameron bowed. "I do appreciate the invitation, my lady. Being new in town, I haven't had the opportunity to meet many new people."

"I'm sure our Mr. Newland will take care of that," Lady Myerson said. "Please come with me. We'll have an aperitif in the parlor."

She guided Cam to a small divan and sat down beside him as a maid brought their drinks. The earl was nowhere in sight.

"Will Lord Myerson be joining us later?" Cameron asked.

"Oh no, I'm afraid not. He had an engagement that he couldn't miss this evening."

"I see." He was beginning to see very well. So much for Newland's promise that he wouldn't have to trade his services for donations. "Tell me, my lady. Why did you invite me here?"

"My, you do like to get right to the point, don't you?" Lady Myerson smiled.

She was a very pretty woman with cinnamon-colored hair and eyes, a perky round face and a firmly curved body. Cameron guessed her to be in her early thirties. Her mouth was definitely her most intriguing feature. Her lips were a spicy coral color, and the top lip was slightly fuller than the bottom, giving her a pouty look that was distinctive and, well, tempting. For a moment, Cameron imagined sucking on it.

"You're staring, Mr. Price."

"Pardon? Forgive me. My mind was elsewhere."

"I think I may know where."

He laughed nervously. "Opening night is less than a week away. I can't seem to focus on anything except my music these days."

"Zachary has assured me that you are extremely gifted. I doubt you need to worry about your compositions."

"I worry nonetheless. This is my first full-time post. I want to make sure that I do the best job possible."

"Zachary says that you are extremely dedicated."

"Yes, I am."

"I'm looking forward to discussing your work with you. Shall we head to the dining room?"

"Of course." He stood and offered her his arm.

She led him not to a formal dining area but to a small sitting room where a table for two had been set.

"Since it's just the two of us this evening, I thought a more...*intimate* setting would be appropriate."

Indeed. "It looks very nice." Cameron held her chair and took his place next to her.

"May I offer you some wine?" Lady Myerson asked. "This is a late Burgundy. One of my favorites."

Yes, he would need a drink to get through this evening. "Thank you." He took the bottle and poured her glass and then his own.

"I must tell you, Mr. Price, I've taken quite an interest in the new Regal Theatre."

"We all appreciate your support."

"You have that. I've been a fan of Zachary's for years. He's brilliant."

"Yes, he certainly is."

"From what he tells me, you are brilliant as well."

"He has shown a lot of confidence in my work, which I appreciate."

"I'm so looking forward to opening night. I'm sure your work will be inspired."

"I hope I don't disappoint you."

"I don't imagine you could." She motioned to an upright pianoforte in the corner of the small room. "Might you play something for me now?"

"If you wish, I suppose I could. But isn't dinner going to be served soon?"

"In a half hour or so. I thought we'd enjoy a glass of wine first." She rose and took his hand, leading him to the pianoforte. "Please. I'd love to hear something."

Cameron sat down. "You'll have to forgive my playing," he said. "I've a decent hand, but I'm really more of a composer than a performer." He began to play *Lily's Waltz*.

"Oh, that's lovely," Lady Myerson said. "Why have I never heard it before?"

"It was a private commission for the Duke of Lybrook."

"Really? How nice."

"He commissioned it for his wife, for their first dance together at their wedding ball."

"Myerson and I missed the wedding. We were on the continent. It must have been quite a gala."

"It was. A very extravagant affair." He finished the piece.

"That was beautiful," Lady Myerson said. "Could you play something else?"

"Yes, of course." The only piece better than *Lily's Waltz* was *Wandering Rose*. If he was going to impress this woman, that was the piece he should play. His heart wasn't in it, but he began stroking the keys softly, letting the melody and harmony of Rose flow through his body and into the pianoforte. He imagined Rose's unique touch giving life to the music she inspired. To hear her play his music, just once more, would be heaven. He came to the end of the piece and stopped playing abruptly.

"Now that was truly brilliant," Lady Myerson breathed. "It was haunting, yet joyous. Who inspired that piece?"

Cameron cleared his throat. "It was another private commission."

"Indeed? I could have sworn it was a love song."

"No," Cameron lied.

"You're a remarkable talent, Mr. Price."

"You're too kind."

"Rubbish. I am never kind, as those who know me will attest." She smiled. "In fact, I'm rather wicked."

"Indeed?" Cameron eyed Lady Myerson's seductive mouth.

"Oh, yes." She looked up as a footman entered the room. "Ah, I believe our meal is ready to be served. Come join me, won't you?"

Cameron stood up and followed Lady Myerson to the table, seated her, and then himself. A footman placed a steaming bowl of carrot soup before him. The meal was delicious, and Cameron enjoyed Lady Myerson's company. She was interested in his work, and was not at all surprised or bothered by the fact that he was self-taught. He told her of his family, and she told him a bit about hers. She had been a commoner before she married Myerson, so the two of them shared similar philosophies about life. After dessert, when the footman had cleared the table, Lady Myerson poured two glasses of port and bade Cameron to join her on a cozy loveseat. As the dinner conversation had been free of innuendo, he did so, thinking that her interest in him was solely as a composer. It became apparent, however, that he was mistaken.

"Mr. Price," Lady Myerson began, "you probably know that I have made several generous contributions to Zachary's fledgling theatre."

"As I've only been with the theatre for little more than a week, my lady, I'm afraid I'm not aware of all of our benefactors. However, I personally thank you for your support. I hope you won't find it misplaced."

"Oh, surely not. If anyone can make a go of it, Zachary can. Of that I am certain. In the meantime, however, I might be willing to make another gift."

"Your generosity is very much appreciated."

"Just how *much* do you appreciate my generosity, Mr. Price?"

"My lady?"

"Cecilia, please."

"If you wish." Cameron's throat constricted. He had an urge to loosen his cravat, but he sat stiffly. What to do with his hands?

"Do you know where Myerson is this evening?"

"Why would I know that?"

"He's with his mistress," Lady Myerson said. "He sees her several times a week. I'm afraid he doesn't see to my needs as he should."

"I'm...sorry, my lady."

"I find you very attractive, Mr. Price." She ran her fingers lightly over his hand. "I think we could get along very well together."

"You're not suggesting..."

"No, I'm not suggesting. I'm asking. I'd like you to take me to bed."

Cameron jerked backward. He hadn't expected her to be so blunt.

"Do you find me attractive, Mr. Price?"

"Well, yes. Of course I do, but—"

"Surely you're not so naive as to think I invited you here merely for dinner?"

"I was under the impression that I would be dining with you and your husband," Cameron said. "But when I found him absent, I had a pretty good idea what you were after."

"Good. Then let's get to it." She began to loosen his cravat.

"However," Cameron continued, "I make it a point never to sleep with married women."

"I see." She traced his jawline. "How about two married women then? My friend the Viscountess of Homington indicated that she might be interested in joining us this evening."

His cock tightened. Her sexy mouth beckoned to him, and two women at once? He'd never imagined that. He was still a farm boy at heart. The idea aroused him. He cleared his throat, willing his body not to betray his head and his heart. "I don't sleep with married women period, my lady, whether one or ten at a time."

"I could win you over, I think."

"I doubt it. I view marriage as sacred. And I have no desire to be pummeled by a jealous husband."

"Good Lord. Myerson doesn't care what I do, as long as I'm discreet."

"As tempting as your offer is, my lady, I'm afraid I must decline."

Lady Myerson took his hand in her own and led it to her breast. She wasn't wearing a corset, and her taut nipple brushed against his fingers. "I can see you will take some convincing."

"Your charms are exquisite indeed." Cameron drew his hand away. "However, I'm afraid I'll not be sampling them tonight."

"You are devilishly handsome, Mr. Price," Lady Myerson said. She began unbuttoning his shirt. "I bet you're an animal in bed, and I bet you're hung like—"

Cameron removed her hand before she could finish her thought. If she only knew! But she never would. "I'm sorry."

"Goodness, what on earth is wrong with you? Don't tell me you like men?"

He laughed. "No. I assure you that is not the case."

"Then come now, I won't bite." She giggled. "Well, I will, but you'll like it."

"I have every confidence that I would enjoy myself immensely in your bed," he said. "I'm flattered that you desire me. However..." He cleared his throat.

"However, what?" She leaned into him. "You like my mouth, don't you? I've seen you staring."

"As I said, I am aware of your charms."

"Then"—she brushed her lips over his—"taste me."

He ran his tongue over her sensual upper lip, gently

sucked on it. As he readied to plunge into her delicious mouth, Rose's pink lips flashed into his mind. He backed away. "I'm sorry. You are beautiful, but I can't."

"Why on earth not?"

"I...love another."

"Goodness, I'm not asking for your love."

"I understand that. But I...want to remain faithful to her." His statement, although truthful, was ridiculous. Rose was no doubt betrothed to Xavier by now and had possibly already gone to his bed. Bile rose in his throat at the thought of another man touching Rose. He quickly banished the image from his mind.

He regarded the woman next to him. Lady Myerson was beautiful and desirable, but Cameron didn't want to make love to any woman but Rose. He would pledge her his fealty, even though it would not be returned. Was he really condemning himself to a life of celibacy? For the moment, at least, he was.

"Are you betrothed to your lady?" Lady Myerson asked.

"No."

"Then there's no reason why we can't enjoy each other. She'll never know."

"No, she won't. But *I* will."

"My. You are smitten, aren't you? She's a lucky woman. Tell me, who is she?"

"I'd rather not say."

"Why?"

"She's a lady of the peerage."

"Oh. Doesn't she return your feelings?"

"She does, but I fear we may never be together. It won't work out. We're from two different worlds."

"Are you planning to propose to her?"

"No, actually."

"Oh?"

"I'd rather not discuss this." He rose. "Thank you for the meal and your company. I enjoyed both very much. And I hope..."

"Yes?"

"I hope there won't be any...discomfort between us."

"Of course not."

"And I hope you won't withdraw your support of the Regal because of...how this evening ended."

"No, Mr. Price. Zachary and I go way back, and I believe in his endeavor. As a matter of fact, it took me several attempts before *he* landed in my bed." She smiled. "I don't think I'll give up on you just yet."

"Are you and Newland still involved?"

"No. We tired of each other. But it was fun while it lasted."

"I see." He took her hand and brushed his lips lightly over her fingers. "You've been a pleasant diversion this evening. Part of me wishes I could stay."

"I'm flattered."

"Good evening. I'll see myself out."

CHAPTER THIRTEEN

Rose awoke to pounding on her chamber door. She stood, nearly falling over from dizziness. She was coming down with something. She had been nauseated and dizzy for the past several days, and she couldn't stand the sight of food. She had decided to sleep most of the day. Aunt Iris's wedding was only four days away, and she wanted to be well by then.

The pounding continued.

"I'm coming, I'm coming," she said.

She opened the door.

"Rose!" her sister cried.

"Lily, what on earth? You weren't supposed to be home until the solstice."

"That's only three days from now, dear. You might be a bit happier to see me."

"Oh, I am, I am." Rose hugged her sister, pulling her into the room. "You have no idea how happy I am to see you. I've been dying to talk to you. When did you get in?"

"Late last night. Daniel and I were so fatigued we just fell into bed. But I was up with the birds this morning. I couldn't wait to see everyone."

"Why did you come home early?"

"The duchess—that is, the dowager duchess—*I'm* the duchess, good God! Anyway, she sent word of Auntie Iris's impending nuptials, so Daniel and I decided to come home a few days earlier than originally planned."

"That's wonderful, but I'm sure Aunt Iris didn't want to cut your trip short."

"No, no. We were glad to come home. We did have a splendid time though. I have finally seen the Louvre! France is absolutely wonderful."

"I want to hear all about it."

"You shall. But first, I have the most wonderful news!"

"What?"

"I've been feeling wretched!"

"So have I," Rose said dryly. "Why is that wonderful news?"

"Because," Lily smiled, "I've missed my courses!"

"Oh! Lily, you don't mean... That's perfectly marvelous! I'm so happy for you." Rose embraced her sister. Then, "Oh my God."

"What is it?"

"Your courses. You've missed your courses."

"Yes."

"And you're feeling wretched."

"Yes. I've never been so happy to feel so terrible!"

"Of course, I'm thrilled for you, but..."

"What is it, Rose?"

"I've been feeling terrible too, Lily. I haven't even thought about my courses. I never even imagined..."

"Rose?"

"But it's been a while since I last... Oh my God, it was way before..."

"Rose, what are you trying to say?"

"Oh no." Tears welled in Rose's eyes.

"Rose, you didn't..."

"Yes, I did. What am I going to do?"

Lily took her sister's hand. "Who was it?"

"Cameron, of course. There was never anyone else."

"What of Lord Evan?"

"He and I have ended our relationship."

"You mean he didn't propose?"

"Oh, he did. But I turned him down. I don't love him, and he doesn't love me. He admitted it. I just couldn't marry one man when I love another."

"You and Cameron are in love? That's wonderful!"

"Not exactly." Rose buried her face in her sister's shoulder. "Oh, Lily. I don't know what to do!"

"It's going to be all right. I've already sent word to Dr. Blake. He should come out later today if he's not too busy. We'll simply have him examine you also, and then we'll go from there."

"Lily, no one can know."

"Blake will be discreet, dear. I trust him. I will speak to him privately when he comes."

"You can't tell anyone. Not even Daniel."

"Of course. You have my word." Lily took a small handkerchief out of her pocket and wiped away Rose's tears. "Now stop crying. We don't even have any answers yet. It's possible that you're not with child. Neither of us may be."

Rose sniffled loudly. "What will become of me?"

"If you are pregnant, I'm sure Cameron will do the right thing by you."

"No," Rose sobbed. "He won't."

★ ★ ★ ★

Dr. Blake's examination had been humiliating. Only Cameron

had seen and touched her intimate parts. Yet she could have borne it, had she been happily married like Lily. She had felt cheap and used. The doctor was a perfect gentleman, yet Rose felt soiled and ugly. Then the blow. The truth she already knew. She was expecting a child.

So was Lily. Rose hated herself for being in this situation, and hated even more the fact that Lily couldn't rejoice in her own pregnancy because of Rose's state of affairs. Instead, Lily sat in her private sitting room with Rose cradled in her arms, when she should have been running to tell her husband he was going to be a father.

"How can you ever forgive me for this?" Rose said. "I've ruined your good news."

"Don't be silly. I'll tell Daniel later, and I'll ask him to keep it to himself for a little while. I...I'll tell him that I'm afraid of losing the babe, that I want to keep it quiet for a bit. You know Mummy lost a few. And I might have lost one after my fall. He'll believe that."

"This is horrible. Just horrible. Wonderful for you, of course."

"We'll figure it out."

"Papa, Mummy, and Thomas are arriving tomorrow. So are Evan's brother and sister." Rose wept quietly. "How on earth did I manage this? I was always the good girl."

"Sleeping with the man you love doesn't mean you're no longer a good girl."

"It was a terrible mistake. There's only one thing to do."

"What?"

"I...I'll tell Evan that I changed my mind. I'll tell him that I love him and I want to marry him. He'll probably still have me. Then I'll tell him I can't wait and I want to go to Gretna

Green. We'll...consummate the union and no one will be the wiser."

"Rose..."

"It's the only way, Lily."

"And what exactly are you going to tell Evan when his child is born with coal-black hair?"

"I don't know. I'll cross that bridge when I come to it. It's just as likely that the babe will be blond."

"I suppose so."

"And if it's not, I'll remind him that you and Papa and Thomas are all dark. It could have come from there."

"You can't be serious."

"I am, Lily. There's no other way to deal with this." Rose shook her head. "I'll wait until after Auntie Iris's wedding. I don't want to rain on her parade. She's waited long enough for happiness. But after, I'll ask Evan to take me to Gretna Green."

"What if he refuses?"

"He won't. He...he wanted me. Of course, he refused to bed me..."

"What?"

"I was just trying to... Lord, I must sound like a little strumpet! It wasn't like that. It wasn't."

"I know, I know. Tell me."

"Cameron—he rejected me."

"He did what?"

"You heard me. He made love to me, and then he sent me away. He told me he loved me. He was so gentle and tender. But the next day, he told me he had lied to me so I would sleep with him."

"That scoundrel! I'll have Daniel throttle him!"

"No. No, you couldn't anyway. He's gone." Rose wiped her

nose. "But what I started to tell you is that I... Well, I wanted to feel that way again, so I tried to seduce Evan. He responded at first, but he wouldn't take me to bed."

"He's a gentleman. Unlike some others."

"I'm glad he didn't, Lily. I really didn't want to sleep with him."

"But you'll have to now, if you insist on going through with this ridiculous plan of yours."

"Yes. I will. It won't be so bad. He's very attractive and very kind."

"Rose, you're talking in fragments. I think it might be best if you told me the whole story, from the beginning. I'll order some tea."

Between gulps, sobs, and a bit of laughter, Rose poured out the whole story, beginning with meeting Cam by the stream and Kat's illness up to their last encounter in the hired man's cabin and Evan's proposal.

"He left me, Lily. He and his mother and the girls are gone. They took everything. Everything except the bed where we made love."

"We'll find him."

"No, we won't. He doesn't want to be found."

"If they've vacated the Lybrook land, they must have sent notice to Daniel. Likely it's buried in his correspondence somewhere. Perhaps they left forwarding instructions. I'll have him look for it."

"No. Don't. I don't want Daniel to know about this."

"Rose dear, Daniel is a very powerful man. If anyone can find Cameron and make him do right by you, it's Daniel."

"I don't want to force him to marry me. I...I'd rather have Evan. He'll be kind and gentle. Cameron will hate me for trapping him."

"You haven't trapped anyone. This is just as much his responsibility as it is yours."

"I'm afraid society doesn't see it that way, Lily. You know I'm right."

"Nonsense. I don't give two figs what society thinks. You are the sister of the Duchess of Lybrook. I dare any of them to say one vile word against you!"

"Please, I can't have you ruining your own reputation in a futile attempt to save mine. What will Daniel think?"

"Daniel loves me, Rose. You know that. And he doesn't care about reputations. Remember, he had a renowned one himself before I made an honest man of him."

"But—"

"If Cameron won't do right by you, you can stay here. Make your home with Daniel and me. We have plenty of room."

"And become the next spinster aunt? I suppose that would be tolerable, but my situation isn't the same as Lucy's. I'll have a bastard child, Lily."

"That child is my niece or nephew, and you're my sister. I won't see you put out."

"I still think Evan is the best alternative."

"But you don't love him, and you're carrying another man's child."

"He'll never know it's not his, and I can be happy with him. I'll be a loving and devoted wife. He won't suffer by marrying me."

"Of course he won't, but...you love another."

Rose sighed. "Another whom I can't have."

"Are you sure Cameron doesn't love you? I know he said

as much, but his actions speak otherwise, as does his mother."

"He left, didn't he?"

"Yes, but he may have had reason, which is why you should let Daniel find him."

"No. I don't want him found. I shall deal with this on my own. Seeing him is like torture for me. I need your word."

"All right. You have my word. I won't look for him. But I think you're making a mistake."

"Then it's mine to make. After Auntie Iris's wedding, I'll tell Evan that I've reconsidered his proposal."

Lily took her hand. "If that is your wish."

★ ★ ★ ★

Rose did her best to appear delighted at dinner that evening. It was a jovial affair, with Lily and Daniel telling stories about their wedding trip. Daniel gazed lovingly at Lily's midriff several times during the evening, so Rose guessed Lily had told him her news and asked that he not speak of it to anyone yet. She felt as if she had been pricked with a sharp thorn. Her sister's happiness was being quashed because of her own situation.

All around her, love was in the air. Lily and Daniel hardly took their eyes off of each other. Iris spoke of her impending marriage to Lord Brighton with a smile Rose wasn't sure she had ever seen on her aunt's pretty face. Ally gossiped of Mr. Landon's business dealings in Scotland, where he had been for several weeks. Even sweet conservative Sophie's eyes lit up when Lord Van Arden's name came up in conversation. Although he wasn't officially courting her, he still came by now and then to visit. Other than Aunt Lucy and Aunt Maggie,

Rose was the only one not paired off. Nausea nagged at her, and she wasn't sure whether it was her condition or her emotions. Most likely a combination of both.

"Rose, aren't you listening to me?" Ally nudged her.

"What? I'm sorry, Ally."

"I said, aren't you excited about the Midsummer festival?"

"Oh. Of course. But Papa is coming tomorrow. He may not allow me to attend. You know how he feels about pagan rituals."

"I'll speak to Papa, Rose," Lily said.

"It's not important," Rose said. "I...may not even want to go."

"Of course you'll go," Daniel said. "I want my entire family there to see me take the archery championship away from Cameron Price." He laughed boisterously. "I'll not be bested again."

Lily winced ever so slightly, almost imperceptibly, at her husband's reference to Cameron. She had obviously kept her word to Rose, otherwise Daniel wouldn't have mentioned him. Not that she had doubted her sister's promise for a moment.

"You'll always be my champion." Lily smiled at her husband. "You don't need to shoot an arrow into a little dot to prove that."

"That's the only championship that matters to me, love," Daniel said, winking at her. "But I'll outdo him anyway."

Rose's heart lurched in happiness for her sister and in sadness for herself. If only she could be bantering with the man she loved, the father of her child.

"That reminds me," Daniel went on. "There's a new theatre opening the evening of the solstice. I made a sizeable contribution, and the proprietor has asked that we be his guests for the evening. A box has been reserved for us. I hope you'll all join Lily and me."

"That sounds heavenly, Daniel," Lily said.

"Oh, yes," Ally agreed. "It's been so long since we've been to the theatre."

"Ally, we've *never* been to the theatre," Sophie said.

"That's certainly a long time, don't you think?" Alexandra giggled.

Soon the whole table was laughing. Ally had that effect on people.

"I think that sounds wonderful," Maggie said. "You must be speaking of Zach Newland's new enterprise."

"The actor?" Alexandra asked.

"The one and only," Daniel said. "And yes, Mother, the Regal is his venture."

"Oh, he is absolutely to die for!" Alexandra exclaimed.

"Have you seen his work?" Maggie asked.

"Heavens, no," Alexandra said. "Sophie is correct. We've never been to the theatre. But I've seen portraits of him. He is exquisite."

"Goodness, Ally," her mother admonished.

"I'm right, Mother."

"Of course you're right, but goodness," Iris said again.

"There will be plenty of room in the box if you would like to ask Lord Brighton to join us," Daniel said to Iris.

"That is very generous of you," Iris replied. "I'll speak to him when he arrives tomorrow."

"And Xavier too," he said to Rose.

Rose's cheeks burned. "That is kind of you, Daniel, but Lord Evan and I aren't...that is...we have discontinued our courtship."

"I didn't know," Daniel said. "I'm sorry."

"No, I'm sorry, Daniel," Lily said. "I haven't had a chance to fill you in on everything yet."

"It's fine, Lily," Rose said. Then, to Daniel, "It was a mutual decision." *Good Lord, would someone please change the subject?* She didn't want to go into any more detail about Evan, especially since she planned to marry him anyway after his father's wedding. She gave Lily a pleading glance.

Lily cleared her throat. "The theatre sounds wonderful. What are they opening with, Daniel?"

"*A Midsummer Night's Dream.*"

"One of my favorites!" Alexandra gushed. "Mr. Newland will make a wonderful Oberon."

"I don't know which part he chose for himself," Daniel said, "but I've no doubt the production will be a hit."

"I can't wait," Alexandra said. "You are too kind to all of us, Your Grace."

"No more Your Grace," Daniel said. "We're all family now."

"Heavens, yes," Lily agreed. "Unless you'd like to start calling me Your Grace, Ally. I think I could get used to that."

Everyone at the table erupted in cheerful laughter. Everyone except for Rose. Unseen by the others, she ran her palm smoothly across her abdomen, thinking about Cameron's babe slumbering inside. How happy she should be, to be carrying the child of the man she loved. How happy indeed.

CHAPTER FOURTEEN

Two days later, everyone rose at dawn to attend the Midsummer Celebration outside of Bath. The Earl and Countess of Ashford, who had arrived the previous day, chose to forgo the celebration, not to anyone's surprise. However, the earl did concede to let Rose attend, so she and Thomas rode with Lily and Daniel in their carriage. The rest were divided among other carriages, including Evan who rode in Lord Brighton's carriage with Aunt Iris and the girls. Rose sighed heavily. She had asked Thomas to be her escort at the festival. She had to talk to Evan eventually, to tell him she had changed her mind about marrying him, but she didn't plan to do it today. She would not cloud Aunt Iris's day in the sun.

She resisted the urge to clutch at her stomach, despite the nausea she felt. It would alert Thomas and Daniel to her condition. Lily sat next to her husband, her hand clasped in his, looking radiantly healthy. She was apparently adjusting to pregnancy a lot better than Rose was. Of course, her situation was quite different.

"Next year I want to watch the sun rise at Stonehenge," Lily said.

"Whatever you wish, my love," Daniel replied.

Thomas rolled his eyes at Rose, and then said, "God, man, she has you wrapped around her little finger."

Daniel laughed.

"Do shut up, Thomas," Lily said. Then, "I suppose we

shall miss the bonfires tonight as well, since we'll be going to the theatre."

"I didn't know you wanted to see the bonfires, Lily," Daniel said. "Most of them were last night, on the eve, but there will likely be a few tonight."

"No, I'd much rather go to the theatre," Lily said. "I love Shakespeare."

"There will be another festival in a few days for the Feast of St. John," Daniel said. "This one today is the true pagan celebration. We'll likely see the spiral dance, fortune tellers, candle boats, maybe even a dragon or two." He smiled.

"What's a candle boat?" Rose asked.

"Wait and see." Daniel smiled.

They arrived amidst children and adults dressed in peasant finery, jeweled in flower garlands and crowns.

"Much like the May Day festival," Lily remarked.

"Yes, a lot of the traditions are similar," Daniel said.

"Why, there's a May Pole." Rose pointed.

"It's called the Midsummer Tree," Daniel explained. "Although it is the same dance."

Dozens of women walked about veiled in white, their hair flowing freely, scattering flower petals.

"Who are they, Daniel?" Lily asked.

"Druids."

"Druids still exist?" Lily asked incredulously.

"Yes, especially here in Wiltshire. You'd be amazed how many haven't embraced Christianity."

"What would Papa say?" Lily said to Rose and Thomas.

"We'd best not tell him," Thomas replied, chuckling. "He may significantly lower his opinion of your husband if he learns of the heathen practices that he has subjected us all to today."

As they walked toward a rolling stream, Daniel said, "There are your candle boats, Rose."

They watched as people folded pieces of paper into boats, filled them with flowers, set them on fire, and sailed them down the rolling waters.

"How lovely." Rose watched intently. "What are they for?"

"The tradition comes from Austria," Daniel said. "It's not commonly practiced in England, so I'm not sure how it made its way here to Wiltshire. The boats are said to carry prayers to the deities."

"May we sail one?" Lily asked.

"Of course."

Daniel led them forward. He gave several coins to a young maiden and returned with two matches and two pieces of paper. "Here you are." He showed them how to fold the paper into a boat. "Now gather the flowers and petals from the ground and put them in your boat."

When the boats were full, Daniel led them to the edge of the stream. "Think of your wish before we light them," he said. "You must pray to the Goddess as the boat hits the water."

"The Goddess?" Rose asked. Her father would not approve.

"To the Christian God, if you wish," Daniel said. "Whatever deity works for you."

"I'm ready, Daniel," Lily said.

Daniel lit Lily's boat on fire and she quickly placed it in the rolling water. It burned as it sped downstream.

"What did you wish for Lily?" Rose asked.

"She can't tell you," Daniel said. "It's private, between her and the Goddess."

"I see. I guess I'm ready then."

Daniel lit Rose's boat, and as she placed it in the water, she closed her eyes and prayed as hard as she could. *Dear God. And G-Goddess, please bring Cameron back to me and our babe.* When she opened her eyes, her boat was gone.

"What a fun little custom," Lily said.

"I'm famished, Lybrook," Thomas said. "Where are the eats around here?"

"Look around. They're everywhere." Daniel pointed. "My favorite is beef on a stick. They sell it at that little kiosk. Come on. My treat."

While the others relished their snack, Rose choked hers down, fighting the ever-present nausea. Daniel brought two tankards of ale for himself and Thomas and watered-down wine for Lily and Rose. What Rose really wanted was some fresh water, but she drank her beverage, not complaining.

"Look, there's a dragon!" Lily pointed to a parade of musicians being led by a large dragon head. Behind the musicians, several gypsies dragged a large wooden man.

"I told you, love," Daniel said. "See that giant coming behind the dragon? He's made of wicker. He'll be burned tonight in one of the bonfires as a sacrifice to the Goddess."

"Fascinating," Lily said. "Are the rest of you finished? I'm dying to walk around a bit more. I feel like we haven't even scratched the surface of what there is to see here."

Rose handed her unfinished meat to Thomas. "I can't possibly eat another bite."

"Are you feeling well, Rose?" Thomas asked.

Lily gave Rose a sideways glance.

"I'm fine," Rose replied. "I had a large breakfast is all."

They continued walking, browsing through the merchants' wares. After spending some time looking at oriental silk, a gypsy crone beckoned them.

"Ah, two little maidens on the verge of motherhood," she said. "I can tell you the gender of your babe."

Rose's heart thundered. She sent a pleading look to Lily.

"You must be mistaken, madam." Lily raised her eyebrows at the crone and jiggled her reticule.

The crone smiled. "My mistake, my lady. Would you care to have your fortune told? You and your sister?"

"No, thank you."

"Oh, go ahead, Lily," Daniel urged. "It's tradition."

"Well, all right, if you say so."

"I'll see only the ladies at this time," the crone said to Daniel and Thomas, gesturing them to stay where they were.

Lily grabbed Rose and pulled her into the crone's tent. "I'm sorry about this, Rose."

"It's all right. I'm just glad you were able to keep her quiet."

"Now, now." The crone sat down behind a small table laden with stones, a crystal sphere, and a deck of cards. "My name is Melina. Do have a seat, both of you."

"I must thank you for your discretion," Lily said, pulling several shillings out of her reticule and handing them to Melina.

"Then I am correct. You are both with child."

"Yes," Lily said. "How did you know we were sisters?"

"Melina knows all. So you both expect bairns, but only one of you is married."

"Yes."

Again, Rose's eyes welled. Goodness, had she not cried

every tear in England yet?

"Don't cry, little one," Melina said. "Your man is returning for you."

"I'm afraid you're mistaken," Rose said.

"Melina is never mistaken. Shall we see what the cards have to say?"

"I thought you were going to tell us the gender of our babes," Lily said.

"Yes, yes. We'll get to that. But your sister is hurting. She needs the wisdom of the cards." Melina took the stack of cards from her table, shuffled them quickly, and handed them to Rose. "You cut them, dear."

Rose obliged.

Melina drew the first card. "Ah, the nine of swords. You are worrying. Suffering. It is a burden you have been carrying alone."

"Lord, she didn't need you to tell her that," Lily said dryly.

"Your sister is protective of you," Melina continued. "Know then, that you do not suffer alone."

"My sister is helping to carry my burden, I know."

"I talk not of your sister. Another suffers as you do. Another feels helpless."

"Who?"

"The father of your babe, of course."

Rose widened her eyes as Melina drew another card.

"The eight of pentacles. You have a talent with your hands."

"Yes," Rose said. "I play the pianoforte."

"Don't help her, Rose," Lily said.

"Melina needs no help." The crone drew the next card. "The ace of cups. Wonderful! This is the cup of life. You are the cup of life. You give life to your babe. Your babe is a miracle and a blessing."

"But my babe will be a bastard," Rose said, weeping softly.

"Every babe is a blessing. A miracle. And your babe will not be a bastard. He returns to you."

"I wish I could believe you."

"Believe Melina. She knows. I will draw your last card. The moon." Melina sighed.

"What? Is it bad?" Rose asked.

"No. Not necessarily. But something is not as it seems. Someone has lied to you."

"Yes, that is true. The father of my babe lied to me."

"Yes, it was he. But something is still amiss. All is not as you think it. He will return."

"How do you know?"

"The cards know no falsehoods, my lady," Melina said. "Your suffering will cease. He will return."

Rose nodded, sniffling into her handkerchief. "Your turn, Lily."

"Heavens no, I don't want my cards read," Lily said. "But I would like to know the gender of my babe."

"Of course." Melina reached for a crystal on a leather cord. "I will read for your sister first, to ease her suffering."

"How is knowing the sex of her babe going to ease her suffering?" Lily asked, rolling her eyes.

"Trust Melina." She motioned to Rose and pointed to a pile of pillows on the ground. "You must lie down."

Rose hesitantly lay down on the pillows as Melina held the crystal over her belly. "Now we wait for the spirits to guide us." The crystal began to weave slowly back and forth, until it established a pattern. "You carry a girl, my lady. A beautiful girl. She has hair like her father, and eyes like yours. She will be beautiful, the light of his eye."

"A little girl?" Rose said, her lips curving upward. "A girl. How wonderful."

"Melina knew it would help ease your suffering. Now you." She motioned to Lily.

Lily assumed the position as Melina held the crystal over her abdomen. "A boy for you, my dear. An heir for the duke."

"An heir! How marvelous!" Lily exclaimed. "Wait a minute. How did you know my husband was the duke?"

"Melina knows."

Lily sat up and fumbled with her reticule. "I don't know if you're right, Melina, but you've certainly been entertaining." She handed the crone several more coins. "For your time and trouble. And your discretion," she added.

"The duchess is generous," Melina said. "Melina thanks you." Then, turning to Rose, "Do not despair. Your man loves you and will return." The crone pulled a pink rose out of a vase behind her table. "Take this rose. Scatter the petals at midnight tonight. Your man will catch the scent and return to your arms."

Lily rolled her eyes, but Rose was desperate.

"Yes, I will," she said, taking the flower. "Thank you so very much." She fumbled with her reticule.

Melina stopped her. "The duchess has paid more than necessary. You keep your coins."

"No, I insist." Rose placed a sovereign in the crone's wrinkled hand. "I don't know whether I believe you, but I do feel better."

"I cannot take so much." Melina shook her head.

Rose folded the old woman's fingers around the gold coin.

"Please. You've helped me more than you know."

"Rose, you don't actually believe this nonsense, do you?" Lily said.

"No," Rose said, "but I do feel better. I'm not sure why. Bless you, Melina."

"Bless you, my lady." Melina smiled. "Blessed be to you and yours and to the Goddess."

★ ★ ★ ★

When the ladies had left the tent, a large gypsy man entered from a hidden door behind Melina's chair. "Do you really think her man will return to her?" he asked.

"Hell if I know," Melina said. "Thank you for telling me who they were." She tossed him a few shillings.

He put the coins in his pocket. "How did you know they were both with child?"

"I don't need the sight for that. A woman gets a look about her. When you've lived as many moons as I, it's easy enough to recognize."

"Poor thing."

"Yes. Keep it to yourself. We've been highly compensated for our discretion." Melina smiled.

★ ★ ★ ★

"It's about time for the archery, isn't it?" Lily said to Daniel.

"I believe you're right." He turned to Thomas. "What do you say, Jameson? Would you care to let me best you in contest?"

"I've a rotten aim I'm afraid," Thomas said, "but Lily tells me you're amazing."

"Yes, and he's great with a bow and arrow, too," Lily teased.

Thomas rolled his eyes as Daniel raised Lily's hand to his lips and kissed it lightly, smiling at his adoring wife. "I assume Price will be here. I won't let him beat me again."

Rose swallowed. Her heart still thundered at the thought of seeing Cam. Of course, Daniel didn't yet know that Cameron had left the Lybrook land and would probably not be at the festival.

Cameron wasn't there, as Rose suspected, but Evan was, and he nearly beat Daniel.

"Good show, Xavier," Daniel said.

"You as well, Lybrook," he said.

"Yes, Evan," Rose said with a smile. "I had no idea you were such a fine archer." She purposefully used his Christian name again. After all, he was the man she had decided to marry.

"We oarsmen have our other hobbies as well," Evan said, chuckling. "I heard you got bested on May Day, Lybrook."

"Yes, I'm afraid so. My only regret is that Price wasn't here today to lose to me." His laughter rang across the festival.

Sophie and Alexandra hurried toward them. "I'm sorry we didn't see your archery contest, Evan," Sophie said.

Sophie's use of his Christian name startled Rose, but of course, he would be her stepbrother soon. Family always addressed each other informally.

"That's quite all right," Evan said. "Lybrook won, although I took a close second."

"Oh, that's wonderful," Sophie said. "We would have gotten here sooner, but Ally insisted on speaking to a fortune teller."

"Yes, I apologize," Alexandra said, hardly sparing Evan a glance. "But I got the most delicious news about Mr. Landon from an old gypsy crone named Melina."

"Oh dear, Ally, not you too," Lily said.

"Indeed," Rose said. "What did she say?"

"She said that my true love is closer than I think," Alexandra gushed. "Isn't that terrific? Mr. Landon must be on his way home to me!"

"Have his letters indicated that he's coming home soon?" Lily asked.

"No, but perhaps he's planning to surprise me."

"I suppose that's possible." Lily rolled her eyes. "What shall we do now?"

"How about a pint?" Thomas said amiably.

"I'm with Jameson," Evan said. "I fear my thirst needs quenching."

"Admittedly, that sounds good," Daniel agreed, "but the ladies—"

"Oh for goodness' sake, go on with them," Lily said. "You're allowed a few carefree remnants of your bachelor days." She shooed the men off. "The girls and I will shop. I want to look at the oriental silk some more. Let's meet back here in an hour. I don't want to miss the spiral dance."

"Perfect," Daniel said. "Buy whatever you want, love."

"Do you hear yourself, Lybrook?" Thomas chortled. "I'm not sure you need another drink."

The three men laughed as they tottered off together.

Alexandra sighed. "I do believe those are the three best-looking men in England," she said thoughtfully. "My cousin, my cousin-in-law, and my future stepbrother. Of all the rotten luck!"

"Ally, do you ever think of anything but men?" Sophie shook her head.

"Come now, they're splendid, and you know it."

"I have to agree with her," Lily said. "Especially the one in the middle. Now come on, let's shop! I want to get some of that incredible silk."

"I still can't believe you aren't marrying Evan, Rose," Ally said. "I admit he isn't my favorite person in the world, but he's damned good-looking!"

"Ally! Your language." Sophie sighed.

"I'm beginning to regret our mutual decision," Rose said.

"Really?" Alexandra raised her eyebrows. "So you feel more for him than you thought?"

"I'm thinking about it," Rose said, "and that's all I'm saying." She shot Lily a look telling her to keep quiet.

"Well, I certainly can't blame you," Ally said. "He is spectacular."

Spectacular indeed. Alexandra was right. All three of them were. But one existed who put them all to shame, who stole her breath with a single glance.

Cameron. The father of her child.

★ ★ ★ ★

The men returned from their jaunt to the tavern, pleasantly relaxed. The ladies awaited them, their arms full of parcels.

"Dear God, Lybrook," Thomas said, approaching. "Do you see what you've done? They've gone and bought out the place."

"I'm sorry, Daniel," Lily said. "We didn't have time to

deliver our purchases to the carriage or we would have been late to meet you."

"No problem, love. We'll take them for you." He motioned to Thomas and Evan.

"You're kidding, right?" Thomas said, winking. "She's your problem now. Once you married her, all big brother duties officially ceased."

"Thomas, you fool," Lily laughed.

"You're still her brother," Daniel said. Then, to Evan, "and you're her cousin, almost. Come on."

"To be fair, it's not all Lily's," Ally chimed in. "Rose and I both purchased the most beautiful scarves, and Sophie found a wonderful shawl."

By the time the men returned from their errand, the spiral dance had begun. The druids, clad in white diaphanous veils and flower garlands and crowns, moved slowly in a circle, their arms outstretched. A flautist accompanied them as they spiraled toward the center of the circle, never colliding.

"During the dance," Daniel explained, "each dancer faces each other dancer at least once. As they spiral, they raise energy to call the Goddess."

"It's beautiful," Lily sighed.

"Yes, it is," Rose agreed.

"Oh my!" Sophie exclaimed, as the leader of the spiral joined hands with another woman and kissed her on the mouth.

"That's just part of the dance," Daniel said. "Physical contact helps them raise energy. Sometimes they do this dance during a full moon. It's called drawing down the moon. They raise energy from the moon to work their magick."

"Magic?" Rose queried. "They hardly look the smoke and

mirrors type."

"Magick with a K, Rose," Daniel said. "It's how the pagans pray."

"How do you know so much about this, Daniel?" Lily asked.

"My parents brought Morgan and me to all the festivals when we were lads."

"It's really beautiful, isn't it," Rose said. "Who would have thought pagan rituals could be so inspiring?"

"Not Papa, that's for sure," Lily said. "He's as devout a Christian as there is."

"This is all new to you then?" Evan asked.

"Oh, yes," Rose replied. "Papa never allowed us to participate in any of the pagan celebrations. No May Day, no Midsummer, no Samhain, no Yule."

"We saw some in Scotland," Alexandra interjected. "Especially where the Celtic clans settled. Sophie and I didn't go often, but when our father was out of town, which, unfortunately, wasn't near enough, mother sometimes took us. It was quite a treat."

"I don't know much about your father," Evan said. "My father hasn't enlightened me much about Iris's past."

Alexandra shook her head nonchalantly. "Believe me, you're better off not knowing." She turned to Daniel. "Shouldn't we be leaving soon, if we're to dine and change for the theatre?"

"Yes, you're absolutely right. I'm sorry you won't see the bonfires, Lily."

"Oh, don't worry a smidge about that. This has been a wonderful day." Lily waved her hands. "And I can't wait for tonight. Imagine, being present for a new theatre's debut!"

Daniel took her hand and kissed it, and they headed toward the awaiting carriages.

Rose's heart hurt. As much as she relished the fact that her sister was in love with the man of her dreams, she couldn't help feeling sorry for herself. She imagined Cam kissing her hand, carrying her parcels, pulling her body close to his from behind and whispering in her ear. She clutched the rose from Melina tightly and touched her abdomen, hoping her unborn daughter could feel her love.

I promise you, Rose told her child silently, *that I will love you as much as any mother and father combined have ever loved a child. You'll want for naught. As God, or the Goddess, is my witness, I promise you.*

CHAPTER FIFTEEN

"I do wish we could have gone to the festival," Kat said as her sister helped her into her new dress.

"Yes, me too," Tricia agreed, "but you know Cam didn't have time to take us. He's been at the theatre all day preparing for opening night."

"I don't like his new job," Kat pouted.

"Why in the world not? It's because of his new job that you have this lovely little gown to wear this evening."

"I'd rather have Cam," Kat whined. "We hardly ever see him anymore. He's never here for dinner, and I'm asleep by the time he gets home. Then he's gone in the morning before I wake up."

"I know." Tricia sighed, fastening the last button on her sister's pink gown. "It will get better, Kitty-Kat. He only had two weeks to write the music for the play. He'll have more time for his next composition so he won't have to work such long hours."

"I think he misses Lady Rose."

Tricia arched her eyebrows. Her little sister was observant. "I think it's you who miss Lady Rose, Kat."

"Yes, I do. I wish she could be our governess instead of Miss Penney."

"Goodness, Kat, Lady Rose is a lady of the peerage. She would never be someone's governess. Besides, Miss Penney is a jewel. Aren't you fond of her?"

"She's pretty, but not as pretty as Lady Rose."

"No one's as pretty as Lady Rose," Tricia said.

"You are."

Tricia laughed softly. "That's a fine compliment, Kat. Thank you."

"And Lady Lily is too."

"And someday you will be, I've no doubt. Turn around now." Tricia brushed Kat's soft dark hair. While Tricia and Cameron possessed hair black as night, Kat's was a rich brown that fell in soft curls around her shoulders. Her cocoa-colored eyes and pretty round face would one day mature into true beauty. "Would you like to wear your hair up tonight, Kitty-Kat?" she asked.

"Could I, Trish?"

"Just this once, I think you could."

"What will Mum say?"

"She won't say anything. We'll stay up here until it's time to go." Tricia piled Kat's soft curls on top of her head. "You have lovely hair. One day the boys are going to flock to you."

"Like they flock to you?"

"Well, they're hardly flocking now."

"They did at our old house."

Tricia smiled. Yes, she had garnered her share of attention from the tenants and village men. But here, in the city, without a recognized name or dowry, she would have a more difficult time. Her sixteenth birthday was less than a month away, and Cameron still felt she was too young to be courted anyway. "We're no longer at our old house." She placed the last pin in her little sister's hair. "Now, come to the looking glass."

"I love it!" Kat squealed.

"I'm glad." Tricia kissed Kat and gave her cheeks a pinch.

"There, now you have some color. That's what ladies do so they'll have a rosy complexion."

Kat giggled and pinched them again.

"Not so much, Kat, or you'll bruise yourself. Just a little." Tricia pinched her own cheeks. "See? Like that. Now you sit down on the bed, and you can watch me get ready."

Tricia had already donned her periwinkle-blue evening gown, so she sat down to begin work on her hair.

"Your dress is the color of your eyes," Kat said.

"More the color of Cam's eyes," Tricia replied. "Mine are considerably darker."

"No, Cam's are more like silver," said Kat. "Mum says he has our papa's eyes."

"Yes, he does."

"I wish I could remember Papa."

"I know, Kat. He was a good papa. I'm sorry you didn't get to know him."

"Oh well." Kat sighed softly, fanning out her skirt on Tricia's bed. "My skirt makes noise." She giggled.

"It's made of taffeta. It rustles."

"I like the sound of it."

"So do I."

"I never imagined I'd have such a fine dress."

"Nor did I, Kat."

"Do you think I'll ever have another dress like this one?"

"I'm sure you will. The way you're growing, that one will no longer fit you by the end of the summer."

"What of yours?"

"Mine will fit me for a while," Tricia said, giggling, "unless I grow fat."

"You won't," Kat said. "Mum isn't fat."

"True." Tricia put the finishing touches on her hair. "There." She turned to face her sister. "How do I look?"

"Like a princess," Kat breathed. "Now pinch your cheeks and bite your lips."

"Bite my lips?" Tricia smiled. "How did you know about that little trick?"

"I've seen you do it."

"You are the observant one." In more ways than one. Tricia turned her attention back to the looking glass and was pleased with the results. Her mind wandered for a moment to the handsome Lord Jameson, Lady Rose's brother. She would no doubt never see him again. Well, it was just a silly fantasy anyway.

She quickly glanced at the clock on her night table. "We'd best go down," she said to Kat. "Cam said the coach was coming for us promptly at eight. Are you ready, Miss Katrina?"

"Yes, Miss Price." Kat put her small pink hand into Tricia's and skipped alongside her down the hallway to the staircase.

★ ★ ★ ★

Rose stared out her chamber window as two carriages pulled away from the Lybrook mansion. She had begged out of the theatre this evening, and but for her parents and Evan's brother and sister, was alone in the house. The earl and countess had decided to stay in as well, as the countess was feeling a bit poorly. Rose used her mother's illness as an excuse, stating that she must be coming down with the same thing. Truthfully, although she wasn't feeling her best, due no doubt to her condition, she could hardly say she felt ill. In fact, her nausea had lessened a bit today, after her encounter with the gypsy crone. Melina's ramblings had no merit, of course, but Rose's heart wanted to be here at midnight to scatter the rose petals to bring her love home to her. She would scatter them off the back terrace, over the area where she and Cameron had nearly made love.

After a small supper, she bathed and changed into her nightdress. She wasn't going anywhere anyway, and she desired the comfort of her night clothes while she played the grand piano in the conservatory. She ran through her repertoire and played through a few new pieces that she was working on. After two hours, she went to look in on her mother, and finding her well, returned to her chamber to read.

★ ★ ★ ★

Daniel led the group consisting of himself and Lily, the dowager duchess and Lucy, Iris and Lord Brighton, Alexandra, Sophie, Evan, and Thomas to their reserved box at the new Regal Theatre.

"My, this is divine!" Alexandra gushed, caressing the red velvet chairs with her gloved fingers. "Are all theatres this elegant?"

"They are all elegant, though perhaps not quite this elegant," Daniel said. "Newland really pulled out all the stops, I'd say."

"If your contribution helped pay for this, I'm all for continuing our patronage," Lily said. "This is wonderful."

The ladies took the front row of seats, while the gentlemen sat behind them. "A box that seats twelve," Lucy said. "This is decadent."

"Newland built two large boxes to accommodate his patrons," Daniel explained. "The other boxes seat six."

"I'm so sorry Rose isn't here," Sophie said. "She would love this."

"Yes, she would," Lily agreed.

"I hope she and Auntie Flora are feeling better for the wedding tomorrow." Sophie worried her hands.

"I'm sure they'll be fine," Iris said.

"Yes, yes, they'll be fine," Lily said. "Neither would miss your wedding for anything in the world, Auntie."

Lily thumbed through her program, reading the biographies of the actors. Zachary Newland's list of accomplishments was impressive, as was the director's. Most of the other actors were not as well-known, although she did recognize a few of their names. She skimmed through their histories, noting the highlights, and then nearly jumped out of her seat when she came to a familiar name.

Cameron Price, Composer.

Quickly she returned to the front page of her program and read through every word. At the bottom, in small print, under choreography but above set design was written: Original Score by Cameron Price. Lily exhaled sharply and went back to the biography page. Cameron's bio was shorter than most.

Mr. Price is a published composer of two works, a ballad and a waltz, and has also written several private commissions. He hails from Wiltshire County. A country boy at heart, he is the son of Mrs. Colton Price of Bath. Cameron thanks Mr. Zachary Newland and the Duke of Lybrook for this chance to compose for the Regal. He dedicates his part in opening night to his beloved sisters, Patricia and Katrina, and to the memory of his father.

The Duke of Lybrook? Lily turned around to her husband who was conversing with Evan. "Daniel?"

"Yes?"

"I'm sorry to interrupt, but you need to read this." She handed him the program and pointed to the relevant entry.

Daniel read it quickly. "Yes?" he said again.

"Why is he thanking you?" Lily asked.

"I'm not sure, although it probably has something to do with the fact that I sent Newland a copy of your waltz."

"You did?"

"Yes. It was quite good, as you know, and I thought Newland might be able to use a composer for his venture. It seems I was right."

"Oh my."

"Good for Price," Daniel continued. "I always thought he was made for more than mere tenancy on our land."

"I must speak with him." Lily started to rise.

Daniel put his hands on her shoulders. "Not now, love. The show is about to start."

"I don't care. He's here somewhere. I need to speak with him now!"

"No, Lily," Daniel said sharply.

"Don't you dare raise your voice to me!" Lily whispered angrily.

"Calm down, love. I'm not raising my voice to you. But the play is going to start. Look, there go the lights."

"Daniel, you don't understand. It's a...matter of grave importance!" She wanted to tell him more, but Evan's presence next to Daniel made that impossible.

"We'll find him at intermission," Daniel said. "Come

on, you don't want to miss the play. Besides, he's most likely extremely busy right now."

Her husband was right, of course. It was aggravating, how right he usually was. She couldn't help smiling to herself. Her impulsiveness was one of the things Daniel loved about her, but he curbed it when necessary. As the curtain lifted to strains of what must have been Cameron's music, she reached behind her. Daniel's hand met hers, and she squeezed gently, saying, without words, how much she loved him.

Lily sighed as the curtain descended for intermission. The performance so far had been amazing, and the music inspiring. Cameron was indeed gifted. A perfect match for Rose. She was determined to find him and make sure he did right by her sister.

"Daniel"—she stood—"I'll return shortly. I need to... powder my nose."

"I'll come with you," he said.

"You're going to help her powder her nose?" Evan asked, smiling.

"Er...no."

"Don't tell me you're going to powder your own nose," Thomas joined in, chuckling.

"Can the two of you ever stop giving me grief?" Daniel asked. "Is it such a crime to be in love with one's wife?"

"It's no crime at all," Lily giggled. "Come, my love."

When they were free of the box, Lily said urgently. "We must find Mr. Price."

"Can you tell me why it's so important now?" Daniel asked.

"Yes. I need to find him for Rose. She's...in love with him."

"What?"

"It's true. The Prices have left our land, by the way."

"That's apparent, given his work here," Daniel said. "I'm sure they sent notice. I still haven't gotten through all the correspondence that came in during our trip. But that's not the issue. How can Rose be in love with him? She was with Xavier up to recently."

"She just is. We don't choose whom to fall in love with, Daniel. You and I ought to know that."

"True." He smiled. "But does Price return Rose's feelings?"

"Well..."

"Lily."

"He says he doesn't. But I don't believe it. Besides it doesn't matter anyway."

"Why doesn't it matter?"

"Because Rose is with child, damn it!" Lily quickly clasped her hand over her mouth.

"She's what?"

"Keep your voice down," Lily urged. "She's with child. Dear Lord, I promised her my confidence."

"Come on." Daniel grabbed her hand. "We're going backstage to find that blackguard and make him do right by your sister."

"No, Daniel. Not that way. I promised Rose I wouldn't tell anyone. If we tell Mr. Price, she'll never forgive me. I shouldn't have told you. It just sort of...came out."

"Rubbish. Rose is staying on my estate. She's under my protection. I have a duty to see that this fool takes care of his mess."

"Daniel, please..."

"Lady Lily!"

Lily turned to see young Katrina Price running toward her.

Patricia walked briskly after her. "No, Kat," she said. "She's the duchess now. You must address her as Your Grace."

"No, no, don't worry about that," Lily said. "It's wonderful to see you both. May I present my husband, the Duke of Lybrook. Daniel, Misses Patricia and Katrina Price."

"It's an honor, Your Grace," Patricia said, and curtsied.

"The honor is mine." Daniel bowed politely.

"We're looking for your brother," Lily said. "Have you seen him?"

"He's backstage," Tricia replied. "He told us not to come back until after the show. He said he'd be too busy during intermission."

"Oh. I hadn't thought of that." Lily looked at Daniel. "We may as well go back. We'll find him after the show."

"I'll tell him you're looking for him," Tricia said.

"No," Lily said abruptly. "We would rather...surprise him."

"All right. Come on, Kat. We should get back to our seats." Tricia took Kat's hand and led her away.

"Lovely young ladies," Daniel said. "Too bad their brother is a scoundrel."

"I recall when many used that word to describe you, myself included." Lily took his arm.

"I suppose even the worst can reform. All right. I won't say anything about Rose's condition. But he had better come back with us tonight. If he won't come willingly, I *will* tell him and I will force him to marry her or he'll feel the heat of my dueling pistol."

"Dear God," Lily said. "You don't actually approve of

that barbaric custom do you? I can't believe dueling is still practiced."

"It's still practiced because of situations like this."

"Well, you're not dueling him. He beat you with the bow, remember? Who's to say he won't beat you with a pistol? And I'm way too young to be a widow. Besides...I'd miss you too much."

"Fine, I won't call him out." Daniel kissed her cheek and then caressed it with his thumb. "Is Rose really with child?"

"I'm afraid so."

"My, you Jamesons are a fertile lot, aren't you?" Daniel lovingly touched Lily's midriff and then walked her back to their box.

★ ★ ★ ★

After the curtain calls for the actors, Newland pushed Cameron on stage to take a bow as composer. His music had been very well received. As he stood on the stage, after bowing to thunderous applause, the harsh lights heating his brow, he scanned the audience. The stage lights made it almost impossible to see any single face among the spectators, yet he searched. He bowed again politely and left the stage when the applause died down. He hadn't been looking for his mother or his sisters. It had been Rose's face he sought. He had scanned the orchestra section, the balcony, the boxes, but he couldn't find her. Sighing, he walked slowly toward his office in the back of the theatre. He would continue his work. He would be a success and make a good life for his family. He would do it, and he would do it well.

But it wouldn't mean anything without Rose.

His mother and sisters were waiting for him in his office, where he had told them to meet him.

"Cameron, it was absolutely wonderful," his mother said, taking both of his hands in hers.

"I'm glad you enjoyed it, Mum." He kissed her cheek.

"And you"—he swept Kat up in his arms—"how did you like it, Kitty-Kat?"

Kat yawned. "I'm afraid I'm frightfully tired, Cam. But I loved it. I really loved it! I think I might be an actress someday."

"Then you shall have the best training my money can buy," Cameron said. "You look quite the young lady tonight. That coiffure is very grown up."

"Tricia did it," Kat said.

"Yes, and I'm not sure I approve," Mrs. Price added.

"Don't be silly. She looks like an elfin princess." Cameron set his sister down. He groaned as the Duke and Duchess of Lybrook entered his small vestibule.

"Lady Lily!" Kat squealed.

"Kat, I told you, it's Your Grace," Tricia admonished.

Mrs. Price curtsied politely. "How nice to see you, Your Grace and...Your Grace."

"It's very nice to see you as well, Mrs. Price," Lily said. "The duke and I need to have a word with your son."

"I'm afraid I'm busy," Cameron said dryly.

"Cameron!" Mrs. Price turned to Lily. "Do excuse him, Your Grace. The girls and I will leave you alone. Come, Tricia, Kat." She ushered them out of the office.

"My mother needn't make apologies for me," Cameron said. "I honestly am busy."

"Congratulations on your post, Price," Daniel said. "The music was inspiring."

"I'm glad it pleased you, Your Grace. I wouldn't have gotten this position if you hadn't sent my waltz to Newland. I owe you my gratitude."

Daniel arched his eyebrow. "Perhaps there's a way for you to repay me."

Cameron groaned softly. Of course. Now the payback. No such thing as a free ride and all that. He took a deep breath. "I doubt there's anything I can do that is of value to you, Your Grace, but I'll certainly do what I can."

"You can come home with the duchess and me tonight," Daniel said.

"Pardon me?"

"He didn't stutter, Mr. Price," Lily said. "You must come with us. Rose is suffering. She needs to see you."

Cameron closed his eyes, his heart breaking yet again. Rose was suffering. He could hardly bear the thought. "I have nothing to offer her," he said, opening his eyes. "She's better off with Xavier. Hasn't he proposed yet?"

"Yes, he did," Lily said. "She turned him down."

"She what?" Cameron shook his head in disbelief.

"You heard me."

"But why?"

"Because she doesn't love him, Mr. Price. She loves you."

"Dear God." That Rose might not marry Xavier had never occurred to him. Yet his heart leaped at the thought that she was still, in some small way, his.

"She loves you. And you love her, do you not?"

Cameron didn't reply.

"Do you love my sister or do you not?" Lily demanded again.

"My feelings don't matter," Cameron said. "I have nothing

to offer her."

"Don't be silly. Look at what you've done tonight. You have plenty to offer her."

"No," Cameron said. "She deserves better. Perhaps I'm not a pauper anymore, but I will never be able to give her the kind of wealth she was raised with. And I'm responsible for my mother and sisters as well. I can never give her what she deserves."

"You can give her one thing that no one else can," Lily said.

"And that would be?"

"Your love."

"I...c-can't," Cameron stammered.

"Nonsense," Lily said. "You are absolutely not going to stand there and tell me that you do not love my sister. You do. I can see it in your face."

"But she's better off with a husband of the nobility. So she didn't marry Xavier. There will be dozens of other young lords waiting for a chance at her. With her gentleness and her beauty, she won't lack for attention. She is the most wonderful woman alive."

"You *do* love her."

He said nothing for a moment. Then, "I can't give her what she requires."

"For God's sake. Stop being an idiot!"

"Lily, the man does have his pride," Daniel said gently.

"Yes, yes, the male pride. Of course. I understand completely." She fidgeted with her skirts. "You're both idiots."

"Lily..."

"You dark brooding types are all the same," she said to Cameron. Then, turning to her husband, "Thank goodness I fell for a blond rakish type. Much more fun."

"Price," Daniel said, "I understand that you don't think you can offer anything of significance to my sister-in-law. But I'm going to insist that you accompany us to Laurel Ridge. Tonight."

"And if I don't?"

"Then I shall take you by force," Daniel said. "Don't underestimate me. I will see Rose happy."

"Please, Mr. Price," Lily urged. "Rose needs you."

"And I need her, damn it." Cameron pounded his fist on his desk. "All right. I'll go. God, I hope it's not too late."

They hurried toward the side entrance to the theatre, but were waylaid by Zachary Newland who was pushing an elderly woman in a wheelchair. The countess of Myerson walked beside them.

"Price," Newland called. "Just the man I was looking for. I want you to meet the Dowager Marchioness of Denbigh."

"It's an honor, my lady." Cameron took the old woman's hand. "I'm sorry I can't stay and chat with you, but I've some pressing business—"

"I quite enjoyed your compositions, Mr. Price," Lady Denbigh said, staring into his eyes. "You're a splendid talent."

"Thank you." Then, remembering his companions. "I'm sorry. May I present the Duke and Duchess of Lybrook. Lady Denbigh, Lady Myerson, Mr. Newland."

"We're so pleased to see all of you," Lily said, "but I'm afraid Mr. Price is correct. We do have some pressing business to attend to."

"What must you attend to at this hour?" Newland asked.

"It's—" Cameron heaved a sigh. "I'm going after the woman I love, Newland, and no one on this earth will stop me!"

Lady Myerson smiled. "The woman you told me about?"

"Yes, yes. She's the duchess's sister."

"Then go get her, Mr. Price. Go get her."

"Yes, do," Lady Denbigh agreed. "Don't ever let love get away."

"Thank you both for your understanding." Cameron kissed each of their hands and turned to Newland. "Could you see that my mother and sisters get home safely?"

"Yes, Price, of course."

"Thank you," he said, stumbling toward the door. "Thank you very much!"

He stopped abruptly as one of the actresses crossed his path carrying a bouquet of pink roses. "Lorna, those are lovely," he said, pulling one bloom away from the others. "May I?"

He didn't wait around for a response.

Rose stood on the back terrace, inhaling the sweet fragrance of the rose petals as they drifted over the soft grass where she and Cameron had lain together. Following the aroma, she drifted down the stairs and out onto the cool, dry lawn, spinning around slowly, her pink nightdress catching the soft breeze. She lowered to the ground, stretching out on the spot where she and Cam had nearly made love. She inhaled, exhaled, caressing her abdomen and whispering sweet words to her slumbering babe. She closed her eyes, the breeze slapping her tresses across her cheeks gently.

If only...

★ ★ ★ ★

When Lily and Daniel's carriage finally reached the house, it was near two in the morning and the house was quiet. Lily led Cameron into the main parlor and bade him wait.

"I'll fetch Rose for you," she said. "Get him a brandy or something." She motioned to Daniel.

"What will it be, Price?" Daniel asked.

"Anything with alcohol in it. God, what will I say to her?"

"I'll not tell you that I'm an expert on matters of the heart," Daniel said. "I'm not, that's for certain. And I'm not at all comfortable talking about this."

"Nor am I."

"But I will give you this one piece of advice. Tell her the truth. Don't ever lie to her. Don't ever keep something from her. You never know when she may not be around to hear it."

"Your Grace?"

"I nearly lost Lily before I confessed my love to her," Daniel said. "If I had... Well, it turned out fine, thank God."

"Yes, I see." He took the brandy Daniel offered and downed it in one gulp.

"Another?"

"No, I need my wits about me." He paced back and forth. "Maybe one more. I'll drink it slowly this time."

Daniel refilled Cameron's snifter as Lily strode in briskly.

"Rose isn't in her chamber, Daniel."

"She's not?"

"No, and no one upstairs has seen her. I checked with Sophie and Ally, even Evan. I didn't want to wake my parents or your mother. It would just worry them."

"She's likely not with any of them anyway," Daniel said.

Cameron's heart thumped, his nerves on edge. Was his beloved in danger? "We've got to find her."

"My God, where could she be, Daniel?" Lily queried. "She's been so upset about...everything."

"This is all my fault." Cameron tugged at his hair. "Where the devil is she?"

"Price," Daniel said, "why did you leave her in the first place?"

"It's a long story," Cameron said. "I'd rather explain it to Rose before I explain it to anyone else."

"All right," Daniel said. "Well, we can't just stand here, let's look for her."

"You stay here, Mr. Price," Lily said. "You don't know your way around the estate."

"I can't just wait here when she's out there somewhere."

"All right, all right, come with me then," Lily said.

"I'll check the stables and kennels, although what she'd be doing there at this hour is beyond me," Daniel said. "You two look through the house."

Lily and Cameron checked the conservatory, the library, the art gallery, the chapel. No Rose. "I suppose we should check all the vacant guest chambers, but that will take hours."

"What about the ballroom?" Cameron asked.

"Why not?" Lily said, and they descended.

Rose was not in the ballroom. "My God," Cameron said, shaking. "What if someone took her?"

"We have lots of servants, Mr. Price. They're on duty at all hours. It would be nearly impossible for someone to kidnap a person under this roof."

"Then if she's gone, she went of her own accord?"

"Most likely."

"Oh my God." Cameron sat down in one of the chairs on the side of the ballroom. "What the hell have I done?"

"If she left, Mr. Price, someone would have seen her go. Yet when I questioned the servants, none of them had any knowledge."

"They could have been paid off."

"Our servants are very loyal."

"Damn it!" Cameron stood and paced around the room. "I need some air." He strode toward the double doors at the back of the ballroom, unlatched the lock, and went outside onto the terrace. He paced back and forth across the terrace, and then settled his elbows on the ledge and looked down.

There, lying under the stars, bathed in the glow of the moon, sleeping peacefully, was Rose.

CHAPTER SIXTEEN

"Rose, my love. Rose. Wake up."

Rose stirred and opened her eyes. What a lovely dream. She was under the stars, and Cameron was gazing down at her with love in his eyes. He held a rose. She reached for him, closing her eyes again tightly, willing the dream to last. He wrapped his arms around her and lifted, carried her away...

"Wake up, sweetheart. Wake up."

"No." Rose refused to open her eyes. "Not yet. Don't want to wake up."

"Yes, sweetheart. Please."

Rose opened her eyes, her vision slowly clearing. She was sitting in a chair. Was that Cameron kneeling before her? And where was she? "What is going on?"

"You're in the ballroom, sweetheart. You fell asleep on the lawn," Cameron said.

"Yes, yes, of course." Rose remembered now. "What are you doing here?"

Cameron took her hands in his. "Your sister and the duke found me. They insisted I come see you. And Rose, I'm so glad I did."

"Oh, no." Rose exhaled. Lily had told him.

"I've been a fool." Cameron brushed a piece of grass out of her hair. "Why did I ever try to live without you? You're my muse, the other side of my song. I need you. I love you."

"Cameron, what is this about?" Rose brushed his hand

away. She couldn't take more of his lies. Her mind was still muddled with sleep...

"No, please don't push me away." He reached for her hands again and brought both to his lips. "Can you ever forgive me?"

Rose shook her head. "Cameron, don't do this. Please."

"Tell me you still love me. Please tell me you still love me."

"Stop." She pushed him away. "I can't listen to any more of this. You won't hurt me again. I swear it!"

"I will never hurt you again." Cameron's face was twisted in anguish. "God, I'm so sorry. I love you, sweetheart. I love you."

Rose's lips trembled, but she willed herself to remain strong. "This isn't fair. I know you're just here because of... what Lily told you."

"What Lily told me?" Cameron arched his eyebrows. "She said only that you loved me, that you were suffering."

"For God's sake, Cameron, I may be young and innocent but I'm not a ninny. You're here because of the babe. How could Lily do this to me?"

"Do what?" Lily said, entering the room. "Rose, thank God you're all right."

"Lily, how could you? How could you tell him?"

"I didn't," Lily said. "I would never betray you Rose. How could you think it?"

"The *babe*?" Cameron stared into Rose's eyes. "You mean, you and I, we made..."

"Then how did he know?" Rose asked.

"You clearly just told him, dear," Lily said. "Now if you'll excuse me, I think you two should talk. Alone." She strode up out of the room.

"You didn't know?"

"No." Cameron cupped Rose's cheek in his hand, gently caressing it with his thumb. The toothy smile that Rose loved spread across his face. "Are you feeling all right? You're not... ill, are you?"

"No, Cameron. I'm fine. I just get a little dizzy and a little nauseated sometimes."

"My angel. Why didn't you tell me?"

"You didn't want me. I wasn't going to trap you. And you left anyway. I had no idea where you went or where to find you."

"I went to Bath. I got a job there. I'm the house composer for the new Regal Theatre."

Rose couldn't help smiling. He was finally doing what he loved. "That's wonderful, Cameron. I always knew you could—" She stopped herself from gushing. "So that's how Lily found you."

"Yes."

"How did she get you to come here then? Bribery? Force?"

"Of course not. She simply told me you were suffering. And that you weren't marrying Xavier." He exhaled sharply. "I...never wanted to leave you. There were circumstances. I'm so sorry."

"Cameron, I can't think right now," Rose said. "Can we talk about this tomorrow? I'll see that a guest chamber is made up for you."

"Please, let me explain," he begged. "I did lie to you, but not in the way you think. I always loved you. That was never a lie, sweet. I swear it. The lie was that I didn't love you. Please, hear me out. I swear on my life I'll never lie to you again."

Rose sighed, closing her eyes. She wanted nothing more than to pull him to her and never let him go. "All right. Tell me the truth."

He was still kneeling before her. He cleared his throat. "Xavier came to me before Kat's illness and asked me to write a song for you. I agreed to the commission because after you ran from me that first night, I didn't think we had a future." He took a deep breath. "Then, after we made love, I meant to cancel the commission. But then Kat had to be hospitalized."

Rose reached out and pushed a strand of Cam's hair behind his ear. "Yes?"

"I needed money, Rose. Xavier's commission was the easiest and fastest way to get it. I had to choose between my sister's life and the woman I love most in the world. I knew Xavier would take care of you and you would want for naught. That you'd have a much better life than I could give you. It killed me to do it, but I...let you go."

"Cameron..."

"I knew the only way you would leave me is if I convinced you that I didn't love you and I told you to go." He raked his hand through his hair. "I must be a hell of an actor."

"Cameron, none of this was necessary."

"I didn't see an option at the time. I'm sorry."

"I would have helped you. I would have done anything for you and for Kat."

"I didn't want to take your money. What kind of man would that make me?"

"The kind who lets the woman who loves him share his burdens, Cam."

"Cam. You called me Cam." His smile lit up his face. Then, "I'm the man, Rose. I'm supposed to take care of you, not the other way around."

"We're supposed to take care of each other," Rose said,

caressing his cheek. "That's the way of things. Didn't your mother and father share their burdens?"

"I suppose so...but that's different."

"How so?"

"Well...they never really had anything of value... It was just different, that's all."

"That's ridiculous and you know it."

"I still can't offer you much, Rose. Not what you're used to. But I have my position at the Regal. It's only three hundred fifty pounds per year, but I can still take private commissions. I've made some great contacts. And I have a townhome in Bath. My mother and sisters will have to stay with us though. And then there's the issue of the song Xavier commissioned. I have to give him a refund. I...I don't think I can live with myself if I don't. That will be a lot of money, two hundred pounds. Oh, bloody hell. What was I thinking? You deserve so much more than I have to offer."

Rose threaded her fingers through his black locks. "You trimmed your hair."

"Yes, for the opening."

"I liked it long."

"Then I'll grow it back."

Rose laughed. "It doesn't matter," she said. "I'd love you even if you were bald as a billiard ball."

"I love you too, sweetheart. I love you. I love you." He pushed the rose into her hands and buried his head in her lap as she stroked his hair.

"It's all right." She stroked the stem of the flower lovingly. "There are no thorns."

"I carved them off with my jackknife during the ride here."

"That was sweet," Rose said.

He looked up at her. "Please marry me, Rose. I want nothing more than to spend my life making you happy. Making our child happy. I'm sorry that we'll have to pinch pennies for a while, at least until I can pay back Xavier."

"Cam," Rose said, "I can pay Xavier."

"No."

"Yes. I have an income from my father's estate. I'll have it until I die."

"I can't take your money."

"If we marry, it will be your money."

"I can't."

"Now you're just being stubborn. Do you think Xavier wouldn't have taken my income if I'd married him? Or any other peer for that matter? Why do you think there are such a thing as dowries? And by the way, I have a substantial one."

"I don't care about that."

"Neither do I. And my father may not give it to me anyway if I don't marry a peer."

"That's another thing."

"I don't care. Dowry be damned. I still have my income. It's mine. He can't take it away from me. The trust is very specific on that."

"How much is your income, Rose?"

She smiled, stroking his stubbled cheek. "Two thousand pounds per year."

"Good God."

"So you see, I can pay Evan, and I can help you take care of those you love, and nothing would make me happier."

"I still don't feel right—"

"Cam, you're being foolish. Do you know how many

271

peers are in dire straits, with their estates dwindled down to nothingness due to poor management and excess spending? Do you think any one of them would have a problem taking my money? They certainly would not. Why do you think so many peers marry American heiresses? To replenish their coffers. So why do you have such a problem with it?"

"I don't know. Foolish pride, I guess. I want to do everything for you, give you everything. I don't want to take from you."

"Then you deprive me of the joy of giving to you," Rose said. "I never cared that you had nothing. I love you. I would have lived in a shack with you. I would have cooked your meals and cleaned your house and scrubbed your back when you came in from a hard day's work. Don't you see?" Rose began to weep. "All I wanted was to be with the man I love."

She left the chair and knelt beside him on the floor. "I love you, Cam. There will never be another for me. I want your name. I want our child to have your name."

"Oh, sweetheart."

Cameron lowered his mouth to hers and kissed her passionately, their teeth clashing, their tongues plunging, until they were both gasping for air.

"Marry me, Rose. Please marry me."

"Yes," Rose said. "I will."

Cameron touched his lips to hers, and then stood with Rose in his arms and whirled her around the ballroom. "I can't believe it," he said. "I can't believe you're mine again!"

"I always was, Cam."

He kissed her lips, her nose, her cheeks, ran his tongue down her neck to her shoulder and nipped it lightly. "We'll have to marry quickly, due to your condition. I'll take you to

Gretna Green tomorrow."

Rose laughed lightly. "It *is* tomorrow, Cam."

"Then we'll leave today. Now. I'll borrow a carriage from the duke."

"No, no," Rose said. "We can't. My aunt is getting married today. I need to be here. And you have a job, Mr. Price. You have responsibilities. You need to be at the theatre in the evening."

"Damn. We need to marry quickly. We can't wait for the banns to be read."

"We'll get a special license."

"I wouldn't have the first clue how to do that."

"Daniel will know. We'll ask him."

"But what of the cost?"

"Who cares?" Rose laughed. "We both have money, you silly. We can take care of it. Together."

Her heart melted as Cameron smiled down into her face, the smile that she had seen so seldom, and that she hoped she would see much more now.

"Yes, together, sweetheart."

They both looked toward the stairway as Lily came bustling down. "I've had the maids prepare a chamber for Mr. Price, Rose. You'd best be getting some sleep. It will be a big day around here tomorrow with the wedding and all."

"Mr. Price will be staying in my chamber, Lily."

"Good Lord. I take it your conversation went well then? As if I have to ask, with you in his arms as though you're going to be carried over the threshold."

"We're getting married!" Rose exclaimed.

"Thank God." Lily sighed. "I'll turn a blind eye tonight. Thank goodness Papa and Thomas are already abed. Good night now."

★ ★ ★ ★

Cameron gently laid Rose down on her bed and sat down beside her. "Are you sure we can do this with you in your condition? I don't want to hurt you."

"Cam, you'll hurt me if you don't." Rose pulled him toward her and kissed him, untied his cravat, and unbuttoned his formal shirt. "Take your clothes off. I don't want anything between us."

"Nor do I," he said, smiling. He eased her nightdress over her head. "You are an angel. Heaven couldn't have created a more perfect being if they'd tried." He slid his hands over her body. "You are so beautiful, Rose, and you're mine. I still can't believe that you're really mine."

"I'm yours," Rose whispered. "And you're mine. Now let me see that sensational body of yours."

Cameron's smile lit up his face as he began to disrobe.

"I love your smile, Cam," Rose said. "I love the way your one front tooth overlaps the other one."

He laughed softly. "You do?"

"Yes."

"Why?"

"I don't know. I love to run my tongue over it."

"I see." He tossed his trousers on the floor. "I had no idea that my flaws were so attractive. I fear my body is covered with imperfections, sweet. Perhaps you should run your tongue over all of them."

"Oh no, your body is perfect, Cam." Rose grinned. "But I shall run my tongue over it anyway."

He lowered himself on top of her and took her mouth, exploring her with his tongue and lips, kissing her face, her neck, her breasts. He took each swollen nipple between his lips and tugged delicately as she moaned beneath him. "I've missed you," he said huskily. "I can't imagine ever kissing another woman."

"You'd better not," Rose said wickedly.

"You don't have to worry." Cameron trailed tiny kisses over her stomach, pausing for a moment to run his hands over her abdomen. "The fact that you're carrying my child makes you even more beautiful."

She smiled. "I'll be big as a house soon enough."

"You'll still be beautiful, sweetheart." He kissed between her thighs, trailed down her shapely legs, caressing and kissing until he reached her ankles.

Rose's breath caught as he tongued the inside of her ankle then blew on the wetness.

"Do you like that?" he asked.

"Oh yes, it's wonderful." Rose sighed.

Cameron kissed the instep of her foot, each of her toes, gently turned her over and kissed up her calves to the back of her knees, tickling her sensually with his tongue and breath.

"Cam, please, make love to me," Rose breathed.

"Soon," he said.

He kissed the back of her thighs and glided his tongue over the wetness of her sex, kissed her back and her neck. "I'll love you until the end of time, Rose. I promise you."

"Love me now, Cam!"

He thrust inside her from behind. Rose bucked under him, trying to meet him with her hips, as he maneuvered one hand beneath her and rubbed her sensitive peak. Rose exploded quickly, sobbing his name and writhing against his nimble fingers. Cameron followed, pulsating within her as he climaxed.

He rolled over onto his side. "I'm sorry, sweet. I wish I could have lasted longer. I just wanted you so badly."

"It's all right," Rose said. "I don't mind. It felt wonderful, Cam."

He leaned toward her and kissed her lips. "I'm glad." He tangled his fingers in her long tresses. "Next time I'll make it better for you."

"It will always be wonderful with you. I love you."

"I love you too, sweetheart. Forever."

★ ★ ★ ★

Rose awoke when the soft rays of dawn peeked through her window. Cameron rested next to her, his arm strewn across her body, his breathing slow and steady. She leaned over and kissed his nose, and then gently moved his arm so she could rise. She wrapped an extra sheet around her and strode to her window, gazing out upon the bright new day. Smiling, she hummed softly to herself.

"Sweetheart?" Cam's voice was husky.

Rose turned. "I'm sorry. I didn't mean to wake you."

"I knew as soon as you left the bed," he said. "I don't think I'll ever be able to sleep again without you beside me."

Her lips curled. "You won't have to." She walked back to the bed and sat down. A tingle of excitement pulsed through her as he reached out and stroked her bare arm. His hair was tousled and sexy, his night beard a shadow on his strong jaw.

"You were humming your song," he said.

"My song?"

"The song I wrote for you."

"Was I?"

"Yes. It came to me in a dream. I dreamed of you one night. Well, actually, I dreamed of you every night."

She smiled and tousled his hair.

"But one night, I dreamed that you were a flower, floating across the breeze. The song came to me, so I got up in the middle of the night and wrote it all down. It was the easiest composing I've ever done. But it became the hardest. I had to give it to Xavier for him to give it to you."

"When he gave it to me, I knew you had written it."

"How?"

"I saw some of your drafts at the pianoforte the day I visited Kat. But I would have known it was yours anyway. I know you. You're in my heart. In my soul."

He closed his eyes and pressed her hand to his heart. "As you are in mine. Everything I've ever written has been for you. It will always be. You're my muse, Rose. My inspiration. You're everything. Everything."

Rose let the sheet fall from her bosom and then climbed in bed next to Cameron. Slowly she slid her tongue over his throat and down to his chest, flicking his hard nipples and then sucking them into her mouth. She drifted downward to his stomach, pushing her tongue into his navel, smiling as his breathing quickened.

"What are you doing?" he asked, grinning.

"I'm running my tongue over all your imperfections," she said. When she reached his erection and began nibbling, she giggled.

"Sweet," he said teasingly, "don't ever laugh when you're pleasuring that part of a man's body. It's likely to lead to a feeling of inferiority."

"I'm sorry." She continued giggling. "Believe me, I didn't mean it that way. It's just...I was thinking that there's absolutely nothing imperfect about this part of you. In fact, it's rather...majestic."

"That's better," he said, pulling her toward him. "Come here."

He rolled her over and kissed her deeply, his tongue exploring the innermost parts of her mouth. He covered her face with moist kisses, his breath massaging her as he moved to her breasts and pleasured them slowly. "You're full of imperfections too," he teased, licking small circles around her nipple. He continued lower, licking and nibbling, parted her legs, and kissed her wetness. "This part of you is extremely imperfect. I think I shall have to give it special attention."

He pushed her thighs forward, grasping the cheeks of her bottom so she was completely bared to him. Rose opened her mouth to protest, but he hushed her and resumed his delicate assault on her. The soft velvet of his tongue teased her peak as he slowly glided his strong hands up the planes of her body and squeezed her breasts. He pinched her nipples while his mouth worked on her sex, sucking her swollen flesh and releasing it.

Rose writhed beneath him, and she soared toward climax when his tongue swiped lower, over her most private opening.

"Cam!"

"Shh, sweet."

She calmed. She was his. Every single part of her. Even that part. And as he tongued her, she shivered. It felt wonderful. When he breached her anus with a finger, she jolted. The intensity shocked her for a moment, but he slid his tongue over her pussy and soon the penetration turned to pleasure. Profound and shimmery pleasure unlike anything she'd imagined. To her complete surprise, she was thrilled to share this with him. He nipped at her clitoris, sucked it between his lips, all while working her bum with his long finger. Her body raced toward climax with a vengeance that she hadn't yet known.

"Cam!" she cried. "Cam, yes, Cam, yes!" An explosion of whirling waves crashed into her, as he continued to plunder her, bringing her to the crest once more.

"Again, sweet. Come for me again."

Fingers slid in and out of both openings now, his tongue still working her peak, and bliss raged through her, catapulting her to the crest again. Joy. Pure joy.

"Now, Cam. Come inside me now!"

He crawled forward, his silver eyes smoking as they gazed into hers. As he pushed into her, she wrapped her legs around his back, pulling him closer.

"I love you, Rose," he said as he thrust. "Only you."

"And I love only you, Cam."

He thrust and he thrust, and as she fell into climax again, he plunged into her deeply.

"You're mine, Rose!" he roared, as his body shuddered against hers. "Mine!"

He collapsed against her, and she rubbed his muscular back, tracing soothing patterns with her fingers.

"Mine," he continued to whisper. "Always mine."

"Yes," she soothed. "Yours."

"I love you. I love you." His breathing slowed, returning to normal.

"I love you, too," Rose said. "Forever."

They lay silently for a few moments, their legs tangled together intimately.

Cameron softly caressed Rose's abdomen and broke the silence. "Do you want a boy or a girl?"

"A gypsy crone at the festival yesterday told me it was a girl," Rose said. "A little girl with your hair and my eyes. Won't she be a beauty, Cam?"

"Any child from you is bound to be a beauty," he said, chuckling softly. "But it could just as easily be a boy."

"It's a girl," Rose murmured.

"My sweet, you've never struck me as the type of person to believe in fortune telling."

"I never thought I did," Rose said seriously. "But she also told me that if I scattered rose petals at midnight last night, my true love would come back to me. And you did."

"Is that why you were outside last night?"

"Yes. I scattered the petals over the place where we had our first...encounter. Then I lay down. I didn't mean to fall asleep."

"You looked like an angel when I found you." Cameron stroked her cheek. "Your hair was fanned out on the grass, and your face was glimmering in the moonlight."

"You make me feel beautiful, Cam."

"You are beautiful. The most beautiful woman alive."

"I think you're biased." She ran her fingers through his silky hair.

"Hardly. Any man would agree with me."

"Not the duke. He has eyes only for Lily."

"He'd better. I'll pummel any man who looks at you the way I do."

"Cam..."

"Yes, sweetheart?"

Did she dare ask the question? "If you love me that much,

how could you have let Evan have me?"

"It was the most difficult thing I ever had to do, Rose." He moved away from her slightly, almost imperceptibly, but she felt it. "The thought of him touching you, of any man touching you that wasn't me... I can't bear to think of it. Don't make me go back to that place. Please."

"I didn't mean to upset you." She stroked his arm lightly.

"I didn't feel I had a choice at the time. I was shortsighted. I'm sorry."

"You've already explained all of that. You don't need to go through it again."

"Tell me then. If you truly thought I was gone from your life, why didn't you accept Xavier? You had feelings for him, didn't you?"

"Yes, I did," she said. "I cared for him as a good friend. And to be honest, I had thought to accept him after you... Well, there's no other way to say it. After you jilted me."

Cameron winced. "God, I'm sorry."

"It's all right." She kissed his mouth. "But I didn't love him. And he didn't love me. Still, I might have accepted him except for one thing."

"What is that?"

"Well, his father and my aunt are getting married. They met twenty years ago and fell in love. But both were in loveless marriages to others, so they weren't free to be together. I didn't want the same thing to happen to me or to Evan."

"Did he take it well?"

"He seemed to. I think he was just as glad that I said no."

Cameron toyed with her nipple. "I find that hard to believe."

"It's true. We're on good terms. He's going to be my

stepcousin soon anyway, so he will always be in our lives."

Cameron grimaced a bit. "I'm not sure how I feel about that."

"It's a fact, Cam. Neither of us can change it. My aunt and his father are very much in love."

"Then I suppose I shall have to tolerate him."

"He's a very nice person, Cam. I think the two of you could be friends."

"That's reaching a little too far, sweet. But I'll be cordial."

"That's all I ask."

"How could I not be? I got the prize and he didn't." Cameron lightly stroked Rose's abdomen again.

She smiled, chills racing to her core. "That feels nice." Then, "I've been thinking, Cam."

"About what?"

"Well, I have two mares you know. My favorite is Junie. She's a beauty, nearly black. The other is a bit younger and gentler. Her name is Nora. I'd like to give her to Kat and teach her how to ride."

"I can't let you give Kat a horse."

"But I want to. You have Apollo, and Tricia has Mary. I'll have Junie, and Nora is for Kat. We can all go riding together. Won't that be wonderful?"

"You are wonderful, sweet. You're the most kind and unselfish person I've ever met. Kat will love that."

"Good." Rose smiled. "Are you hungry?"

"Famished, actually."

"I'll send for a tray and have a bath readied. We have a lot to do today. You should...speak to my father."

"He's here?"

"Of course. For the wedding."

Cameron rubbed his forehead. "Dear God."

"It won't be so bad. I'll go with you."

"I have nothing to wear, Rose. I can hardly put my formal clothes back on. They're completely ruined." He pointed to the heap of garments on the floor.

Rose giggled. "My father is very conventional. He might be impressed if you wear formal attire to speak with him."

Cam rolled his eyes.

"Don't worry. I'll get some clothes from Thomas. You're about his size."

"Just don't tell him where I spent the night."

"Of course I won't. You're of much more use to me in one piece."

★ ★ ★ ★

After sharing breakfast and bathing each other, Rose and Cameron went downstairs and asked Lily to arrange a meeting with the Earl and Countess of Ashford. With an hour to spare, Cameron led Rose into the conservatory.

"I want to hear you play your song," he said. "I never did it justice."

"I can't believe that," Rose said. "You play very nicely."

"I've a decent hand is all. I can't make the piano sing like you can. Please."

"Of course. I'd do anything for you." Rose sat down on the cushioned bench and arranged the pieces of parchment in front of her. "I can help you with your work, you know. I would love nothing more."

"I can't say I relish the idea of my wife working, but if it means spending more time with you, I shall bear it."

Cam's lips curved into the smile that Rose loved, as he sat next to her on the bench.

He spoke as she played. "You're at your most beautiful when you play, Rose. The keys are like extensions of your fingers."

"I think it's the music," Rose said. "It's beautiful, Cam. I've never heard a lovelier piece."

"You were as much a part of its creation as I." He caressed her cheek and penetrated her gaze with his silvery eyes. "I love you so very much."

"I love you too." Rose kissed his lips and slid against his chest into his embrace.

As the kiss deepened, Rose climbed onto Cameron's lap, hiking up her skirts and straddling him. His arousal poked her through his trousers, and as she kissed him she moved subtly, grinding against him as her pussy began to pulse.

"I can't believe I want you again," Cameron whispered, nibbling on her ear. "I can't get enough of you."

"Mmm," was Rose's only comment, as she moved on him, purring like a kitten and rubbing her sensitive peak against him.

"Rose?"

No response.

"Sweetheart?"

"Hmm?"

"Is this room soundproof?"

No response again.

"Is this room soundproof, sweet?"

"Mmm. Yes, I think so. It's a conservatory. It should be." She brushed her lips over his cheeks and chin, his rough stubble tickling her.

Cameron stood, Rose still in his arms, strode briskly to the door of the conservatory, turned the key in the lock, and brought her back to the piano. He lowered the lid of the grand piano while still holding Rose, then set her atop the piano.

"What are you doing, Cam?"

"Shh." He removed her shoes and stockings, kissing and licking her legs and making her skin tingle, and then pulled her drawers down over her ankles. He lowered his head between her legs and licked her pussy, softly at first, and then more ferociously.

Rose writhed beneath him. So wicked to be making love in the conservatory, yet somehow this was where they belonged. She wiggled her bottom against the cool wood of the pianoforte, begging and pleading, until he finally filled her emptiness with a finger, and then two.

Cam moved his fingers in a slow circular rhythm, and then increased his speed and pressure, all the while tantalizing her peak with his silky tongue.

"So good, Cam." Rose lifted her hips, moaning his name as she succumbed once again to the ecstasy of climax. He forced her to the summit again, and then again, until she screamed in joyful torment.

He brought his face to hers and kissed her mouth, plunging his tongue into her.

"Cam," she said between gasps. "God, Cam."

"See why I wanted to know if it was soundproof?" He smiled lazily as he fumbled with the buttons of his trousers and freed his beautiful cock. "I'm going to sink myself into your body, sweet."

"Yes, please," Rose begged.

He thrust into her.

Cam pulled her legs up over his shoulders as he pounded her, kissing her calves and ankles, running his tongue over the arch of her foot. "You were made for me, Rose. God, you fit me perfectly." He continued his rhythm of thrusts while sensually caressing the curves of her long, slender legs.

Rose sobbed, calling his name, begging him to take her, as each sensational thrust nudged her swollen tip. Soon she came again.

At last Cameron plunged into her, his sex pulsating, his body shuddering. "Mine," he said. "My Rose."

"Yes, yours," Rose whispered. "Always."

Cameron gathered Rose into his arms and kissed her, deeply and slowly, whispering his love to her. Rose relished the closeness, the giddiness, until she looked at the clock on the mantel.

"We need to meet my parents," she said.

Cam groaned. "Can't we just stay here? I want to love you again."

"How many times has it been this morning? Are you steam powered?"

"Love powered." He gently set her down on the brocade sofa and gathered her discarded garments. "I need to take care of you. But I don't have anything to clean you with."

"Here, just use these." She handed him her drawers.

"What are you going to wear then?" He gently wiped the semen and juices from her body.

"I guess I'll just have to go without." She winked.

Cam's eyes widened into saucers. "You expect me to sit across from your father and ask for your hand, knowing that you're not wearing any undergarments?"

"Yes, yes," Rose said. "That should make you very

persuasive indeed."

Cam chuckled, helping Rose with her stockings and shoes. "Persuasive? I'm likely to be a blathering idiot. I won't be able to think straight."

Rose stood and straightened her dress. "Is my hair all right?"

Cam tucked a few stray ends behind her ears. "I think you should pass muster."

"Very well, then. Shall we?"

As they walked out of the conservatory and toward Daniel's study where they were to meet her parents, Rose summoned a housemaid. "Meghan," she said, "the piano in the conservatory needs to be polished and dusted." Then, tossing her soiled drawers, "And put these in the laundry."

CHAPTER SEVENTEEN

The Earl of Ashford sat behind the duke's mahogany desk. The countess and Lily were on the red velvet settee next to the desk. The tension hit Rose as she and Cameron entered. Lily gave Rose a calming grin and stood.

"No, Lily, please stay." Rose gestured.

"All right." Lily sat back down next to her mother.

Ashford cleared his throat. "Mr. Price, Rose. It's not every day that I'm summoned to a meeting by a commoner. Exactly what is your business with me?"

Cameron inhaled deeply and looked at Rose. She showered him with all the love she possessed, hoping he could see it in her eyes.

"My lord, I wish to marry your daughter."

Lady Ashford inhaled sharply.

"Pardon me?" Ashford raised his brow.

"I want to marry Rose," Cameron said again.

"I have little time for jokes, Mr. Price."

"This is no joke, Papa." Rose took Cam's hand. "We are in love and we wish to marry."

"Do be quiet, Rose," Ashford said. "This is no concern of yours."

"No concern of mine? Are you serious?" Rose's nerves vibrated under her skin.

Lady Ashford pleaded with her eyes for Rose to be quiet. Rose inhaled, trying to calm herself.

"I'm afraid I cannot allow my daughter to marry a commoner," Ashford said to Cameron.

Cam wiped his free hand nervously on his trousers. "My lord, I assure you that I can take care of her."

"Really? Just what do you have to offer my daughter?"

"My love, most importantly."

Ashford rolled his eyes. "You can't live on love, Price."

"Papa—"

"Enough, Rose. Let him speak his piece," Ashford said.

Cameron cleared his throat. "I have a post as the house composer for the new Regal Theatre."

"We heard his music last evening, Papa," Lily said. "It was very well received."

"And I can take private commissions."

"And you expect to support my daughter in the manner she has become accustomed to as a theatre composer?"

"Well, perhaps not in the manner you have supported her, but—"

"I'm sorry, Price. It's out of the question."

"Papa," Rose said. "We are in love, and we are going to marry."

"You would defy my decision?"

"To be with the man I love, yes, I would," Rose said.

"Well, that's all fine and well," Ashford said, "but you're forgetting one tiny detail. You're not of age, Rose."

"I'll be twenty-one in two months!"

"Until then, you require my permission to marry, and I will not give it."

Rose looked pleadingly at Lily.

"Papa," Lily said, "Daniel and I are acquainted with Mr. Price and his family. He is a good man, and he loves Rose."

"I don't need anyone to defend me," Cameron said.

"Lily was just trying to—" Rose began.

"Yes, I know," he said. "I mean no offense, Your Grace. I'm not used to having to sell myself." He turned to Ashford. "I may not have been born a peer, my lord, but I love Rose more than anything in the world. She refused Xavier because she's in love with me."

"You are no doubt aware of her dowry?"

"I don't give a damn about her dowry!"

Rose squeezed his hand, hoping he understood.

"Forgive me, my lord. I should have controlled that outburst."

"You're saying that you would marry her if she didn't have a dowry?"

"I would marry her if she didn't have a farthing. I love her!"

"I see." Ashford removed his spectacles and turned to his wife. "Flora, have you any opinion on this?"

"I wish only to see Rose happy," Lady Ashford said.

Ashford cleared his throat. "Then I will give permission if you wait for two months, when Rose reaches the age of twenty-one."

"But, Papa—"

"If your love is true, it can survive for two months. You won't need my permission anyway after that."

"But we can't wait."

"Why not?"

Rose took a deep breath. She had no choice but to tell the truth. "Because I'm with child."

Lady Ashford fanned herself with her hands. "Dear Lord, Rose."

"I'm sorry, Mummy," Rose said. Then, "Well, no, I'm actually not."

"Well," Ashford said, "I can see that the matter is settled then. I suppose you have my permission. I'll not see my daughter a societal outcast."

"Oh, thank you, Papa!"

"Don't thank me yet, Rose," Ashford said. "Now you, your sister, and your mother must leave this room. Your...*intended* and I need to have a chat."

Rose embraced Cameron protectively. "No, Papa. I'll not leave him."

"It's all right, Rose. I'll be fine."

"Yes, it's fine. Now go on, all of you—"

A knock on the door interrupted Ashford. "What is it?" he bellowed.

Crawford opened the door. "My apologies, Your Grace, my lord, my ladies. Mr. Price has a visitor."

"Mr. Price is otherwise engaged, Crawford," Lord Ashford said.

"I know. I informed our visitors as much, but they insist on seeing him straight away."

"I'll handle this, Papa," Lily said, rising.

"The duke has been informed already, Your Grace. He insists that Mr. Price come to the main parlor."

"Who are these mysterious visitors, Crawford?" Lily asked.

"The Marquess of Denbigh and his mother, the dowager marchioness."

"Do you know them, Cameron?" Rose asked.

"I just met the marchioness last evening. But why on earth would they come all the way here to see me?"

"Mr. Newland is with them," Crawford said, "as are your mother and sisters."

"I'm flummoxed," Cameron said. "I have no idea what this could possibly be about."

"Go ahead," Ashford said. "Denbigh outranks me. I shan't keep you from your business."

"Papa, really." Lily rolled her eyes. "Your obsession over rank is so— Oh, never mind. Come now," she said to Rose and Cameron. "Let's see what this is about."

★ ★ ★ ★

The elderly Lady Denbigh sat in her wheelchair with a cup of tea. Cameron strode forward and took her hand.

"It's a pleasure to see you again, my lady," he said.

"The pleasure is mine, Mr. Price." Lady Denbigh smiled. "I would like to introduce my son, Beauregard Adams, the ninth Marquess of Denbigh."

Cameron raised his head to regard the older gentleman standing behind his mother's wheelchair. He was tall, about Cameron's own height, with a shock of thick white hair and a finely chiseled jawline, devoid of the wrinkles of age. As Cameron readied himself to bow politely, his heart nearly stopped.

His own silver eyes stared back at him.

CHAPTER EIGHTEEN

Cameron gulped down his surprise. "My lord, it's a pleasure." He motioned to Rose and Lily, "May I present my betrothed, Lady Rose Jameson, and her sister, the Duchess of Lybrook."

"I'm charmed," Lord Denbigh said. "What rare beauties you both are."

"You're a flatterer, my lord," Lily said flirtatiously. "I'm not sure the duke would approve."

"I'd have given him a run for his money in my day," Denbigh laughed.

Kat squealed and ran to Cam. "You're betrothed? You mean Lady Rose will be my sister?"

"Yes, Kitty-Kat." Cam scooped the little girl into his arms. "Lady Rose will be your sister. She's going to come live with us."

"Oh! You'll love our townhome, Lady Rose. And Tricia and I have our own governess, Miss Penney. But maybe you can be our governess now."

"Kat, Lady Rose is going to be my wife, not your governess," Cameron said.

"But we'll spend all sorts of time together, I promise." Rose tousled the little girl's hair.

Newland cleared his throat. "Price, the marquess and marchioness need to speak to you. It's a matter of some importance."

"I can't imagine what it would be," Cam said.

"Oh Cam"—Mrs. Price strode forward—"it's the most amazing story."

"All right. It must be important if you came all this way."

"Perhaps I should take Kat and Tricia out to the kennels to see the puppies," Lily said.

"What a lovely idea, Your Grace," Mrs. Price said. "We'd be obliged."

"No trouble at all." Lily ushered the girls out.

"May we speak in private, Mr. Price?" the marchioness asked.

"Of course, but I want Lady Rose to stay. Anything that concerns me concerns her as well."

"Very well," Denbigh said. "Newland and your mother are already aware of all the details, so let me get straight to the point then. I believe you are my grandson."

Cameron jolted backward but caught himself. Rose tightened her hold on his arm.

"I beg your pardon?"

"I fathered a child some years ago on a young housemaid. I'm not proud of it, but please know that I did not force her, and I would have done right by her had I known of the pregnancy. Unfortunately, my father had her put out when he discovered her condition, and it wasn't until years later that my mother and I learned the reason behind his action."

Cameron swallowed, Rose's fingers digging into his arm.

"The housemaid's name was Joy. Joy Price. And her child was your father."

"I don't understand." Cameron turned to his mother. "You said my grandfather was an earl, Mum."

"I was, at the time," Denbigh said. "I didn't become the marquess until my father passed on."

"I see." Cameron's legs shook. He put his arm around Rose to steady himself.

"A little over a decade later, my father's valet sent for me on his deathbed and told me that Joy had been carrying my child. I began to search for her, but my search proved fruitless. I found out that she had died several months earlier, and I wasn't able to locate the child. It never occurred to me to look among the gentry. I searched the workhouses and orphanages. However, as I learned from your mother this morning, your other grandfather took my son in as a stable boy." Denbigh sighed. "Of course, I am saddened to learn of his fate at your grandfather's hands."

"Cam, what is he talking about?" Rose asked.

"My lord," Cameron said to Denbigh, "do you mind if I take a moment to explain my father's fate to my fiancée?"

"Not at all."

Cameron told the story of his father, Colton, as Rose listened intently.

"That's so horribly sad," she said. "Please, my lord. Continue."

Lord Denbigh coughed. "When I was unable to locate my son, I decided to marry. My wife was not able to give me any children, and she passed on ten years ago."

"I'm sorry," Cameron said.

"She was a good woman and a good wife. However, without an heir, my marquessate will cease to exist upon my passing."

"You don't have any brothers with children?" Rose asked.

"No, my lady. I am an only child."

"My husband was a tyrant," Lady Denbigh said. "I was barely sixteen when I married him, and he was twenty years my senior. I produced an heir within the first year, and he never touched me again."

"Why on earth not?" Rose asked. "It's clear that you must have been quite a beauty."

"You are indeed kind, my dear. Unfortunately, I didn't have the right equipment, so to speak, to please my husband."

"That doesn't make any sense," Rose said.

"I'll explain it to you later, sweetheart," Cameron said.

"My mother is quite correct," Denbigh said. "My father was a tyrant, which is evidenced by the harsh treatment that Joy received. I have never been able to forgive myself for taking advantage of her. Not only was it inexcusable, it also led to her demise. She was a lovely little thing."

"Yes, she was." Lady Denbigh nodded.

"Last evening, when my mother returned from the theatre, she mentioned meeting you briefly and that you bore a striking resemblance to me as a young man. Then, when she told me your surname was Price, I knew I had to meet you. We went to your home this morning and had a long talk with your mother. After learning her story, we came here to find you."

"It's an amazing tale," Cameron said. "I'm nearly speechless."

"I think you'll be even more speechless by the time I'm done." Denbigh cleared his throat again. "I would like to make you my heir."

Cameron shook his head, his nerves exploding. "Excuse me?"

"My heir. Heir to the marquessate. Without an heir, my holdings will return to the crown upon my death. Right now I don't have one."

"But you can't pass title to a bastard," Cameron said.

"Can you?"

"Need I remind you, Price, that you're *not* a bastard. You are the legitimate son of my son. He was a bastard, not you."

"Of course, I know that, but—"

"And I do have the right to name an heir. I have an imbecile second cousin who's hoping I'll name him, but I'd rather my estate go to the crown. In the Middle Ages, members of the nobility often passed their titles to illegitimate offspring. It is still an option today. But I'll say it again, you're not illegitimate. And you are my blood issue."

"I'm grateful," Cameron said, "but I have no desire to become a pampered aristocrat."

"Trust me, you wouldn't be pampered," Denbigh said. "My estate is intact, but I'm afraid I've not been as thorough in my affairs as I should have been during the last decade. Not having an heir, I didn't see much point in securing our holdings. If you'll be my heir, Price, I promise I'll get things in order before my time on earth is over. But it will take a lot of work on both our parts."

"I have a job," Cameron said.

"Price, don't be a fool," Newland said. "I don't want to lose you, but this is an incredible opportunity."

"But I'm finally able to work on my music full time and make a living at it. That's been my dream forever."

Lady Denbigh smiled. "There was a time, Beau, when music was important to you. Do you remember?"

"Yes, yes, I do. I composed music myself as a lad. My father felt his heir shouldn't concern himself with such frivolities, so I stopped when I became a teen."

"How terrible," Rose said.

"I survived. Of course, had I had other ways to occupy my

free time, perhaps I wouldn't have chased after housemaids."

"But then Cam wouldn't be here, nor Kat and Tricia," Rose said. "That would have been a huge loss."

Denbigh smiled. "You've a bright and kind young lady there, Cameron. You're very lucky indeed."

"I agree." Cam gave Rose a chaste kiss on the cheek.

"Perhaps there's a way for young Cameron to pursue his musical interests and be your heir," Lady Denbigh said.

"I suppose you can stay in Bath during the six months the theatre is open," Denbigh said. "Would that work for you, Newland?"

"Of course. I'd love to have Price stay on."

"Then for the other six months of the year, you and your family will live on my estate."

"Where is your estate, my lord?" Cameron asked.

"In Hampshire."

"My father's estate is in Hampshire," Rose said.

"Then your lovely wife will be close to her parents. What do you say?"

"I'm sorry," Cameron said, raking his fingers through his hair. "This is all a bit overwhelming."

"My lord," Mrs. Price said, "tell him about the title."

"Yes, of course," Denbigh continued. "As my heir, you will carry the title of Earl of Thornton, and your lovely lady here will be a countess."

Cameron's knees nearly buckled.

"I also plan to offer you a yearly allowance. As I said, my estate is not in the best condition, but I can give you three thousand pounds per year. Plus, I've already talked to Newland about purchasing your townhome from him. He has agreed to my offer, and the papers will be drawn up posthaste, with the deed in your name."

"I can't allow you to buy me a house."

"Of course you can. You're my grandson. Consider it a betrothal gift."

"I think I need to sit down."

Rose led Cameron to a settee and sat down next to him.

"I will also be giving your sisters small dowries, and your mother will receive a modest allowance as well. One thousand pounds per year."

"My lord?" Mrs. Price said. "This is the first you've mentioned of that."

"My dear, I wish it could be more. Your kindness and faithfulness to my son has earned you far more than that," Denbigh said. "I thank God that you were in his life and stood by him, even after he lost much of the use of his brain."

"He was a good man, my lord, and a fine husband. I loved him very much, and he gave me my beautiful children. I think you would have been proud of him."

"I've no doubt of that. I wish I could have been a father to him."

"I don't know what to say," Cameron said.

"Just say yes, Cameron," Denbigh said. "I can never atone for the havoc that my behavior wreaked on the lives of your grandmother and father, but at least let me care for their loved ones."

"Rose?" Cameron said. "What do you think?"

"I think it's your decision, Cam." She took his hand. "I love you, and I shall stand by you no matter what. You know that."

"Mum?"

"I agree with Lady Rose. It's your decision."

Cameron looked at his beautiful fiancée, and then at his mother. It would be selfish of him to deprive them of the life that this title could provide for them. "All right, my lord," he said to Denbigh. "I will be your heir."

"Good, very good." Denbigh smiled and strode forward to shake Cam's hand. "There is one other small thing, though."

"Yes?"

"You'll have to take my surname. It should have been yours anyway, had I had the chance to do right by your grandmother."

"Well...I suppose that's all right. It will be difficult to get used to a new name."

"You'd have to anyway," Denbigh said. "As the Earl of Thornton, you'll be known as Thornton, not Price. Your surname won't make much of a difference."

"I suppose that's true." Cameron paced through the parlor. "This will no doubt please your father," he said to Rose.

"No doubt," Rose said, "but that doesn't matter to me."

"I know it doesn't, sweet."

"Ashford has a problem with my grandson?" Denbigh asked. "I'll speak to him."

"I don't think it's me personally, my lord," Cameron said. "It's my common status. He wants better for Rose."

"There's no one better than you, Cam," Mrs. Price said.

"Your mother is quite correct." Rose chuckled. "As an earl though, you'll be his equal, and when you inherit the marquessate, you'll outrank him."

Cameron couldn't help laughing at the absurdity of it all. "I'm sorry I can't make you a duchess, sweet, like your sister."

"The only thing you need to make me is your wife, Cam," Rose said. "That's all I ever wanted."

Newland stepped forward. "I hate to break up this party, but I'm afraid I need to return to Bath. I have a play to put on this evening."

"Yes, of course," Cameron said. "I should return as well."

"No, no, take the next two evenings off," Newland said. "The music went flawlessly last night. No changes were necessary. Take a few days and ponder this new development in your life."

"That's big of you, Newland. Thank you."

Once Newland left, Lily returned and invited Cameron's family, both old and new, to stay for the wedding on the morrow.

"Now, Cam," Rose said. "I believe you have an appointment with my father."

"Yes," Lily said, laughing. "This will just knock the pompous air right out of him, won't it?"

"I'm sorry, but I find the whole concept ridiculous," Cameron said. "I'm exactly the same man I was an hour ago."

"Of course you are, Mr. Price," Lily said. "Or should I say, my lord. But to Papa, you're an equal now. May I accompany you? I really want to see the look on Papa's face."

"I'll accompany you as well," Lord Denbigh said. "I'll be proud to tell Ashford that you're my grandson and heir."

"Really, none of this is necessary," Cameron said. "I'm not afraid of Ashford."

"We know you're not, my love," Rose said. "We just all want in on the fun!"

CHAPTER NINETEEN

"Will you ever stop giggling?" Cameron squeezed Rose's hand as they walked along the estate.

"I'm sorry. Just the look on my father's face when we told him the whole story... It was absolutely priceless!" Rose leaned into him.

His body twitched. A slight touch from her, and he was an adolescent schoolboy again. "Yes, I'm now worthy to father your children."

"You always were, Cam."

"What do you want to name our child?" he asked. "Are you fond of family names?"

Rose shook her head and laughed. "I love my parents dearly, but I would never saddle a poor innocent child with the name Crispin or Flora."

Cameron joined in. "And I love my mother, but no, I'll not name a sweet little girl Clementine. If it's a boy, though, I'd like to name him after my father. Colton. Would you mind?"

"Cam, that's a wonderful idea. But as you know, the gypsy I met on Midsummer said we're having a girl."

"And you believed her, sweet?"

Rose smiled. "I wanted to. I wanted to believe her because she said you were coming back to me. And you did, so she was right about that."

"I'd like to think I would have made it back to you no matter what. And of course once I found out about the babe,

302

nothing would have kept me away."

"Well, it's all in the past now, thank goodness," Rose said. "And if the gypsy was right, and we do have a girl, what would you like to name her?"

"What about my grandmother's name? Joy?"

Rose smiled. "That's lovely. And since the first name will come from your family, might I choose the second name?"

"Of course, sweet." He was at her mercy. He'd give her whatever she wanted, even if she wanted to name the child Colton Crispin or Joy Clementine.

"Perfect, then. If it's a boy, Colton Thomas, for my brother, and for a girl, Joy Lily, for my sister."

Cameron choked back a sob. Two more perfect names could not have tumbled from her lips. "I love them both, truly. And whether little Colton or little Joy slumbers within you, I know the other isn't far behind."

Rose giggled. "I'm in the best mood, Cam. Would you like to go riding? I know Apollo isn't here, but you could ride one of Daniel's horses. I know he wouldn't mind."

Cam inhaled. Fresh summer air and a ride with his beloved. Perfect. "I'd love that, sweet. Lead the way."

They arrived at the stables and Rose picked out a gelding for Cameron to ride. They readied their horses and chattered about nothing in particular. Cam reached for a saddle, but jerked when he heard a soft click of a door locking. He turned.

"I figured you'd be here," Lord Evan Xavier said.

"Xavier"—Cam cleared his throat—"what can I do for you?"

Rose peeked around from Begonia. "Evan?"

"Leave us, Rose," Evan said, his eyes dark and grim.

"What on earth—"

"I said leave us!"

Anger bit at the back of Cameron's neck. "Don't speak to her that way, Xavier. What is it that you want? And why in God's name did you lock the door to the stables?"

"I've heard your good news. You and I are going to have it out, Price." Evan pulled out a dueling pistol and aimed it at Cameron.

Cameron's heart leaped into his throat and his bowels cramped. What the hell? This was Xavier. He wasn't a madman. What had gotten into him?

"Evan!" Rose shrieked.

"Leave, Rose," Cameron said, willing his voice not to crack. "Let her go, Xavier. Unlock the door and let her go."

"No!" Rose ran in front of Cameron. "If you want him, my lord, you have to go through me."

"This doesn't concern you, my lady," Evan said. "It's between Price and me."

"Of course it concerns me. What other business could you possibly have with Cameron?"

"Rose, leave," Cameron pleaded. "I'll be fine."

"I won't. I won't leave you."

"Think of the babe," Cam whispered into her ear.

She softened against him.

"Please," he said. "I'll be all right. I promise." He prayed he wasn't lying to her.

She nodded. "If you say so, Cam. I'll bring help." Rose inched along the wall, never taking her gaze off of Evan, until she reached the door. She unlocked it and scurried outside.

Cameron held up his hands, his heart pounding. "Come on, Xavier. You don't expect to fight an unarmed man, do you?" The man was a mountain, but a pummeling was preferable to being shot. *Stay calm, Cameron. Stay calm.*

"She was supposed to be mine," Evan said.

"Look, if this is about the commission, I plan to give you your money back. You can ask Rose. She knows."

"Do you think I give a damn about the money?" Evan took a step forward, and his face twisted in anguish. He exhaled and then lowered the pistol and deposited it back in his pocket. "My God, man, I'm sorry."

Cameron walked toward him, his nerves skittering. "Xavier, what is this really about?"

"I don't know. Rose, I guess. My foolish pride. My father's impending nuptials. Everything's changing so quickly. I thought I knew where I was headed." Evan raked his hands through his blond hair. "I wasn't going to do anything. Just scare you a little." He let out a nervous laugh. "The pistol's not even loaded."

"You accomplished your objective. I very nearly shat myself." Cameron held back a shudder. Oddly, he felt a sort of kinship with the other man. His own life had changed dramatically in the past month.

"My father. It's difficult to see him with another woman. Yet he's so happy."

"Then you need to be happy for him."

Evan nodded, his eyes sunken. "I haven't found that happiness. I wanted it with Rose, but it wasn't there. It was never there. I envy you, Price. And I envy my father. You're right, of course. I need to be happy for him. And I know that, in my heart."

"It will take a little time to get used to. But you will. Listen, I—"

"Mr. Price, I presume?"

Cam and Evan both looked toward the door as it locked again with a click. Cameron inhaled a sharp breath. A balding man stood, gun in his hand, and this was no dueling pistol.

"Who are you?" Cameron asked, his stomach churning again.

"You are Cameron Price?" the stranger said again.

Cameron gulped. "I am."

"Then I suppose I'm your cousin. Or second cousin once or twice removed or some such. Dorrance Adams."

"Ah. You're the imbecile." The words popped out before Cameron could stop them.

"Seeing as how you're the one with a gun pointed at you, I'd say it's debatable who the imbecile is here." Adams advanced. "I've no concern with you"—he gestured to Evan—"but as I can't have witnesses, I have no choice but to dispose of you both. And I plan to do a better job than I did with your father all those years ago."

"My father?" Cameron shook his head, his ears ringing. "You've got it all wrong. My father only died seven years ago."

"Yes, unfortunately, I found that out recently. The men I hired were supposed to kill him."

"The men *you* hired?" Cameron's mind raced. Was his grandfather not responsible? "I was told my mother's father—"

"I'm afraid not. I've done some research over the past couple weeks. All the good baronet did was throw your parents out of his house. The beating was my doing, though obviously those I entrusted it to didn't get the job done. Which is why I came for *you* myself. You won't be getting out of this stable alive, Price."

"What's this about, Price?" Evan asked, slowly moving along the wall of the stable, farther away from Cameron.

"I'll explain later, God willing," Cameron said, his heart hammering. *Keep him talking. Think of Rose and the babe.* "Look," he said to Adams, "if it's the marquessate you want, you can have it. I don't even want it." *Don't mention Rose. If he knows about the babe—* Cameron couldn't complete the thought.

Adams let out a sigh. "If only it were that simple, Price. But it isn't. You're going to have to go." He raised his hand.

Like a cyclone, Evan flew toward Adams and tackled him to the ground with a thundering thud. Adams thrashed around under Evan's mass, unable to move, and a shot fired from the gun into the ceiling. The horses thrashed and whinnied in their stalls. Cameron stood, immobile, his body numb.

"Get the bloody gun, Price," came Evan's muffled voice.

Cameron jolted back into awareness and ran toward the mass of limbs. Where was the gun? When he finally spied it in Adams's right hand, he focused on it and kicked as hard as he could. The gun rattled across the dirt. Cam scurried forward, grabbed it, and held it on the still-thrashing duo.

"I've got it, Xavier. You can get off him."

Evan landed a few ham-fisted punches to Adams's face and then rose. Adams writhed on the dirt.

"Your bravery was humbling," Cam said to Evan. "I'm in your debt."

Evan shook his head as he rubbed his hands together. "Call it even. I'm not sure what got into me earlier. I'm truly sorry."

"Price, are you all right?" The Duke of Lybrook burst in with three servants in tow.

"Yes, yes, I'm fine." Cam brushed off his jacket. "Thanks to Xavier."

"But Rose said—"

"That was a misunderstanding," Cameron said. "But you'll need to summon the authorities." He pointed to the ground. "This man is Dorrance Adams, and he tried to kill both Xavier and me."

"What? I don't understand."

"Find the marquess, too. I believe he's acquainted with this man. Evidently he's our second cousin."

Adams grunted, blood squirting from his nose. Two of the servants bound his hands behind his back and lifted him to his feet. "It's off to the ice house with you," one of them said, and they led him out of the stable.

"I say, Xavier," Cameron said, slapping him on the back with more nerve than he felt. "I always knew I wanted you on *my* side."

"I'm glad I could help. Can you forgive my earlier actions?"

"It's already forgiven. If you hadn't acted earlier, both Rose and I would have been here when Adams showed up, and we'd both surely be dead by now." Cam smiled, his shuddering finally starting to subside. "Now let's get cleaned up. I believe there's supposed to be a wedding here on the morrow."

EPILOGUE

After Auntie Iris and the Earl of Brighton became husband and wife, Rose and Cameron sneaked outside.

Rose sighed as Cameron drew her into his arms and kissed her. "You know," she said, "this is the exact spot where we nearly made love after Lily's wedding."

Cameron trailed tiny kisses over her jaw line, the nape of her neck, and her shoulders, which were nearly bare in her summer ball gown. She shivered at his touch, and her nipples tightened under her corset.

"And here we are, after yet another wedding." Cam nibbled on her skin. "Whatever shall we do?"

"I've an idea." Rose guided Cam's hand underneath her dress. Her pussy quivered as she anticipated his heated touch.

Cameron gasped, and then chuckled. "Naughty girl. No drawers?" He slid his fingers through her folds. "And so wet, my lady. So wet for me."

"For you, my lord." She sighed against his neck, inhaling his salty scent. "Only for you."

THE END

Continue The Sex and the Season Series
with Book Three

LADY ALEXANDRA'S LOVER
THE STORY OF ALEXANDRA AND EVAN

AVAILABLE NOW
KEEP READING FOR AN EXCERPT

CHAPTER ONE

Brighton Estate, Wiltshire, England July, 1853

"I'm going to sleep with Mr. Landon."

Lady Sophie MacIntyre abruptly straightened her back and dropped her crocheting to the floor with a soft thud. "Excuse me?"

"There's not a thing wrong with your hearing, Sophie dear." Lady Alexandra MacIntyre smiled. "I said I'm going to sleep with Mr. Landon."

Sophie picked up her crocheting and let out a sigh. "I'm not in the slightest mood for one of your jokes, Ally."

"Who is joking?"

"For goodness' sake. You don't expect me to believe—"

Alexandra stood, held up a hand to stop her sister's words, and placed her own knitting in the basket next to her. She wasn't joking. She'd been waiting months now for Mr. Nathan Landon to propose marriage to her, and she was damned tired of his foolish trifling. "I certainly do expect you to believe it. I've allowed him so many liberties I'm beginning to feel like I've already lost my virginity. Yet nothing. No promises from him, not even a bloody 'I love you.'"

"Have you considered," Sophie said, "that perhaps it's because you've allowed him so many liberties that he's not taking you more seriously?"

"Don't be silly. I haven't allowed him liberties to get him to propose marriage. I've allowed him the liberties because I wanted to."

"Ally..."

"Have you never been curious, sister dear?"

Sophie's cheeks reddened. "I'm as curious as anyone, but I know my place."

"You and Van Arden never...?"

"Of course not!" Sophie said hotly. "Not even a kiss."

"You're missing out on life's pleasures, then."

"I've no interest in—"

"Oh, Sophie, please spare me the self-righteous drivel. You just admitted to curiosity. We're all interested. Lily and Rose both slept with their husbands before marriage. And while it might have been behavior to expect from Lily, it was not from Rose. Yet she did it."

"Still, Ally, if it's marriage you're after, perhaps you should not have let him have so many liberties."

"And you think he would have proposed by now if I hadn't allowed the kissing?"

"I think it's a distinct possibility."

Ally rolled her eyes. No man in the world would marry a woman just to get into her drawers. There were places one could go to get *that*. And with Mr. Landon's money, he could have as much as he wanted. "I disagree, dear, but it's quite a moot point. I've allowed the liberties, and I can't take them back. Nor do I want to. I enjoyed it."

"And now you think to give him the ultimate liberty?"

"Yes."

"Whatever for?"

Ally smiled deviously. "So you can catch us, of course."

Lord Evan Xavier entered his father's mansion on the Brighton Estate, handing his riding gloves to the butler.

"I trust your ride was pleasant, my lord?"

"Yes, thank you, Graves. Are my stepsisters at home?"

"Ladies Sophie and Alexandra are in the front parlor."

"Thank you." Evan turned and headed up the long staircase to the second level, his goal to get as far away from the front parlor as possible. He didn't want to deal with his stepsisters at the moment, especially Alexandra, who had lately turned into the very bane of his existence.

Their newly wedded parents had left for the continent nearly a month ago, and while they were abroad, the girls were Evan's responsibility. His father, David, the Earl of Brighton, and his new stepmother, Iris, the girls' mother, were desperately in love with each other, and Evan didn't expect them home anytime soon. He normally enjoyed having the estate to himself when his father was away, but now... Well, he was no longer alone.

He found sanctuary in his own suite of rooms on the third level. The girls would never dream of setting foot there. He dismissed Redmond, his valet, and stripped off his riding clothes himself. After cleaning up, he lay on his bed and closed his eyes. Only a bloody hour until dinnertime...

★ ★ ★ ★

"Catch you?" Sophie said, her green eyes wide. "Have you lost your mind?"

"Of course not. You catch us, and you tell our new stepfather, the esteemed Earl of Brighton, and he will force Mr.

Landon to do right by me." Ally smiled. The plan was brilliant. No one would think for a moment that her sweet and prudish older sister had made up the tale. And their new stepfather had already proven himself to be vastly overprotective.

"Absolutely not." Sophie vehemently shook her head. "I'll not take part in this ridiculous scheme."

"But you must, Sophie. Everyone will know you're telling the truth."

"This is a truth I want no part of. Please reconsider, Ally. You'll be ruined."

"Do you think I care about being ruined? I want to be married, and Mr. Landon is my choice."

"Do you love him?"

"What does that matter?"

"It's the only thing that matters. Just ask Lily or Rose."

"Lily and Rose both made fine matches," Ally said, "and I'm thrilled for them. But I'm not going to wait around forever. I want Mr. Landon."

"You want his million pounds."

"I've made no secret of that. But I do care for him. He's kind, and he makes me laugh."

AUTHOR'S NOTE

The Theatre Royal in Bath, England opened in 1805. It is one of the more important theatres outside London, with a capacity to seat nine hundred. It is still open today and underwent a major renovation in 2010.

Since Zachary Newland is fictional and consequently never performed there, he also never opened the Regal Theatre. I needed a place for Cameron to compose, so I created the Regal.

Performers of the arts were often backed by benefactors. Thomas Attwood, the composer and organist, truly was a student of Mozart, and his expenses were paid by the Prince of Wales—later King George IV—who had been impressed by his talent at the harpsichord.

So in Rose and Cam's fictional world, the Marchioness of Denbigh took young Zach Newland under her wing. Zach paid it forward by offering Cameron a job as a composer, even though he lacked formal education, and also because Zach hoped to maintain the Duke of Lybrook's support for his venture.

Based on history, something similar just might have happened in a comparable place—and perhaps lives were changed, as they were in *Rose in Bloom*.

MESSAGE FROM HELEN

Dear Reader,

Thank you for reading *Rose in Bloom*. If you want to find out about my current backlist and future releases, please like my Facebook page: **www.facebook.com/HelenHardt** and join my mailing list: **www.helenhardt.com/signup/**. I often do giveaways. If you're a fan and would like to join my street team to help spread the word about my books, you can do so here: **www.facebook.com/groups/hardtandsoul/**. I regularly do awesome giveaways for my street team members.

If you enjoyed the story, please take the time to leave a review on a site like Amazon or Goodreads. I welcome all feedback.

I wish you all the best!

Helen

ALSO BY HELEN HARDT

The Sex and the Season Series:
Lily and the Duke
Rose in Bloom
Lady Alexandra's Lover
Sophie's Voice
The Perils of Patricia (Coming Soon)

The Temptation Saga:
Tempting Dusty
Teasing Annie
Taking Catie
Taming Angelina
Treasuring Amber
Trusting Sydney
Tantalizing Maria

The Steel Brothers Saga:
Craving
Obsession
Possession
Melt (Coming December 20th, 2016)
Burn (Coming February 14th, 2017)
Surrender (Coming May 16th, 2017)

Daughters of the Prairie:
The Outlaw's Angel
Lessons of the Heart
Song of the Raven

DISCUSSION QUESTIONS

1. The theme of a story is its central idea or ideas. To put it simply, it's what the story means. How would you characterize the theme of *Rose in Bloom*?

2. Rose starts out as the traditional "good girl." Is she still a "good girl" at the end of the story? Why or why not?

3. Cameron and Evan are both obsessed with Rose's station. Compare and contrast the two characters. How are they alike, and how are they different?

4. How might Cameron's life have been different if his father hadn't died after Kat was born?

5. Discuss the character of Mrs. Price. What kind of woman is she? What kind of relationship does she have with each of her children? What kind of relationship do you think she had with her late husband?

6. We learn a little more about Rose's father, the Earl of Ashford, in this book—he's a devout Christian, and he's obsessed with his rank in society. Like a lot of nobility of the time period, he seems to see things in black and white. What do these things say about him? About his relationship with his wife and children? About his reaction when Cameron asked

for Rose's hand?

7. How did you feel when Rose decided not to sleep with Cameron on the night of Lily's wedding? What do you suppose made her change her mind?

8. If Cameron's father hadn't been beaten and brain damaged, what do you think his life would have been like? How would Mrs. Price's and the children's lives have differed, if at all?

9. Discuss the scene with Melina, the gypsy crone. She seems to be dead on with her predictions, yet we learn later that she knew who Rose and Lily were. Do you think any of her predictions were accurate? Which ones and why? How do you feel about fortune telling? Did Melina have any real ability, or was she simply drawing on what she knew to be true?

10. Evan behaves quite out of character at the end of the book. What do you suppose motivates this?

11. The subplot of Iris and David is a beautiful story of love later in life. What do you think the future holds for them?

12. What do you think the future holds for Cam's sisters, Tricia and Kat?

13. Cameron's father, Colton, clearly had a difficult life. What do you think his life was like before his mother, Joy, died? How did they make ends meet?

14. This book is full of colorful supporting characters: Zachary Newland, the dowager Marchioness of Denbigh, Dorrance Adams, and Lady Myerson, to name a few. Discuss the roles of these characters. What is their purpose in the story?

15. Who do you think Alexandra's hero will be? Or have we yet to meet him?

ACKNOWLEDGEMENTS

Thank you to everyone at Waterhouse Press for your continued belief in me and my work. I look forward to getting the rest of the Sex and the Season series into the world with your help. David, Jon, Kurt, Shayla, Yvonne, Robyn—it wouldn't happen without you. And to Meredith Wild, thank you for your unwavering support. It means more than you know.

To my talented editor, Michele Hamner Moore, thank you for your diligent work.

And thanks to all of you who read *Lily and the Duke* and who looked forward to Rose and Cam's story. I hope you enjoyed it. Alexandra is up next...and it's going to be a hot one!

ABOUT THE AUTHOR

New York Times and *USA Today* Bestselling author Helen Hardt's passion for the written word began with the books her mother read to her at bedtime. She wrote her first story at age six and hasn't stopped since. In addition to being an award winning author of contemporary and historical romance and erotica, she's a mother, a black belt in Taekwondo, a grammar geek, an appreciator of fine red wine, and a lover of Ben and Jerry's ice cream. She writes from her home in Colorado, where she lives with her family. Helen loves to hear from readers.

Visit her here:
www.facebook.com/HelenHardt

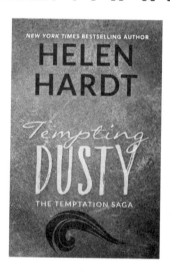